THE DEEP RANGE

ARTHUR C. CLARKE

THE DEEP RANGE

UNABRIDGED

PAN BOOKS LTD : LONDON

First published 1968 by Victor Gollancz Ltd.
This edition published 1970 by Pan Books Ltd,
33 Tothill Street, London, S.W.1

ISBN 0 330 02570 8

2nd Printing 1971

*All the characters in this story are
fictitious except the giant grouper
in Chapter Three.*

*Printed in Great Britain by
Cox & Wyman Ltd, London, Reading and Fakenham*

For Mike
who led me to the sea

AUTHOR'S NOTE

In this novel I have made certain assumptions about the maximum size of various marine animals which may be challenged by some biologists. I do not think, however, that they will meet much criticism from underwater explorers, who have often encountered fish *several times* the size of the largest recorded specimens.

For an account of Heron Island as it is today, sixty-five years before the opening of this story, I refer the reader to *The Coast of Coral*, and I hope that the University of Queensland will appreciate my slight extrapolation of its existing facilities.

PART ONE

The Apprentice

CHAPTER 1

THERE WAS a killer loose on the range. The South Pacific air patrol had seen the great corpse staining the sea crimson as it wallowed in the waves. Within seconds, the intricate warning system had been alerted; from San Francisco to Brisbane, men were moving counters and drawing range circles on the charts. And Don Burley, still rubbing the sleep from his eyes, was hunched over the control board of Scout-sub 5 as it dropped down to the twenty-fathom line.

He was glad that the alert was in his area; it was the first real excitement for months. Even as he watched the instruments on which his life depended, his mind was ranging far ahead. What could have happened? The brief message had given no details; it had merely reported a freshly killed right whale lying on the surface about ten miles behind the main herd, which was still proceeding north in panic-stricken flight. The obvious assumption was that, somehow, a pack of killer whales had managed to penetrate the barriers protecting the range. If that was so, Don and all his fellow wardens were in for a busy time.

The pattern of green lights on the telltale board was a glowing symbol of security. As long as that pattern was unchanged, as long as none of those emerald stars winked to red, all was well with Don and his tiny craft. Air – fuel – power – this was the triumvirate that ruled his life. If any one of these failed, he would be sinking in a steel coffin down towards the pelagic ooze, as Johnnie Tyndall had done the season before last. But there was no reason why they should fail, and the accidents one foresaw, Don told himself reassuringly, were never those that happened.

He leaned across the tiny control board and spoke into the mike. Sub 5 was still close enough to the mother-ship for radio to work, but before long he'd have to switch to the ultrasonics.

'Setting course 255, speed 50 knots, depth 20 fathoms, full

sonar coverage. Estimated time to target area forty minutes. Will report at ten-minute intervals until contact is made. That is all. Out.'

The acknowledgement from the *Rorqual* was barely audible, and Don switched off the set. It was time to look around.

He dimmed the cabin lights so that he could see the scanner screen more clearly, pulled the Polaroid glasses down over his eyes, and peered into the depths. It took a few seconds for the two images to fuse together in his mind; then the 3-D display sprang into stereoscopic life.

This was the moment when Don felt like a god, able to hold within his hands a circle of the Pacific twenty miles across, and to see clear down to the still largely unexplored depths two thousand fathoms below. The slowly rotating beam of inaudible sound was searching the world in which he floated, seeking out friend and foe in the eternal darkness where light could never penetrate. The pattern of soundless shrieks, too shrill even for the hearing of the bats who had invented sonar millions of years before man, pulsed out into the watery night; the faint echoes came tingling back, were captured and amplified, and became floating, blue-green flecks on the screen.

Through long practice, Don could read their message with effortless ease. Five hundred feet below, stretching out to the limits of his submerged horizon, was the Scattering Layer – the blanket of life that covered half the world. The sunken meadow of the sea, it rose and fell with the passage of the sun, hovering always at the edge of darkness. During the night it had floated nearly to the surface, but the dawn was now driving it back into the depths.

It was no obstacle to his sonar. Don could see clear through its tenuous substance to the ooze of the Pacific floor, over which he was driving high as a cloud above the land, but the ultimate depths were no concern of his; the flocks he guarded, and the enemies who ravaged them, belonged to the upper levels of the sea.

Don flicked the switch of the depth selector, and his sonar beam concentrated itself into the horizontal plane. The glimmering echoes from the abyss vanished, and he could see more clearly what lay around him here in the ocean's stratospheric heights. That glowing cloud two miles ahead was an unusually large school of fish; he wondered if Base knew about it, and made an entry in his log. There were some larger blips at the edge of the school – the carnivores pursuing the cattle, ensuring that the endlessly turning wheel of life and death would never lose momentum. But this conflict was no affair of Don's; he was after bigger game.

Sub 5 drove on towards the west, a steel needle swifter and more deadly than any other creature that roamed the seas. The tiny cabin, now lit only by the flicker of lights from the instrument board, pulsed with power as the spinning turbines thrust the water aside. Don glanced at the chart and noted that he was already halfway to the target area. He wondered if he should surface to have a look at the dead whale; from its injuries he might be able to learn something about its assailants. But that would mean further delay, and in a case like this time was vital.

The long-range receiver bleeped plaintively, and Don switched over to Transcribe. He had never learned to read code by ear, as some people could do, but the ribbon of paper emerging from the message slot saved him the trouble.

AIR PATROL REPORTS SCHOOL 50-100 WHALES HEADING 90 DEGREES GRID REF X186593 Y432011 STOP MOVING AT SPEED AFTER CHANGE OF COURSE STOP NO SIGN OF ORCAS BUT PRESUME THEY ARE IN VICINITY STOP RORQUAL

Don considered this last piece of deduction highly unlikely. If the orcas – the dreaded killer whales – had indeed been responsible, they would surely have been spotted by now as they surfaced to breathe. Moreover, they would never have let the patrolling plane scare them away from their victim, but would have remained feasting on it until they had gorged themselves.

One thing was in his favour; the frightened herd was now heading almost directly towards him. Don started to set the coordinates on the plotting grid, then saw that it was no longer necessary. At the extreme edge of his screen, a flotilla of faint stars had appeared. He altered course slightly, and drove head on to the approaching school.

Part of the message was certainly correct; the whales were moving at unusually high speed. At the rate they were travelling, he would be among them in five minutes. He cut the motors and felt the backward tug of the water bringing him swiftly to rest.

Don Burley, a knight in armour, sat in his tiny, dim-lit room a hundred feet below the bright Pacific waves, testing his weapons for the conflict that lay ahead. In these moments of poised suspense, before action began, he often pictured himself thus, though he would have admitted it to no one in the world. He felt, too, a kinship with all shepherds who had guarded their flocks back to the dawn of time. Not only was he Sir Lancelot, he was also David, among ancient Palestinian hills, alert for the mountain lions that would prey upon his father's sheep.

Yet far nearer in time, and far closer in spirit, were the men who had marshalled the great herds of cattle on the American plains, scarcely three lifetimes ago. They would have understood his work, though his implements would have been magic to them. The pattern was the same; only the scale of things had altered. It made no fundamental difference that the beasts Don herded weighed a hundred tons and browsed on the endless savannahs of the sea.

The school was now less than two miles away, and Don checked his scanner's steady circling to concentrate on the sector ahead. The picture on the screen altered to a fan-shaped wedge as the sonar beam started to flick from side to side; now he could count every whale in the school, and could even make a good estimate of its size. With a practised eye, he began to look for stragglers.

Don could never have explained what drew him at once towards those four echoes at the southern fringe of the school. It was true that they were a little apart from the rest, but others had fallen as far behind. There is some sixth sense that a man acquires when he has stared long enough into a sonar screen – some hunch which enables him to extract more from the moving flecks than he has any right to do. Without conscious thought, Don reached for the controls and started the turbines whirling once more.

The main body of the whale pack was now sweeping past him to the east. He had no fear of a collision; the great animals, even in their panic, could sense his presence as easily as he could detect theirs, and by similar means. He wondered if he should switch on his beacon. They might recognize its sound pattern, and it would reassure them. But the still unknown enemy might recognize it too, and would be warned.

The four echoes that had attracted his attention were almost at the centre of the screen. He closed for an interception, and hunched low over the sonar display as if to drag from it by sheer will power every scrap of information the scanner could give. There were two large echoes, some distance apart, and one was accompanied by a pair of smaller satellites. Don wondered if he was already too late; in his mind's eye he could picture the death struggle taking place in the water less than a mile ahead. Those two fainter blips would be the enemy, worrying a whale while its mate stood by in helpless terror, with no weapons of defence except its mighty flukes.

Now he was almost close enough for vision. The TV camera in Sub 5's prow strained through the gloom, but at first could show nothing but the fog of plankton. Then a vast, shadowy shape appeared in the centre of the screen, with two smaller companions below it. Don was seeing, with the greater precision but hopelessly limited range of light, what the sonar scanners had already told him.

Almost at once he saw his incredible mistake: the two satellites were calves. It was the first time he had ever met a whale with twins, although multiple births were not uncommon. In normal circumstances, the sight would have fascinated him, but now it meant that he had jumped to the wrong conclusion and had lost precious minutes. He must begin the search again.

As a routine check, he swung the camera towards the fourth blip on the sonar screen – the echo he had assumed, from its size, to be another adult whale. It is strange how a preconceived idea can affect a man's understanding of what he sees; seconds passed before Don could interpret the picture before his eyes – before he knew that, after all, he had come to the right place.

'Jesus!' he said softly. 'I didn't know they grew that big.' It was a shark, the largest he had ever seen. Its details were still obscured, but there was only one genus it could belong to. The whale shark and the basking shark might be of comparable size, but they were harmless herbivores. This was the king of all selachians, *Carcharodon* – the Great White Shark. Don tried to recall the figures for the largest known specimen. In 1990, or thereabouts, a fifty-footer had been killed off New Zealand, but this one was half as big again.

These thoughts flashed through his mind in an instant, and in that same moment he saw that the great beast was already manoeuvring for the kill. It was heading for one of the calves, and ignoring the frantic mother. Whether this was cowardice or common sense there was no way of telling; perhaps such distinctions were meaningless to the shark's tiny and utterly alien mind.

There was only one thing to do. It might spoil his chance of a quick kill, but the calf's life was more important. He punched the button of the siren, and a brief, mechanical scream erupted into the water around him.

Shark and whales were equally terrified by the deafening shriek. The shark jerked round in an impossibly tight curve, and Don was nearly jolted out of his seat as the autopilot snapped the sub on to a new course. Twisting and turning with an agility equal to that of any other sea creature of its size, Sub 5 began to close in upon the shark, its electronic brain automatically following the sonar echo and thus leaving Don free to concentrate on his armament. He needed that freedom; the next operation was going to be difficult unless he could hold a steady course for at least fifteen seconds. At a pinch he could use his tiny rocket torps to make a kill; had he been alone and faced with a pack of orcas, he would certainly have done so. But that was messy and brutal, and there was a neater way. He had always preferred the technique of the rapier to that of the hand grenade.

Now he was only fifty feet away, and closing rapidly. There might never be a better chance. He punched the launching stud.

From beneath the belly of the sub, something that looked like a sting ray hurtled forward. Don had checked the speed of his own craft; there was no need to come any closer now. The tiny, arrow-shaped hydrofoil, only a couple of feet

14

across, could move far faster than his vessel and would close the gap in seconds. As it raced forward, it spun out the thin line of the control wire, like some underwater spider laying its thread. Along that wire passed the energy that powered the sting, and the signals that steered the missile to its goal. It responded so instantly to his orders that Don felt he was controlling some sensitive, high-spirited steed.

The shark saw the danger less than a second before impact. The resemblance of the sting to an ordinary ray confused it, as the designers had intended. Before the tiny brain could realize that no ray behaved like this, the missile had struck. The steel hypodermic, rammed forward by an exploding cartridge, drove through the shark's horny skin, and the great fish erupted in a frenzy of terror. Don backed rapidly away, for a blow from that tail would rattle him around like a pea in a can and might even damage the sub. There was nothing more for him to do, except to wait while the poison did its work.

The doomed killer was trying to arch its body so that it could snap at the poisoned dart. Don had now reeled the sting back into its slot amidships, pleased that he had been able to retrieve the missile undamaged. He watched with awe and a dispassionate pity as the great beast succumbed to its paralysis.

Its struggles were weakening. It was now swimming aimlessly back and forth, and once Don had to sidestep smartly to avoid a collision. As it lost control of buoyancy, the dying shark drifted up to the surface. Don did not bother to follow; that could wait until he had attended to more important business.

He found the cow and her two calves less than a mile away, and inspected them carefully. They were uninjured, so there was no need to call the vet in his highly specialized two-man sub which could handle any cetological crisis from a stomach-ache to a Caesarean.

The whales were no longer in the least alarmed, and a check on the sonar had shown that the entire school had ceased its panicky flight. He wondered if they already knew what had happened; much had been learned about their methods of communication, but much more was still a mystery.

'I hope you appreciate what I've done for you, old lady,' he muttered. Then, reflecting that fifty tons of mother love was a slightly awe-inspiring sight, he blew his tanks and surfaced.

It was calm, so he opened the hatch and popped his head out of the tiny conning tower. The water was only inches below his chin, and from time to time a wave made a determined effort to swamp him. There was little danger of this happening, for he fitted the hatch so closely that he was quite an effective plug.

Fifty feet away, a long grey mound, like an overturned boat, was rolling on the surface. Don looked at it thoughtfully, wondering how much compressed air he'd better squirt into the corpse to prevent it sinking before one of the tenders could reach the spot. In a few minutes he would radio his report, but for the moment it was pleasant to drink the fresh Pacific breeze, to feel the open sky above his head, and to watch the sun begin its long climb towards noon.

Don Burley was the happy warrior, resting after the one battle that man would always have to fight. He was holding at bay the spectre of famine which had confronted all earlier ages, but which would never threaten the world again while the great plankton farms harvested their millions of tons of protein, and the whale herds obeyed their new masters. Man had come back to the sea, his ancient home, after aeons of exile; until the oceans froze, he would never be hungry again . . .

Yet that, Don knew, was the least of his satisfactions. Even if what he was doing had been of no practical value, he would still have wished to do it. Nothing else that life could offer matched the contentment and the calm sense of power that filled him when he set out on a mission such as this. Power? Yes, that was the right word. But it was not a power that would ever be abused; he felt too great a kinship with all the creatures who shared the seas with him – even those it was his duty to destroy.

To all appearances, Don was completely relaxed, yet had any one of the many dials and lights filling his field of view called for attention he would have been instantly alert. His mind was already back on the *Rorqual*, and he found it increasingly hard to keep his thoughts away from his overdue breakfast. In order to make the time pass more swiftly, he started mentally composing his report. Quite a few people, he knew, were going to be surprised by it. The engineers who maintained the invisible fences of sound and electricity which now divided the mighty Pacific into manageable portions would have to start looking for the break; the marine biologists who were so confident that sharks never attacked whales would have to think up excuses. Both enterprises, Don was quite sure, would be successfully carried out, and then everything would be under control again, until the sea contrived its next crisis.

But the crisis to which Don was now unwittingly returning was a man-made one, organized without any malice towards him at the highest official levels. It had begun with a suggestion in the Space Department, duly referred up to the World Secretariat. It had risen still higher until it reached the World Assembly itself, where it had come to the approving ears of the senators directly interested. Thus converted from a suggestion to an order, it had filtered down through the Secretariat to the World Food Organization, thence to the Marine Division, and finally to the Bureau of Whales. The whole process had taken the incredibly short time of four weeks.

Don, of course, knew nothing of this. As far as he was concerned, the complicated workings of global bureaucracy resolved themselves into the greeting his skipper gave him when he walked into the *Rorqual*'s mess for his belated breakfast.

'What kind of a job?' asked Don suspiciously. He remembered an unfortunate occasion when he had acted as a guide to a permanent undersecretary who had seemed to be a bit of a fool, and whom he had treated accordingly. It had later turned out that the PU – as might have been guessed from his position – was a very shrewd character indeed and knew exactly what Don was doing.

'They didn't tell me,' said the skipper. 'I'm not quite sure they know themselves. Give my love to Queensland, and keep away from the casinos on the Gold Coast.'

'Much choice I have, on *my* pay,' snorted Don. 'Last time I went to Surfer's Paradise, I was lucky to get away with my shirt.'

'But you brought back a couple of thousand on your first visit.'

'Beginner's luck – it never happened again. I've lost it all since then, so I'll stop while I still break even. No more gambling for me.'

'Is that a bet? Would you put five bucks on it?'

'Sure.'

'Then pay over – you've already lost by accepting.'

A spoonful of processed plankton hovered momentarily in mid-air while Don sought for a way out of the trap.

'Just try and get me to pay,' he retorted. 'You've got no witnesses, and I'm no gentleman.' He hastily swallowed the last of his coffee, then pushed aside his chair and rose to go.

'Better start packing, I suppose. So long, Skipper – see you later.'

The Captain of the *Rorqual* watched his first warden sweep out of the room like a small hurricane. For a moment the sound of Don's passage echoed back along the ship's corridors; then comparative silence descended again.

The skipper started to head back to the bridge. 'Look out, Brisbane,' he muttered to himself; then he began to re-arrange the watches and to compose a masterly memorandum to HQ asking how he was expected to run a ship when thirty per cent of her crew were permanently absent on leave or special duty. By the time he reached the bridge, the only thing that had stopped him from resigning was the fact that, try as he might, he couldn't think of a better job.

CHAPTER 2

THOUGH HE had been kept waiting only a few minutes, Walter Franklin was already prowling impatiently around the reception room. Swiftly he examined and dismissed the deep-sea photographs hanging on the walls; then he sat for a moment on the edge of the table, leafing through the pile of magazines, reviews, and reports which always accumulated in such places. The popular magazines he had already seen –

for the last few weeks he had had little else to do but read –
and few of the others looked interesting. Somebody, he
supposed, had to go through these lavishly electro-printed
food-production reports as part of their job; he wondered
how they avoided being hypnotized by the endless columns of
statistics. *Neptune*, the house organ of the Marine Division,
seemed a little more promising, but as most of the personalities discussed in its columns were unknown to him he
soon became bored with it. Even its fairly lowbrow articles
were largely over his head, assuming a knowledge of technical terms he did not possess.

The receptionist was watching him – certainly noticing
his impatience, perhaps analysing the nervousness and in-
security that lay behind it. With a distinct effort, Franklin
forced himself to sit down and to concentrate on yesterday's
issue of the Brisbane *Courier*. He had almost become
interested in an editorial requiem on Australian cricket, inspired by the recent Test results, when the young lady who
guarded the director's office smiled sweetly at him and said:
'Would you please go in now, Mr Franklin?'

He had expected to find the director alone, or perhaps
accompanied by a secretary. The husky young man sitting in
the other visitor's chair seemed out of place in this orderly
office, and was staring at him with more curiosity than
friendliness. Franklin stiffened at once; they had been dis-
cussing him, he knew, and automatically he went on the
defensive.

Director Cary, who knew almost as much about human
beings as he did about marine mammals, sensed the strain
immediately and did his best to dispel it.

'Ah, there you are, Franklin,' he said with slightly excessive heartiness. 'I hope you've been enjoying your stay here.
Have my people been taking care of you?'

Franklin was spared the trouble of answering this question, for the director gave him no time to reply.

'I want you to meet Don Burley,' he continued. 'Don's
First Warden on the *Rorqual*, and one of the best we've got.
He's been assigned to look after you. Don, meet Walter
Franklin.'

They shook hands warily, weighing each other. Then
Don's face broke into a reluctant smile. It was the smile of a

man who had been given a job he didn't care for but who had decided to make the best of it.

'Pleased to meet you, Franklin,' he said. 'Welcome to the Mermaid Patrol.'

Franklin tried to smile at the hoary joke, but his effort was not very successful. He knew that he should be friendly, and that these people were doing their best to help him. Yet the knowledge was that of the mind, not the heart; he could not relax and let himself meet them halfway. The fear of being pitied and the nagging suspicion that they had been talking about him behind his back, despite all the assurances he had been given, paralysed his will for friendliness.

Don Burley sensed nothing of this. He only knew that the director's office was not the right place to get acquainted with a new colleague, and before Franklin was fully aware of what had happened he was out of the building, buffeting his way through the shirt-sleeved crowds in George Street, and being steered into a minute bar opposite the new post office.

The noise of the city subsided, though through the tinted glass walls Franklin could see the shadowy shapes of the pedestrians moving to and fro. It was pleasantly cool here after the torrid streets; whether or not Brisbane should be air-conditioned – and if so, who should have the resulting multimillion-dollar contract – was still being argued by the local politicians, and meanwhile the citizens sweltered every summer.

Don Burley waited until Franklin had drunk his first beer and called for replacements. There was a mystery about his new pupil, and as soon as possible he intended to solve it. Someone very high up in the division – perhaps even in the World Secretariat itself – must have organized this. A first warden was not called away from his duties to wet-nurse someone who was obviously too old to go through the normal training channels. At a guess he would say that Franklin was the wrong side of thirty; he had never heard of anyone that age getting this sort of special treatment before.

One thing was obvious about Franklin at once, and that only added to the mystery. He was a spaceman; you could tell them a mile away. That should make a good opening gambit. Then he remembered that the director had warned him, 'Don't ask Franklin too many questions. I don't know what his background is, but we've been specifically told not to talk about it with him.'

That might make sense, mused Don. Perhaps he was a space pilot who had been grounded after some inexcusable lapse, such as absent-mindedly arriving at Venus when he should have gone to Mars.

'Is this the first time,' Don began cautiously, 'that you've been to Australia?' It was not a very fortunate opening, and the conversation might have died there and then when Franklin replied: 'I was born here.'

Don, however, was not the sort of person who was easily abashed. He merely laughed and said, half-apologetically, 'Nobody ever tells me anything, so I usually find out the hard way. I was born on the other side of the world – over in Ireland – but since I've been attached to the Pacific branch of the bureau I've more or less adopted Australia as a second home. Not that I spend much time ashore! On this job you're at sea eighty per cent of the time. A lot of people don't like that, you know.'

'It would suit me,' said Franklin, but left the remark hanging in the air. Burley began to feel exasperated – it was such hard work getting anything out of this fellow. The prospect of working with him for the next few weeks began to look very uninviting, and Don wondered what he had done to deserve such a fate. However, he struggled on manfully.

'The superintendent tells me that you've a good scientific and engineering background, so I can assume that you'll know most of the things that our people spend the first year learning. Have they filled you in on the administrative background?'

'They've given me a lot of facts and figures under hypnosis, so I could lecture you for a couple of hours on the Marine Division – its history, organization, and current projects, with particular reference to the Bureau of Whales. But it doesn't *mean* anything to me at present.'

Now we seem to be getting somewhere, Don told himself. The fellow can talk after all. A couple more beers, and he might even be human.

'That's the trouble with hypnotic training,' agreed Don.

'They can pump the information into you until it comes out of your ears, but you're never quite sure how much you really know. And they can't teach you manual skills, or train you to have the right reactions in emergencies. There's only one way of learning anything properly – and that's by actually doing the job.'

He paused, momentarily distracted by a shapely silhouette parading on the other side of the translucent wall. Franklin noticed the direction of his gaze, and his features relaxed into a slight smile. For the first time the tension lifted, and Don began to feel that there was some hope of establishing contact with the enigma who was now his responsibility.

With a beery forefinger, Don started to trace maps on the plastic table top.

'This is the setup,' he began. 'Our main training centre for shallow-water operations is here in the Capricorn Group, about four hundred miles north of Brisbane and forty miles out from the coast. The South Pacific fence starts here, and runs on east to New Caledonia and Fiji. When the whales migrate north from the polar feeding grounds to have their calves in the tropics, they're compelled to pass through the gaps we've left here. The most important of these gates, from our point of view, is the one right here off the Queensland coast, at the southern entrance to the Great Barrier Reef. The reef provides a kind of natural channel, averaging about fifty miles wide, almost up to the equator. Once we've herded the whales into it, we can keep them pretty well under control. It didn't take much doing; many of them used to come this way long before we appeared on the scene. By now the rest have been so well conditioned that even if we switched off the fence it would probably make no difference to their migratory pattern.'

'By the way,' interjected Franklin, 'is the fence purely electrical?'

'Oh no. Electric fields control fish pretty well but don't work satisfactorily on mammals like whales. The fence is largely ultrasonic – a curtain of sound from a chain of generators half a mile below the surface. We can get fine control at the gates by broadcasting specific orders; you can set a whole herd stampeding in any direction you wish by playing back a recording of a whale in distress. But it's not very often we have to do anything drastic like that; as I said, nowadays they're too well trained.'

'I can appreciate that,' said Franklin. 'In fact, I heard somewhere that the fence was more for keeping other animals out than for keeping the whales in.'

'That's partly true, though we'd still need some kind of control for rounding up our herds at census or slaughtering. Even so, the fence isn't perfect. There are weak spots where generator fields overlap, and sometimes we have to switch off sections to allow normal fish migration. Then, the really big sharks, or the killer whales, can get through and play hell. The killers are our worst problem; they attack the whales when they are feeding in the Antarctic, and often the herds suffer ten per cent losses. No one will be happy until the killers are wiped out, but no one can think of an economical way of doing it. We can't patrol the entire ice pack with subs, though when I've seen what a killer can do to a whale I've often wished we could.'

There was real feeling – almost passion – in Burley's voice, and Franklin looked at the warden with surprise. The 'whaleboys', as they had been inevitably christened by a nostalgically minded public in search of heroes, were not supposed to be much inclined either to thought or emotions. Though Franklin knew perfectly well that the tough, uncomplicated characters who stalked tight lipped through the pages of contemporary submarine sagas had very little connexion with reality, it was hard to escape from the popular clichés. Don Burley, it was true, was far from tight lipped, but in most other respects he seemed to fit the standard specification very well.

Franklin wondered how he was going to get on with his new mentor – indeed, with his new job. He still felt no enthusiasm for it; whether that would come, only time would show. It was obviously full of interesting and even fascinating problems and possibilities, and if it would occupy his mind and give him scope for his talents, that was as much as he could hope for. The long nightmare of the last year had destroyed, with so much else, his zest for life – the capacity he had once possessed for throwing himself heart and soul into some project.

It was difficult to believe that he could ever recapture the enthusiasm that had once taken him so far along paths he could never tread again. As he glanced at Don, who was still talking with the fluent lucidity of a man who knows and loves his job, Franklin felt a sudden and disturbing sense of guilt. Was it fair to Burley to take him away from his work and to turn him, whether he knew it or not, into a cross between a nursemaid and kindergarten teacher? Had Franklin realized that very similar thoughts had already crossed Burley's mind, his sympathy would have been quenched at once.

'Time we caught the shuttle to the airport,' said Don, looking at his watch and hastily draining his beer. 'The morning flight leaves in thirty minutes. I hope all your stuff's already been sent on.'

'The hotel said they'd take care of it.'

'Well, we can check at the airport. Let's go.'

Half an hour later Franklin had a chance to relax again. It was typical of Burley, he soon discovered, to take things easily until the last possible moment and then to explode in a burst of activity. This burst carried them from the quiet bar to the even more efficiently silenced plane. As they took their seats, there was a brief incident that was to puzzle Don a good deal in the weeks that lay ahead.

'You take the window seat,' he said. 'I've flown this way dozens of times.'

He took Franklin's refusal as ordinary politeness, and started to insist. Not until Franklin had turned down the offer several times, with increasing determination and even signs of annoyance, did Burley realize that his companion's behaviour had nothing to do with common courtesy. It seemed incredible, but Don could have sworn that the other was scared stiff. What sort of man, he wondered blankly, would be terrified of taking a window seat in an ordinary aircraft? All his gloomy premonitions about his new assignment, which had been partly dispelled during their earlier conversation, came crowding back with renewed vigour.

The city and the sunburned coast dropped below as the lifting jets carried them effortlessly up into the sky. Franklin was reading the paper with a fierce concentration that did not deceive Burley for a moment. He decided to wait for a while, and apply some more tests later in the flight.

The Glasshouse Mountains – those strangely shaped fangs jutting from the eroded plain – swept swiftly beneath. Then came the little coastal towns, through which the wealth of the immense farm lands of the interior had once passed to the world in the days before agriculture went to sea. And then – only minutes, it seemed, after take-off – the first islands of the Great Barrier Reef appeared like deeper shadows in the blue horizon mists.

The sun was shining almost straight into his eyes, but Don's memory could fill in the details which were lost in the glare from the burning waters. He could see the low, green islands surrounded by their narrow borders of sand and their immensely greater fringes of barely submerged coral. Against each island's private reef the waves of the Pacific would be marching forever, so that for a thousand miles into the north snowy crescents of foam would break the surface of the sea.

A century ago – fifty years, even – scarcely a dozen of these hundreds of islands had been inhabited. Now, with the aid of universal air transport, together with cheap power and water-purification plants, both the state and the private citizen had invaded the ancient solitude of the reef. A few fortunate individuals, by means that had never been made perfectly clear, had managed to acquire some of the smaller islands as their personal property. The entertainment and vacation industry had taken over others, and had not always improved on Nature's handiwork. But the greatest land-owner in the reef was undoubtedly the World Food Organization, with its complicated hierarchy of fisheries, marine farms, and research departments, the full extent of which, it was widely believed, no merely human brain could ever comprehend.

'We're nearly there,' said Burley. 'That's Lady Musgrave Island we've just passed – main generators for the western end of the fence. Capricorn Group under us now – Masterhead, One Tree, North-West, Wilson – and Heron in the middle, with all those buildings on it. The big tower is Administration – the aquarium's by that pool – and look, you can see a couple of subs tied up at that long jetty leading out to the edge of the reef.'

As he spoke, Don watched Franklin out of the corner of his eye. The other had leaned towards the window as if following his companion's running commentary, yet Burley could swear that he was not looking at the panorama of reefs and islands spread out below. His face was tense and strained; there was an indrawn, hooded expression in his eyes as if he was forcing himself to see nothing.

With a mingling of pity and contempt, Don understood the symptoms if not their cause. Franklin was terrified of heights; so much, then, for the theory that he was a spaceman. Then what was he? Whatever the answer, he hardly seemed the sort of person with whom one would wish to share the cramped quarters of a two-man training sub . . .

The plane's shock absorbers touched down on the rectangle of scorched and flattened coral that was the Heron Island landing platform. As he stepped out into the sunlight, blinking in the sudden glare, Franklin seemed to make an abrupt recovery. Don had seen seasick passengers undergo equally swift transformations on their return to dry land. If Franklin is no better as a sailor than an airman, he thought, this crazy assignment won't last more than a couple of days and I'll be able to get back to work. Not that Don was in a great rush to return immediately; Heron Island was a pleasant place where you could enjoy yourself if you knew how to deal with the red tape that always entangled headquarters establishments.

A light truck whisked them and their belongings along a road beneath an avenue of Pisonia trees whose heavily leafed branches blocked all direct sunlight. The road was less than a quarter of a mile long, but it spanned the little island from the jetties and maintenance plants on the west to the administration buildings on the east. The two halves of the island were partly insulated from each other by a narrow belt of jungle which had been carefully preserved in its virgin state and which, Don remembered sentimentally, was full of interesting tracks and secluded clearings.

Administration was expecting Mr Franklin, and had made all the necessary arrangements for him. He had been placed in a kind of privileged limbo, one stage below the permanent staff like Burley, but several stages above the ordinary trainees under instruction. Surprisingly, he had a room of his own – something that even senior members of the bureau could not always expect when they visited the island. This was a great relief to Don, who had been afraid he might have to share quarters with his mysterious charge. Quite apart from any other factors, that would have interfered badly with certain romantic plans of his own.

He saw Franklin to his small but attractive room on the second floor of the training wing, looking out across the miles of coral which stretched eastward all the way to the horizon. In the courtyard below, a group of trainees, relaxing between classes, was chatting with a second warden instructor whom Don recognized from earlier visits but could not name. It was a pleasant feeling, he mused, going back to school when you already knew all the answers.

'You should be comfortable here,' he said to Franklin, who was busy unpacking his baggage. 'Quite a view, isn't it?'

Such poetic ecstasies were normally foreign to Don's nature, but he could not resist the temptation of seeing how Franklin would react to the leagues of coral-dappled ocean that lay before him. Rather to his disappointment, the reaction was quite conventional; presumably Franklin was not worried by a mere thirty feet of height. He looked out of the window, taking his time and obviously admiring the vista of blues and greens which led the eye out into the endless waters of the Pacific.

Serve you right, Don told himself – it's not fair to tease the poor devil. Whatever he's got, it can't be fun to live with.

'I'll leave you to get settled in,' said Don, backing out through the door. 'Lunch will be coming up in half an hour over at the mess – that building we passed on the way in. See you there.'

Franklin nodded absently as he sorted through his belongings and piled shirts and underclothes on the bed. He wanted to be left alone while he adjusted himself to the new life which, with no particular enthusiasm, he had now accepted as his own.

Burley had been gone for less than ten minutes when there was a knock on the door and a quiet voice said, 'Can I come in?'

'Who's there?' asked Franklin, as he tidied up the debris and made his room look presentable.

'Dr Myers.'

The name meant nothing to Franklin, but his face twisted into a wry smile as he thought how appropriate it was that his very first visitor should be a doctor. What kind of a doctor, he thought he could guess.

Myers was a stocky, pleasantly ugly man in his early forties, with a disconcertingly direct gaze which seemed somewhat at variance with his friendly affable manner.

'Sorry to butt in on you when you've only just arrived,' he said apologetically. 'I had to do it now because I'm flying out to New Caledonia this afternoon and won't be back for a week. Professor Stevens asked me to look you up and give you his best wishes. If there's anything you want, just ring my office and we'll try to fix it for you.'

Franklin admired the skilful way in which Myers had avoided all the obvious dangers. He did *not* say – true though it undoubtedly was – 'I've discussed your case with Professor Stevens.' Nor did he offer direct help; he managed to convey the assumption that Franklin wouldn't need it and was now quite capable of looking after himself.

'I appreciate that,' said Franklin sincerely. He felt he was going to like Dr Myers, and made up his mind not to resent the surveillance he would undoubtedly be getting. 'Tell me,' he added, 'just what do the people here know about me?'

'Nothing at all, except that you are to be helped to qualify as a warden as quickly as possible. This isn't the first time this sort of thing has happened, you know – there have been high-pressure conversion courses before. Still, it's inevitable that there will be a good deal of curiosity about you; that may be your biggest problem.'

'Burley is dying of curiosity already.'

'Mind if I give you some advice?'

'Of course not – go ahead.'

'You'll be working with Don continually. It's only fair to him, as well as to yourself, to confide in him when you feel you can do so. I'm sure you'll find him quite understanding. Or if you prefer, I'll do the explaining.'

Franklin shook his head, not trusting himself to speak. It was not a matter of logic, for he knew that Myers was talking sense. Sooner or later it would all have to come out, and he might be making matters worse by postponing the inevitable. Yet his hold upon sanity and self-respect was still so precarious that he could not face the prospect of working with men who knew his secret, however sympathetic they might be.

'Very well. The choice is yours and we'll respect it. Good luck – and let's hope all our contacts will be purely social.'

Long after Myers had gone, Franklin sat on the edge of the bed, staring out across the sea which would be his new domain. He would need the luck that the other had wished him, yet he was beginning to feel a renewed interest in life. It was not merely that people were anxious to help him; he had received more than enough help in the last few months. At last he was beginning to see how he could help himself, and so discover a purpose for his existence.

Presently he jolted himself out of his daydream and looked at his watch. He was already ten minutes late for lunch, and that was a bad start for his new life. He thought of Don Burley waiting impatiently in the mess and wondering what had happened to him.

'Coming, teacher,' he said, as he put on his jacket and started out of the room. It was the first time he had made a joke with himself for longer than he could remember.

CHAPTER 3

WHEN FRANKLIN first saw Indra Langenburg she was covered with blood up to her elbows and was busily hacking away at the entrails of a ten-foot tiger shark she had just disembowelled. The huge beast was lying, its pale belly upturned to the sun, on the sandy beach where Franklin took his morning promenade. A thick chain still led to the hook in its mouth; it had obviously been caught during the night and then left behind by the falling tide.

Franklin stood for a moment looking at the unusual combination of attractive girl and dead monster, then said thoughtfully: 'You know, this is not the sort of thing I like to see before breakfast. Exactly what are you doing?'

A brown, oval face with very serious eyes looked up at him. The foot-long, razor-sharp knife that was creating such havoc continued to slice expertly through gristle and guts.

'I'm writing a thesis,' said a voice as serious as the eyes, 'on the vitamin content of shark liver. It means catching a lot of sharks; this is my third this week. Would you like some teeth? I've got plenty, and they make nice souvenirs.'

She walked to the head of the beast and inserted her knife in its gaping jaws, which had been propped apart by a block of wood. A quick jerk of her wrist, and an endless necklace of deadly ivory triangles, like a band saw made of bone, started to emerge from the shark's mouth.

'No thanks,' said Franklin hastily, hoping she would not be offended. 'Please don't let me interrupt your work.'

He guessed that she was barely twenty, and was not surprised at meeting an unfamiliar girl on the little island, because the scientists at the Research Station did not have much contact with the administrative and training staff.

'You're new here, aren't you?' said the bloodstained biologist, sloshing a huge lump of liver into a bucket with every sign of satisfaction. 'I didn't see you at the last HQ dance.'

Franklin felt quite cheered by the inquiry. It was so pleasant to meet someone who knew nothing about him, and had not been speculating about his presence here. He felt he could talk freely and without restraint for the first time since landing on Heron Island.

'Yes – I've just come for a special training course. How long have you been here?'

He was making pointless conversation just for the pleasure of the company, and doubtless she knew it.

'Oh, about a month,' she said carelessly. There was another slimy, squelching noise from the bucket, which was now nearly full. 'I'm on leave here from the University of Miami.'

'You're American, then?' Franklin asked. The girl answered solemnly: 'No; my ancestors were Dutch, Burmese, and Scottish in about equal proportions. Just to make things a little more complicated, I was born in Japan.'

Franklin wondered if she was making fun of him, but

there was no trace of guile in her expression. She seemed a really nice kid, he thought, but he couldn't stay here talking all day. He had only forty minutes for breakfast, and his morning class in submarine navigation started at nine.

He thought no more of the encounter, for he was continually meeting new faces as his circles of acquaintances steadily expanded. The high-pressure course he was taking gave him no time for much social life, and for that he was grateful. His mind was fully occupied once more; it had taken up the load with a smoothness that both surprised and gratified him. Perhaps those who had sent him here knew what they were doing better than he sometimes supposed.

All the empirical knowledge – the statistics, the factual data, the ins and outs of administration – had been more or less painlessly pumped into Franklin while he was under mild hypnosis. Prolonged question periods, where he was quizzed by a tape recorder that later filled in the right answers, then confirmed that the information had really taken and had not, as sometimes happened, shot straight through the mind leaving no permanent impression.

Don Burley had nothing to do with this side of Franklin's training, but, rather to his disgust, had no chance of relaxing when Franklin was being looked after elsewhere. The chief instructor had gleefully seized this opportunity of getting Don back into his clutches, and had 'suggested', with great tact and charm, that when his other duties permitted Don might like to lecture to the three courses now under training on the island. Outranked and outmanoeuvred, Don had no alternative but to acquiesce with as good grace as possible. This assignment, it seemed, was not going to be the holiday he had hoped.

In one respect, however, his worst fears had not materialized Franklin was not at all hard to get on with, as long as one kept completely away from personalities. He was very intelligent and had clearly had a technical training that in some ways was much better than Don's own. It was seldom necessary to explain anything to him more than once and long before they had reached the stage of trying him out on the synthetic trainers, Don could see that his pupil had the makings of a good pilot. He was skilful with his hands, reacted quickly and accurately, and had that indefinable poise which distinguishes the first-rate pilot from the merely competent one.

Yet Don knew that knowledge and skill were not in themselves sufficient. Something else was also needed, and there was no way yet of telling if Franklin possessed it. Not until Don had watched his reactions as he sank down into the depths of the sea would he know whether all this effort was to be of any use.

There was so much that Franklin had to learn that it seemed impossible that anyone could absorb it all in two months, as the programme insisted. Don himself had taken the normal six months, and he somewhat resented the assumption that anyone else could do it in a third of the time, even with the special coaching he was giving. Why, the mechanical side of the job alone – the layout and design of the various classes of subs – took at least two months to learn, even with the best of instructional aids. Yet at the same time he had to teach Franklin the principles of seamanship and underwater navigation, basic oceanography, submarine signalling and communication, and a substantial amount of ichthyology, marine psychology, and, of course, cetology. So far Franklin had never even seen a whale, dead or alive, and that first encounter was something that Don looked forward to witnessing. At such a moment one could learn all that one needed to know about a man's fitness for this job.

They had done two weeks' hard work together before Don first took Franklin under water. By this time they had established a curious relationship which was at once friendly and remote. Though they had long since ceased to call each other by their surnames, 'Don' and 'Walt' was as far as their intimacy went. Burley still knew absolutely nothing about Franklin's past, though he had evolved a good many theories. The one which he most favoured was that his pupil was an extremely talented criminal being rehabilitated, after total therapy. He wondered if Franklin was a murderer, which was a stimulating thought, and half hoped that this exciting hypothesis was true.

Franklin no longer showed any of the obvious peculiarities he had revealed on their first meeting, though he was undoubtedly more nervous and highly strung than the average. Since this was the case with many of the best wardens, it did not worry Don. Even his curiosity about Franklin's past had somewhat lessened, for he was far too busy to bother about it. He had learned to be patient when there was no alternative, and he did not doubt that sooner or later he would discover the whole story. Once or twice, he was almost certain, Franklin had been on the verge of some revelation, but then had drawn back. Each time Don had pretended that nothing had happened, and they had resumed their old impersonal relationship.

It was a clear morning, with only a slow swell moving across the face of the sea, as they walked along the narrow jetty that stretched from the western end of the island out to the edge of the reef. The tide was in, but though the reef flat was completely submerged the great plateau of coral was nowhere more than five or six feet below the surface, and its every detail was clearly visible through the crystal water. Neither Franklin nor Burley spared more than a few glances for the natural aquarium above which they were walking. It was too familiar to them both, and they knew that the real beauty and wonder of the reef lay in the deeper waters farther out to sea.

Two hundred yards out from the island, the coral landscape suddenly dropped off into the depths, but the jetty continued upon taller stilts until it ended in a small group of sheds and offices. A valiant, and fairly successful, attempt had been made to avoid the grime and chaos usually inseparable from dockyards and piers; even the cranes had been designed so that they would not offend the eye. One of the terms under which the Queensland government had reluctantly leased the Capricorn Group to the World Food Organization was that the beauty of the islands would not be jeopardized. On the whole, this part of the agreement had been well kept.

'I've ordered two torpedoes from the garage,' said Burley as they walked down the flight of stairs at the end of the jetty and passed through the double doors of a large air lock. Franklin's ears gave the disconcerting internal 'click' as they adjusted themselves to the increased pressure; he guessed that he was now about twenty feet below the water line.

33

Around him was a brightly lighted chamber crammed with various tyes of underwater equipment, from single lungs to elaborate propulsion devices. The two torpedoes that Don had requisitioned were lying in their cradles on a sloping ramp leading down into the still water at the far end of the chamber. They were painted the bright yellow reserved for training equipment, and Don looked at them with some distaste.

'It's a couple of years since I used one of these things,' he said to Franklin. 'You'll probably be better at it than I am. When I get myself wet, I like to be under my own power.'

They stripped to swim trunks and pullovers, then fastened on the harness of their breathing equipment. Don picked up one of the small but surprisingly heavy plastic cylinders and handed it to Franklin.

'These are the high-pressure jobs that I told you about,' he said. 'They're pumped to a thousand atmospheres, so the air in them is denser than water. Hence these buoyancy tanks at either end to keep them in neutral. The automatic adjustment is pretty good; as you use up your air the tanks slowly flood so that the cylinder stays just about weightless. Otherwise you'd come up to the surface like a cork whether you wanted to or not.'

He looked at the pressure gauges on the tanks and gave a satisfied nod.

'They're nearly half charged,' he said. 'That's far more than we need. You can stay down for a day on one of these tanks when it's really pumped up, and we won't be gone more than an hour.'

They adjusted the new, full-face masks that had already been checked for leaks and comfortable fitting. These would be as much their personal property as their toothbrushes while they were on the station, for no two people's faces were exactly the same shape, and even the slightest leak could be disastrous.

When they had checked the air supply and the short-range underwater radio sets, they lay almost flat along the slim torpedoes, heads down behind the low, transparent shields which would protect them from the rush of water sweeping past at speeds of up to thirty knots. Franklin settled his feet comfortably in the stirrups, feeling for the throttle and jet reversal controls with his toes. The little joy stick which allowed him to 'fly' the torpedo like a plane was just in front of his face, in the centre of the instrument board. Apart from a few switches, the compass, and the meters giving speed, depth, and battery charge, there were no other controls.

Don gave Franklin his final instructions, ending with the words: 'Keep about twenty feet away on my right, so that I can see you all the time. *If* anything goes wrong and you do have to dump the torp, for heaven's sake remember to cut the motor. We don't want it charging all over the reef. All set?'

'Yes – I'm ready,' Franklin answered into his little microphone.

'Right – here we go.'

The torpedoes slid easily down the ramps, and the water rose above their heads. This was no new experience to Franklin; like most other people in the world, he had occasionally tried his hand at underwater swimming and had sometimes used a lung just to see what it was like. He felt nothing but a pleasant sense of anticipation as the little turbine started to whir beneath him and the walls of the submerged chamber slid slowly past.

The light strengthened around them as they emerged into the open and pulled away from the piles of the jetty. Visibility was not very good – thirty feet at the most – but it would improve as they came to deep water. Don swung his torpedo at right angles to the edge of the reef and headed out to sea at a leisurely five knots.

'The biggest danger with these toys,' said Don's voice from a tiny loudspeaker by Franklin's ear, 'is going too fast and running into something. It takes a lot of experience to judge underwater visibility. See what I mean?'

He banked steeply to avoid a towering mass of coral which had suddenly appeared ahead of them. If the demonstration had been planned, thought Franklin, Don had timed it beautifully. As the living mountain swept past, not more than ten feet away, he caught a glimpse of a myriad brilliantly coloured fish staring at him with apparent unconcern. By this time, he assumed, they must be so used to torpedos and subs that they were quite unexcited by them. And

35

since this entire area was rigidly protected, they had no reason to fear man.

A few minutes at cruising speed brought them out into the open water of the channel between the island and the adjacent reefs. Now they had room to manoeuvre, and Franklin followed his mentor in a series of rolls and loops and great submarine switchbacks that soon had him hopelessly lost. Sometimes they shot down to the sea bed, a hundred feet below, then broke surface like flying fish to check their position. All the time Don kept up a running commentary, interspersed with questions designed to see how Franklin was reacting to the ride.

It was one of the most exhilarating experiences he had ever known. The water was much clearer out here in the channel, and one could see for almost a hundred feet. Once they ran into a great school of bonitos, which formed an inquisitive escort until Don put on speed and left them behind. They saw no sharks, as Franklin had half expected, and he commented to Don on their absence.

'You won't see many while you're riding a torp,' the other replied. 'The noise of the jet scares them. If you want to meet the local sharks, you'll have to go swimming in the old-fashioned way – or cut your motor and wait until they come to look at you.'

A dark mass was looming indistinctly from the sea bed, and they reduced speed to a gentle drift as they approached a little range of coral hills, twenty or thirty feet high.

'An old friend of mine lives around here,' said Don. 'I wonder if he's home? It's been about four years since I saw him last, but that won't seem much to him. He's been around for a couple of centuries.'

They were now skirting the edge of a huge green-clad mushroom of coral, and Franklin peered into the shadows beneath it. There were a few large boulders there, and a pair of elegant angelfish which almost disappeared when they turned edge on to him. But he could see nothing else to justify Burley's interest.

It was very unsettling when one of the boulders began to move, fortunately not in his direction. The biggest fish he had ever seen – it was almost as long as the torpedo, and very much fatter – was staring at him with great bulbous eyes.

Suddenly it opened its mouth in a menacing yawn, and Franklin felt like Jonah at the big moment of his career. He had a glimpse of huge, blubbery lips enclosing surprisingly tiny teeth; then the great jaws snapped shut again and he could almost feel the rush of displaced water.

Don seemed delighted at the encounter, which had obviously brought back memories of his own days as a trainee here.

'Well, it's nice to see old Slobberchops again! Isn't he a beauty? Seven hundred and fifty pounds if he's an ounce. We've been able to identify him on photos taken as far back as eighty years ago, and he wasn't much smaller then. It's a wonder he escaped the spear fishers before this area was made a reservation.'

'I should think,' said Franklin, 'that it was a wonder the spear fishers escaped him.'

'Oh, he's not really dangerous. Groupers only swallow things they can get down whole – those silly little teeth aren't much good for biting. And a full-sized man would be a trifle too much for him. Give him another century for that.'

They left the giant grouper still patrolling the entrance to its cave, and continued on along the edge of the reef. For the next ten minutes they saw nothing of interest except a large ray, which was lying on the bottom and took off with an agitated flapping of its wings as soon as they approached. As it flew away into the distance, it seemed an uncannily accurate replica of the big delta-winged aircraft which had ruled the air for a short while, sixty or seventy years ago. It was strange, thought Franklin, how Nature had anticipated so many of man's inventions – for example, the precise shape of the vehicle on which he was riding, and even the jet principle by which it was propelled.

'I'm going to circle right around the reef,' said Don. 'It will take us about forty minutes to get home. Are you feeling OK?'

'I'm fine.'

'No ear trouble?'

'My left ear bothered me a bit at first, but it seems to have popped now.'

'Right – let's go. Follow just above and behind me, so I

can see you in my rearview mirror. I was always afraid of running into you when you were on my right.'

In the new formation, they sped on towards the east at a steady ten knots, following the irregular line of the reef. Don was well satisfied with the trip; Franklin had seemed perfectly at home under water – though one could never be sure of this until one had seen how he faced an emergency. That would be part of the next lesson; Franklin did not know it yet, but an emergency had been arranged.

CHAPTER 4

IT WAS hard to distinguish one day from another on the island. The weather had settled in for a period of prolonged calm, and the sun rose and set in a cloudless sky. But there was no danger of monotony, for there was far too much to learn and do.

Slowly, as his mind absorbed new knowledge and skills, Franklin was escaping from whatever nightmare must have engulfed him in the past. He was, Don sometimes thought, like an overtightened spring that was now unwinding. It was true that he still showed occasional signs of nervousness and impatience when there was no obvious cause for them, and once or twice there had been flare-ups that had caused brief interruptions in the training programme. One of these had been partly Don's fault, and the memory of it still left him annoyed with himself.

He had not been too bright that morning, owing to a late night with the boys who had just completed their course and were now full-fledged third wardens (probationary), very proud of the silver dolphins on their tunics. It would not be true to say that he had a hangover, but all his mental processes were extremely sluggish, and as bad luck would have it they were dealing with a subtle point in underwater acoustics. Even at the best of times, Don would have passed it by somewhat hastily, with a lame: 'I've never been into the math, but it seems that if you take the compressibility and temperature curves this is what happens . . .'

This worked on most pupils, but it failed to work on Franklin, who had an annoying fondness for going into unnecessary details. He began to draw curves and to differentiate equations while, Don, anxious to conceal his ignorance, fumed in the background. It was soon obvious that Franklin had bitten off more than he could chew, and he appealed to his tutor for assistance. Don, both stupid and stubborn that morning, would not admit frankly that he didn't know, with the result that he gave the impression of refusing to cooperate. In no time at all, Franklin lost his temper and walked out in a huff, leaving Don to wander to the dispensary. He was not pleased to find that the entire stock of 'morning-after' pills had already been consumed by the departing class.

Fortunately, such incidents were rare, for the two men had grown to respect each other's abilities and to make those allowances that are essential in every partnership. With the rest of the staff, and with the trainees, however, Franklin was not popular. This was partly because he avoided close contacts, which in the little world of the island gave him a reputation for being standoffish. The trainees also resented his special privileges – particularly the fact that he had a room of his own. And the staff, while grumbling mildly at the extra work he involved, were also annoyed because they could discover so little about him. Don had several times found himself, rather to his surprise, defending Franklin against the criticisms of his colleagues.

'He's not a bad chap when you get to know him,' he had said. 'If he doesn't want to talk about his past, that's his affair. The fact that a lot of people way up in the administration must be backing him is good enough for me. Besides, when I've finished with him he'll be a better warden than half the people in this room.'

There were snorts of disbelief at this statement, and someone asked:

'Have you tried any tricks on him yet?'

'No, but I'm going to soon. I've thought up a nice one. Will let you know how he makes out.'

'Five to one he panics.'

'I'll take that. Start saving up your money.'

Franklin knew nothing of his financial responsibilities when he and Don left the garage on their second torpedo ride, nor had he reason to suspect the entertainment that had been planned for him. This time they headed south as soon as they had cleared the jetty, cruising about thirty feet below the surface. In a few minutes they had passed the narrow channel blasted through the reef so that small ships could get in to the Research Station, and they circled once round the observation chamber from which the scientists could watch the inhabitants of the sea bed in comfort. There was no one inside at the moment to look out at them through the thick plateglass windows; quite unexpectedly, Franklin found himself wondering what the little shark fancier was doing today.

'We'll head over to the Wistari Reef,' said Don. 'I want to give you some practice in navigation.'

Don's torpedo swung round to the west as he set a new course, out into the deeper water. Visibility was not good today – less than thirty feet – and it was difficult to keep him in sight. Presently he halted and began to orbit slowly as he gave Franklin his instructions.

'I want you to hold course 250 for one minute at twenty knots, then 010 for the same time and speed. I'll meet you there. Got it?'

Franklin repeated the instructions and they checked the synchronization of their watches. It was rather obvious what Don was doing; he had given his pupil two sides of an equilateral triangle to follow, and would doubtless proceed slowly along the third to make the appointment.

Carefully setting his course, Franklin pressed down the throttle and felt the surge of power as the torpedo leaped forward into the blue haze. The steady rush of water against his partly exposed legs was almost the only sensation of speed; without the shield, he would have been swept away in a moment. From time to time he caught a glimpse of the sea bed – drab and featureless here in the channel between the great reefs – and once he overtook a school of surprised batfish which scattered in dismay at his approach.

For the first time, Franklin suddenly realized, he was alone beneath the sea, totally surrounded by the element which would be his new domain. It supported and protected him – yet it would kill him in two or three minutes at the most if he made a mistake or if his equipment failed. That knowledge did not disturb him; it had little weight against the increasing confidence and sense of mastery he was acquiring day by day. He now knew and understood the challenge of the sea, and it was a challenge he wished to meet. With a lifting of the heart, he realized that he once more had a goal in life.

The first minute was up, and he reduced speed to four knots with the reverse jet. He had now covered a third of a mile and it was time to start on the second leg of the triangle, to make his rendezvous with Don.

The moment he swung the little joy stick to starboard, he knew that something was wrong. The torpedo was wallowing like a pig, completely out of control. He cut speed to zero, and with all dynamic forces gone the vessel began to sink very slowly to the bottom.

Franklin lay motionless along the back of his recalcitrant steed, trying to analyse the situation. He was not so much alarmed as annoyed that his navigational exercise had been spoiled. It was no good calling Don, who would now be out of range – these little radio sets could not establish contact through more than couple of hundred yards of water. What was the best thing to do?

Swiftly, his mind outlined alternative plans of action, and dismissed most of them at once. There was nothing he could do to repair the torp, for all the controls were sealed and, in any event, he had no tools. Since both rudder and elevator were out of action, the trouble was quite fundamental, and Franklin was unable to see how such a simultaneous breakdown could have happened.

He was now about fifty feet down, and gaining speed as he dropped to the bottom. The flat, sandy sea bed was just coming into sight, and for a moment Franklin had to fight the automatic impulse to press the button which would blow the torpedo's tanks and take him up to the surface. That would be the worst thing to do, natural though it was to seek air and sun when anything went wrong under water. Once on the bottom, he could take his time to think matters out, whereas if he surfaced the current might sweep him miles away. It was true that the station would soon pick up his radio calls once he was above water – but he wanted to extricate himself from this predicament without any outside help.

The torp grounded, throwing up a cloud of sand which soon drifted away in the slight current. A small grouper appeared from nowhere, staring at the intruder with its characteristic popeyed expression. Franklin had no time to bother with spectators, but climbed carefully off his vehicle and pulled himself to the stern. Without flippers, he had little mobility under water, but fortunately there were sufficient handholds for him to move along the torpedo without difficulty.

As Franklin had feared – but was still unable to explain – the rudder and elevator were flopping around uselessly. There was no resistance when he moved the little vanes by hands, and he wondered if there was any way in which he could fix external control lines and steer the torpedo manually. He had some nylon line, and a knife, in the pouch on his harness, but there seemed no practical way in which he could fasten the line to the smooth, streamlined vanes.

It looked as if he would have to walk home. That should not be too difficult – he could set the motor running at low speed and let the torp pull him along the bottom while he aimed it in the right direction by brute force. It would be clumsy, but seemed possible in theory, and he could think of nothing better.

He glanced at his watch; it had been only a couple of minutes since he had tried to turn at the leg of the triangle, so he was no more than a minute late at his destination. Don would not be anxious yet, but before long he would start searching for his lost pupil. Perhaps the best thing to do would be to stay right here until Don turned up, as he would be bound to do sooner or later . . .

It was at this moment that suspicion dawned in Franklin's mind, and almost instantly became a full-fledged conviction. He recalled certain rumours he had heard, and remembered that Don's behaviour before they set out had been – well, slightly skittish was the only expression for it, as if he had been cherishing some secret joke.

So that was it. The torpedo had been sabotaged. Probably at this very moment Don was hovering out there at the limits of visibility, waiting to see what he would do and ready to step in if he ran into real trouble. Franklin glanced quickly around his hemisphere of vision, to see if the other torp was lurking in the mist, but was not surprised that there was no sign of it. Burley would be too clever to be caught so easily. This, thought Franklin, changed the situation completely. He not only had to extricate himself from his dilemma, but, if possible, he had to get his own back on Don as well.

He walked back to the control position, and switched on the motor. A slight pressure on the throttle, and the torp began to stir restlessly while a flurry of sand was gouged out of the sea bed by the jet. A little experimenting showed that it was possible to 'walk' the machine, though it required continual adjustments of trim to stop it from climbing up to the surface or burying itself in the sand. It was, thought Franklin, going to take him a long time to get home this way, but he could do it if there was no alternative.

He had walked no more than a dozen paces, and had acquired quite a retinue of astonished fish, when another idea struck him. It seemed too good to be true, but it would do no harm to try. Climbing on to the torpedo and lying in the normal prone position, he adjusted the trim as carefully as he could by moving his weight back and forth. Then he tilted the nose towards the surface, pushed his hands out into the slip stream on either side, and started the motor at quarter speed.

It was hard on his wrists, and his responses had to be almost instantaneous to check the weaving and bucking of the torpedo. But with a little experimenting, he found he could use his hands for steering, though it was as difficult as riding a bicycle with one's arms crossed. At five knots, the area of his flattened palms was just sufficient to give control over the vehicle.

He wondered if anyone had ever ridden a torp this way before, and felt rather pleased with himself. Experimentally, he pushed the speed up to eight knots, but the pressure on his wrists and forearms was too great and he had to throttle back before he lost control.

There was no reason, Franklin told himself, why he should not now make his original rendezvous, just in case

43

Don was waiting there for him. He would be about five minutes late, but at least it would prove that he could carry out his assignment in the face of obstacles which he was not quite sure were entirely man-made.

Don was nowhere in sight when he arrived, and Franklin guessed what had happened. His unexpected mobility had taken Burley by surprise, and the warden had lost him in the submarine haze. Well, he could keep on looking. Franklin made one radio call as a matter of principle, but there was no reply from his tutor. 'I'm going home!' he shouted to the watery world around him; still there was silence. Don was probably a good quarter of a mile away, conducting an increasingly more anxious search for his lost pupil.

There was no point in remaining below the surface and adding to the difficulties of navigation and control. Franklin took his vehicle up to the top and found that he was less than a thousand yards from the Maintenance Section jetty. By keeping the torp tail heavy and nose up he was able to scorch along on the surface like a speedboat without the slightest trouble, and he was home in five minutes.

As soon as the torpedo had come out of the anticorrosion sprays which were used on all equipment after salt-water dives, Franklin got to work on it. When he pulled off the panel of the control compartment, he discovered that his was a very special model indeed. Without a circuit diagram, it was not possible to tell exactly what the radio-operated relay unit he had located could do, but he did not doubt that it had an interesting repertory. It could certainly cut off the motor, blow or flood the buoyancy tanks, and reverse the rudder and elevator controls. Franklin suspected that compass and depth gauge could also be sabotaged if required. Someone had obviously spent a great deal of loving care making this torpedo a suitable steed for overconfident pupils . . .

He replaced the panel and reported his safe return to the officer on duty. 'Visibility's very poor,' he said, truthfully enough. 'Don and I lost each other out there, so I thought I'd better come in. I guess he'll be along later.'

There was considerable surprise in the mess when Franklin turned up without his instructor and settled quietly down in a corner to read a magazine. Forty minutes later, a great

44

slamming of doors announced Don's arrival. The warden's face was a study in relief and perplexity as he looked around the room and located his missing pupil, who stared back at him with his most innocent expression and said: 'What kept you?'

Burley turned to his colleagues and held out his hand.

'Pay up, boys,' he ordered.

It had taken him long enough to make up his mind, but he realized that he was beginning to like Franklin.

CHAPTER 5

THE TWO men leaning on the rails around the main pool of the aquarium did not, thought Indra as she walked up the road to the lab, look like the usual run of visiting scientists. It was not until she had come closer and was able to get a good look at them that she realized who they were. The big fellow was First Warden Burley, so the other must be the famous mystery man he was taking through a high-pressure course. She had heard his name but couldn't remember it, not being particularly interested in the activities of the training school. As a pure scientist, she tended to look down on the highly practical work of the Bureau of Whales – though had anyone accused her outright of such intellectual snobbery she would have denied it with indignation.

She had almost reached them before she realized that she had already met the smaller man. For his part, Franklin was looking at her with a slightly baffled, 'Haven't we seen each other before?' expression.

'Hello,' she said, coming to a standstill beside them. 'Remember me? I'm the girl who collects sharks.'

Franklin smiled and answered: 'Of course I remember: it still turns my stomach sometimes. I hope you found plenty of vitamins.'

Yet strangely enough, the puzzled expression – so typical of a man straining after memories that will not come – still lingered in his eyes. It made him look lost and more than a little worried, and Indra found herself reacting with a sympathy which was disconcerting. She had already had several narrow escapes from emotional entanglements on the island, and she reminded herself firmly of her resolution: 'Not until *after* I've got my master's degree . . .'

'So you know each other,' said Don plaintively. 'You might introduce me.' Don, Indra decided, was perfectly safe. He would start to flirt with her at once, like any warden worth his calling. She did not mind that in the least; though big leonine blonds were not precisely her type, it was always flattering to feel that one was causing a stir, and she knew that there was no risk of any serious attachment here. With Franklin, however, she felt much less sure of herself.

They chattered pleasantly enough, with a few bantering undertones, while they stood watching the big fish and porpoises circling slowly in the oval pool. The lab's main tank was really an artificial lagoon, filled and emptied twice a day by the tides, with a little assistance from a pumping plant. Wire-mesh barriers divided it into various sections through which mutually incompatible exhibits stared hungrily at each other; a small tiger shark, with the inevitable sucker fish glued to its back, kept patrolling its underwater cage, unable to take its eyes off the succulent pompano parading just outside. In some enclosures, however, surprising partnerships had developed. Brilliantly coloured crayfish, looking like overgrown shrimps that had been sprayed with paint guns, crawled a few inches away from the incessantly gaping jaws of a huge and hideous moray eel. A school of fingerlings, like sardines that had escaped from their tin, cruised past the nose of a quarter-ton grouper that could have swallowed them all at one gulp.

It was a peaceful little world, so different from the battlefield of the reef. But if the lab staff ever failed to make the normal feeding arrangements, this harmony would quickly vanish and in a few hours the population of the pool would start a catastrophic decline.

Don did most of the talking; he appeared to have quite forgotten that he had brought Franklin here to see some of the whale-recognition films in the lab's extensive library. He was clearly trying to impress Indra, and quite unaware of the fact that she saw through him completely. Franklin, on the other hand, obviously saw both sides of the game and was mildly entertained by it. Once, Indra caught his eye, when Don was holding forth about the life and hard times of the average warden, and they exchanged the smiles of two people who share the same amusing secret. And at that moment Indra decided that, after all, her degree might not be the most important thing in the world. She was still determined not to get herself involved – but she had to learn more about Franklin. What was his first name? Walter. It was not one of her favourites, but it would do.

In his calm confidence that he was laying waste another susceptible female heart, Don was completely unaware of the undercurrents of emotion that were sweeping around him yet leaving him utterly untouched. When he suddenly realized that they were twenty minutes late for their appointment in the projection room, he pretended to blame Franklin, who accepted the reproof in a good-natured but slightly absent-minded manner. For the rest of the morning, indeed, Franklin was rather far away from his studies; but Don noticed nothing at all.

The first part of the course was now virtually completed; Franklin had learned the basic mechanics of the warden's profession and now needed the experience that only time would give. In almost every respect, he had exceeded Burley's hopes, partly because of his original scientific training, partly because of his innate intelligence. Yet there was more to it even than this; Franklin had a drive and determination that was sometimes frightening. It was as if success in this course was a matter of life and death to him. True, he had been slow in starting; for the first few days he had been listless and seemingly almost uninterested in his new career. Then he had come to life, as he awoke to the wonder and challenge – the endless opportunity – of the element he was attempting to master. Though Don was not much given to such fancies, it seemed to him that Franklin was like a man awakening from a long and troubled sleep.

The real test had been when they had first gone under water with the torpedoes. Franklin might never use a torp again – except for amusement – during his entire career; they were purely shallow-water units designed for very short-range work, and as a warden, Franklin would spend all

47

his operational time snug and dry behind the protective walls of a sub. But unless a man was at ease and confident – though not overconfident – when he was actually immersed in water, the service had no use for him, however qualified he might be in other respects.

Franklin had also passed, with a satisfactory safety margin, the decompression, CO_2, and nitrogen narcosis tests. Burley had put him in the station's 'torture chamber', where the doctors slowly increased the air pressure and took him down on a simulated dive. He had been perfectly normal down to 150 feet; thereafter his mental reactions became sluggish and he failed to do simple sums correctly when they were given to him over the intercom. At 300 feet he appeared to be mildly drunk and started cracking jokes which reduced him to tears of helpless laughter but which were quite unfunny to those outside – and embarrassingly so to Franklin himself when they played them back to him later. Three hundred and fifty feet down he still appeared to be conscious but refused to react to Don's voice, even when it started shouting outrageous insults. And at 400 feet he passed out completely, and they brought him slowly back to normal.

Though he would never have occasion to use them, he was also tested with the special breathing mixtures which enable a man to remain conscious and active at far greater depths. When he did any deep dives, he would not be wearing underwater breathing gear but would be sitting comfortably inside a sub breathing normal air at normal pressure. But a warden had to be a Jack of all underwater trades, and never knew what equipment he might have to use in an emergency.

Burley was no longer scared – as he had once been – at the thought of sharing a two-man training sub with Franklin. Despite the other's underlying reticence and the mystery which still surrounded him, they were partners now and knew how to work together. They had not yet become friends, but had reached a state which might be defined as one of tolerant respect.

On their first sub run, they kept to the shallow waters between the Great Barrier Reef and the mainland, while Franklin familiarized himself with the controls, and above

48

all with the navigational instruments. If you could run a sub here, said Don, in this labyrinth of reefs and islands, you could run it anywhere. Apart from trying to charge Masthead Island at sixty knots, Franklin performed quite creditably. His fingers began to move over the complex control board with a careful precision which, Don knew, would soon develop into automatic skill. His scanning of the many meters and display screens would soon be unconscious, so that he would not even be aware that he saw them – until something called for his attention.

Don gave Franklin increasingly more complicated tasks to perform, such as tracing out improbable courses by dead reckoning and then checking his position on the sonar grid to see where he had actually arrived. It was not until he was quite sure that Franklin was proficient in handling a sub that they finally went out into deep water over the edge of the continental shelf.

Navigating a Scoutsub was merely the beginning; one had to learn to see and feel with its senses, to interpret all the patterns of information displayed on the control board by the many instruments which were continually probing the underwater world. The sonic senses were, perhaps, the most important. In utter darkness, or in completely turbid water, they could detect all obstacles out to a range of ten miles, with great accuracy and in considerable detail. They could show the contours of the ocean bed, or with equal ease could detect any fish more than two or three feet long that came within half a mile. Whales and the larger marine animals they could spot right out to the extreme limit of range, fixing them with pinpoint accuracy.

Visible light had a more limited role. Sometimes, in deep ocean waters far from the eternal rain of silt which sloughs down from the edges of the continents, it was possible to see as much as two hundred feet – but that was rare. In shallow coastal waters, the television eye could seldom peer more than fifty feet, but within its range it gave a definition unmatched by the sub's other senses.

Yet the subs had not only to see and feel; they also had to act. Franklin must learn to use the whole armoury of tools and weapons: borers to collect specimens of the sea bed, meters to check the efficiency of the fences, sampling devices, branders for painlessly marking un-cooperative whales, electric probes to discourage marine beasts that became too inquisitive – and, most seldom used of all, the tiny torpedoes and poisoned darts that could slay in seconds the mightiest creatures of the seas.

In daily cruises far out into the Pacific, Franklin learned to use these tools of his new trade. Sometimes they went through the fence, and it seemed to Franklin that he could feel its eternal high-pitched shrieking in his very bones. Half-way around the world it now extended, its narrow fans of radiation reaching up to the surface from the deeply sub-merged generators.

What, wondered Franklin, would earlier ages have thought of this? In some ways it seemed the greatest and most daring of all man's presumptions. The sea, which had worked its will with man since the beginning of time, had been humbled at last. Not even the conquest of space had been a greater victory than this.

And yet – it was a victory that could never be final. The sea would always be waiting, and every year it would claim its victims. There was a roll of honour that Franklin had glimpsed briefly during his visit to the head office. Already it bore many names, and there was room for many more.

Slowly, Franklin was coming to terms with the sea, as must all men who have dealings with it. Though he had had little time for nonessential reading, he had dipped into *Moby Dick*, which had been half-jokingly, half-seriously called the bible of the Bureau of Whales. Much of it had seemed to him tedious, and so far removed from the world in which he was living that it had no relevance. Yet occasion-ally Melville's archaic, sonorous prose touched some chord in his own mind, and gave him a closer understanding of the ocean which he, too, must learn to hate and love.

Don Burley, however, had no use at all for *Moby Dick* and frequently made fun of those who were always quoting it.

'We could show Melville a thing or two!' he had once remarked to Franklin, in a very condescending tone.

'Of course we could,' Franklin had answered. 'But would you have the guts to stick a spear into a sperm whale from an open boat?'

Don did not reply. He was honest to admit that he did not know the answer.

Yet there was one question he was now close to answering. As he watched Franklin learn his new skills, with a swiftness which could undoubtedly make him a first warden in no more than four or five years, he knew with complete certainty what his pupil's last profession had been. If he chose to keep it a secret, that was his own affair. Don felt a little aggrieved by such lack of trust; but sooner or later, he told himself, Franklin would confide in him.

Yet it was not Don who was the first to learn the truth. By the sheerest of accidents, it was Indra.

CHAPTER 6

THEY NOW met at least once a day in the mess, though Franklin had not yet made the irrevocable, almost unprecedented, step of moving from his table to the one at which the research staff dined. That would be a flamboyant declaration which would set every tongue on the island wagging happily, and in any case it would not be justified by the circumstances. As far as Indra and Franklin were concerned, the much-abused phrase 'we're just friends' was still perfectly true.

Yet it was also true that they had grown very fond of each other, and that almost everyone except Don was aware of it. Several of Indra's colleagues had said to her approvingly, 'You're thawing out the iceberg', and the compliment had flattered her. The few people who knew Franklin well enough to banter with him had made warning references to Don, pointing out that first wardens had reputations to maintain. Franklin's reaction had been a somewhat forced grin, concealing feelings which he could not fully analyse himself.

Loneliness, the need to escape from memories, a safety valve to guard him against the pressure under which he was working – these factors were at least as important as the normal feelings of any man for a girl as attractive as Indra. Whether this companionship would develop into anything more serious, he did not know. He was not even sure if he wished it to do so.

Nor, for her part, was Indra, though her old resolve was weakening. Sometimes she indulged in reveries wherein her career took very much of a second place. One day, of course, she was going to marry, and the man she would choose would be very much like Franklin. But that it might *be* Franklin was a thought from which she still shied away.

One of the problems of romance on Heron Island was that there were far too many people in too small a space. Even the fragment that was left of the original forest did not provide enough seclusion. At night, if one wandered through its paths and byways, carrying a flashlight to avoid the low-hanging branches, one had to be very tactful with the beam. One was liable to find that favourite spots had already been requisitioned, which would be extremely frustrating if there was nowhere else to go.

The fortunate scientists at the Research Station, however, had an invaluable escape route. All the large surface craft and all the underwater vessels belonged to Administration, though they were made available to the lab for official business. But by some historical accident, the lab had a tiny private fleet consisting of one launch and two catamarans. No one was quite sure who owned the latter, and it was noticeable that they were always at sea when the auditors arrived for the annual inventory.

The little cats did a great deal of work for the lab, since they drew only six inches of water and could operate safely over the reef except at low tide. With a stiff wind behind them, they could do twenty knots with ease, and races between the two craft were frequently arranged. When they were not being used for other business, the scientists would sail them to the neighbouring reefs and islands to impress their friends – usually of the opposite sex – with their prowess as seamen.

It was a little surprising that ships and occupants had always come back safely from these expeditions. The only casualities had been to morale; one first warden of many years seniority had had to be carried off the boat after a pleasure trip, and had sworn that nothing would ever induce him to travel on the *surface* of the sea again.

When Indra suggested to Franklin he might like to sail to Masthead Island, he accepted at once. Then he said cautiously: 'Who'll run the boat?'

Indra looked hurt.

'I will, of course,' she answered. 'I've done it dozens of times.' She seemed to be half-expecting him to doubt her competence, but Franklin knew better than to do so. Indra, he had already discovered, was a very levelheaded girl – perhaps too levelheaded. If she said she could do a job, that was that.

There was still, however, one other point to be settled. The cats could take four people; who would the other two be?

Neither Indra nor Franklin actually voiced the final decision. It hovered in the air while they discussed various possible companions, starting with Don and working down the list of Indra's friends at the lab. Presently the conversation died out into one of those portentous pauses which can sometimes occur even in a roomful of chattering people.

In the sudden silence, each realized that the other was thinking the same thought, and that a new phase had begun in their relationship. They would take no one with them to Masthead; for the first time, they would have the solitude that had never been possible here. That this could lead only to one logical conclusion they refused to admit, even to themselves, the human mind having a remarkable capacity for self-deceit.

It was well into the afternoon before they were able to make all their arrangements and escape. Franklin felt very guilty about Don, and wondered what his reactions would be when he found out what had happened. He would probably be mortified, but he was not the sort to hold a grudge and he would take it like a man.

Indra had thought of everything. Food, drinks, sunburn lotion, towels – she had overlooked nothing that such an expedition might need. Franklin was impressed by her thoroughness, and was amused to find himself thinking that so competent a woman would be very useful to have around

53

the house. Then he reminded himself hastily that women who were too efficient were seldom happy unless they ran their husbands' lives as well as their own.

There was a steady wind blowing from the mainland, and the cat bounded across the waves like a living creature. Franklin had never before been in a sailing boat, and he found the experience an exhilarating one. He lay back on the worn but comfortable padding of the open cockpit, while Heron Island receded into the distance at an astonishing speed. It was restful to watch the twin, creamy wakes trace their passage across the sea, and to caress with the eye the straining, power-filled curves of the sails. With a mild and fleeting regret, Franklin wished that all man's machines could be as simple and efficient as this one. What a contrast there was between this vessel and the crowded complexities of the subs he was now learning to handle! The thought passed swiftly; there were some tasks which could not be achieved by simple means, and one must accept the fact without complaint.

On their left, they were now skirting the long line of rounded coral boulders which centuries of storms had cast up upon the edge of the Wistari Reef. The waves were breaking against the submerged ramparts with a relentless and persistent fury which had never impressed Franklin so much as now. He had seen them often enough before – but never from so close at hand, in so frail a craft.

The boiling margin of the reef fell astern; now they had merely to wait while the winds brought them to their goal. Even if the wind failed – which was most unlikely – they could still make the trip on the little auxiliary hydro-jet engine, though that would only be used as a last resort. It was a matter of principle to return with a full fuel tank.

Although they were now together and alone for almost the first time since they had met, neither Franklin nor Indra felt any need to talk. There seemed a silent communion between them which they did not wish to break with words, being content to share the peace and wonder of the open sea and the open sky. They were enclosed between two hemispheres of flawless blue, clamped together at the misty rim of the horizon, and nothing else of the world remained. Even time seemed to have faltered to a stop; Franklin felt he could lie here forever, relaxing in the gentle motion of the boat as it skimmed effortlessly over the waves.

Presently a low, dark cloud began to solidify, then to reveal itself as a tree-clad island with its narrow sandy shore and inevitable fringing reef. Indra bestirred herself and began to take an active interest in navigation once more, while Franklin looked rather anxiously at the breakers which seemed to surround the island in one continuous band.

'How are we going to get in?' he asked.

'Round the lee side; it won't be rough there, and the tide should be high enough for us to go in across the reef. If it isn't, we can always anchor and wade ashore.'

Franklin was not altogether happy about so casual an approach to what seemed a serious problem, and he could only hope that Indra really did know what she was doing. If she made a mistake, they might have an uncomfortable though not particularly dangerous swim ahead, followed after a long wait by an ignominious rescue when someone came from the lab to look for them.

Either it was easier than it appeared to an anxious novice, or else Indra's seamanship was of a high order. They circled halfway around the island, until they came to a spot where the breakers subsided into a few choppy waves. Then Indra turned the prow of the cat towards the land, and headed straight for shore.

There were no sounds of grinding coral or splintering plastic. Like a bird, the catamaran flew in across the narrow edge of the reef, now clearly visible just below the broken and unsettled water. It skimmed past this danger zone, and then was over the peaceful surface of the lagoon, seeming to gain speed as it approached the beach. Seconds before impact, Indra furled the mainsail. With a soft thud, the vessel hit the sand and coasted up the gentle slope, coming to rest with more than half its length above the water line.

'Here we are,' said Indra. 'One uninhabited coral island, in full working order.' She seemed more relaxed and light-hearted than Franklin had ever before seen her; he realized that she, too, had been working under pressure and was glad to escape from the daily routine for a few hours. Or was it the stimulating effect of his company that was turning her from a serious student into a vivacious girl? Whatever the explanation, he liked the change.

They climbed out of the boat and carried their gear up the beach into the shade of the coconut palms, which had been imported into these islands only during the last century to challenge the predominance of the Pisonia and the stilt-rooted pandanus. It seemed that someone else had also been here recently, for curious tracks apparently made by narrow-gauge caterpillar treads marched up out of the water and vanished inland. They would have been quite baffling to anyone who did not know that the big turtles had been coming ashore to lay their eggs.

As soon as the cat had been made secure, Franklin and Indra began a tour of exploration. It was true that one coral island was almost exactly the same as another; the same pattern was repeated endlessly over and over again, with few variations. Yet even when one was aware of that, and had landed on dozens of islands, every new one presented a fresh challenge which had to be accepted.

They began the circumnavigation of their little world, walking along the narrow belt of sand between the forest and the sea. Sometimes, when they came to a clearing, they made short forays inland, deliberately trying to lose themselves in the tangle of trees so that they could pretend that they were in the heart of Africa and not, at the very most, a hundred yards from the sea.

Once they stopped to dig with their hands at the spot where one of the turtle tracks terminated on a flat-ended sand dune. They gave up when they were two feet down and there was still no sign of the leathery, flexible eggs. The mother turtle, they solemnly decided, must have been making false trails to deceive her enemies. For the next ten minutes, they elaborated this fantasy into a startling thesis on reptile intelligence, which, far from gaining Indra new qualifications, would undoubtedly have cost her the degree she already possessed.

Inevitably the time came when, having helped each other over a patch of rough coral, their hands failed to separate even though the path was smooth once more. Neither speaking, yet each more conscious of the other's presence than they had ever been before, they walked on in the silence of shared contentment.

At a leisurely stroll, pausing whenever they felt like it to examine some curiosity of the plant or animal world, it took them almost two hours to circumnavigate the little island. By the time they had reached the cat they were very hungry, and Franklin began to unpack the food hamper with unconcealed eagerness while Indra started working on the stove.

'Now I'm going to brew you a billy of genuine Australian tea,' she said.

Franklin gave her that twisted, whimsical smile which she found so attractive.

'It will hardly be a novelty to me,' he said. 'After all, I was born here.'

She stared at him in astonishment which gradually turned to exasperation. 'Well, you might have told me!' she said. 'In fact, I really think—' Then she stopped, as if by a deliberate effort of will, leaving the uncompleted sentence hanging in mid-air. Franklin had no difficulty in finishing it. She had intended to say, 'It's high time you told me something about yourself, and abandoned all this silly reticence.'

The truth of the unspoken accusation made him flush, and for a moment some of his carefree happiness – the first he had known for so many months – drained away. Then a thought struck him which he had never faced before, since to do so might have jeopardized his friendship with Indra. She was a scientist and a woman, and therefore doubly inquisitive. Why was it that she had never asked him any questions about his past life? There could only be one explanation. Dr. Myers, who was unobtrusively watching over him despite the jovial pretence that he was doing nothing of the sort, must have spoken to her.

A little more of his contentment ebbed as he realized that Indra must feel sorry for him and must wonder, like everyone else, exactly what had happened to him. He would not, he told himself bitterly, accept a love that was founded on pity.

Indra seemed unaware of his sudden brooding silence and the conflict that now disturbed his mind. She was busy filling the little stove by a somewhat primitive method that involved siphoning fuel out of the hydrojet's tank, and Franklin was so amused by her repeated failures that he forgot his momentary annoyance. When at last she had managed to light the stove, they lay back under the palms, munching sandwiches and waiting for the water to boil. The sun was already far down the sky, and Franklin realized that they would probably not get back to Heron Island until well after nightfall. However, it would not be dark, for the moon was nearing full, so even without the aid of the local beacons the homeward journey would present no difficulties.

The billy-brewed tea was excellent, though doubtless far too anaemic for any old-time swagman. It washed down the remainder of their food very efficiently, and as they relaxed with sighs of satisfaction their hands once again found each other. Now, thought Franklin, I should be perfectly content. But he knew that he was not; something that he could not define was worrying him.

His unease had grown steadily stronger during the last few minutes, but he had tried to ignore it and force it down into his mind. He knew that it was utterly ridiculous and irrational to expect any danger here, on this empty and peaceful island. Yet little warning bells were ringing far down in the labyrinths of his brain, and he could not understand their signals.

Indra's casual question came as a welcome distraction. She was staring intently up into the western sky, obviously searching for something.

'Is it really true, Walter,' she asked, 'that if you know where to look for her you can see Venus in the daytime? She was so bright after sunset last night that I could almost believe it.'

'It's perfectly true,' Franklin answered. 'In fact, it isn't even difficult. The big problem is to locate her in the first place; once you've done that, she's quite easy to see.'

He propped himself up against a palm trunk, shaded his eyes from the glare of the descending sun, and began to search the western sky with little hope of discovering the elusive silver speck he knew to be shining there. He had noticed Venus dominating the evening sky during the last few weeks, but it was hard to judge how far she was from the sun when both were above the horizon at the same time.

Suddenly – unexpectedly – his eyes caught and held a solitary silver star hanging against the milky blue of the sky. 'I've found her!' he exclaimed, raising his arm as a pointer. Indra squinted along it, but at first could see nothing.

'You've got spots before the eyes,' she taunted.

'No – I'm not imagining things. Just keep on looking,' Franklin answered, his eyes still focused on the dimensionless star which he knew he would lose if he turned away from it even for a second.

'But Venus *can't* be there,' protested Indra. 'That's much too far north.'

In a single, sickening instant Franklin knew that she was right. If he had any doubt, he could see now that the star he was watching was moving swiftly across the sky, rising out of the west and so defying the laws which controlled all other heavenly bodies.

He was staring at the Space Station, the largest of all the satellites now circling Earth, as it raced along its thousand-mile-high orbit. He tried to turn his eyes away, to break the hypnotic spell of that man-made, unscintillating star. It was as if he was teetering on the edge of an abyss; the terror of those endless, trackless wastes between the worlds began to invade and dominate his mind, to threaten the very foundations of his sanity.

He would have won the struggle, no more than a little shaken, had it not been for a second accident of fate. With the explosive suddenness with which memory sometimes yields to persistent questioning, he knew what it was that had been worrying him for the last few minutes. It was the smell of the fuel that Indra had siphoned from the hydrojet – the unmistakable, slightly aromatic tang of synthene. And crowding hard upon that recognition was the memory of where he had last met that all-too-familiar odour.

Synthene – first developed as a rocket propellant – now obsolete like all other chemical fuels, except for low-powered applications like the propulsion of space suits.

Space suits.

It was too much; the double assault defeated him. Both sight and smell had turned traitor in the same instant. Within seconds, the patiently built dikes which now protected his mind went down before the rising tide of terror.

He could feel the Earth beneath him spinning dizzily through space. It seemed to be whirling faster and faster on its axis, trying to hurl him off like a stone from a sling by the sheer speed of its rotation. With a choking cry, he rolled over on his stomach, buried his face in the sand, and clung desperately to the rough trunk of the palm. It gave him no security; the endless fall began again ... Chief Engineer Franklin, second in command of the *Arcturus*, was in space once more, at the beginning of the nightmare he had hoped and prayed he need never retrace.

CHAPTER 7

IN THE first shock of stunned surprise, Indra sat staring foolishly at Franklin as he grovelled in the sand and wept like a heartbroken child. Then compassion and common sense told her what to do; she moved swiftly to his side and threw her arms around his heaving shoulders.

'Walter!' she cried. 'You're all right – there's nothing to be afraid of!'

The words seemed flat and foolish even as she uttered them, but they were the best she had to offer. Franklin did not seem to hear; he was still trembling uncontrollably, still clinging to the tree with desperate determination. It was pitiful to see a man reduced to such a state of abject fear, so robbed of all dignity and pride. As Indra crouched over him, she realized that between his sobs he was calling a name – and even at such a moment as this she could not depress a stab of jealousy. For it was the name of a woman; over and over again, in a voice so low as to be barely audible Franklin would whisper 'Irene!' and then be convulsed by a fresh paroxysm of weeping.

There was something here beyond Indra's slight knowledge of medicine. She hesitated for a moment, then hurried to the catamaran and broke open its little first-aid kit. It contained a vial of potent pain-killing capsules, prominently labelled ONLY ONE TO BE TAKEN AT ANY TIME, and with some difficulty she managed to force one of these into Franklin's mouth. Then she held him in her arms while his tremors slowly subsided and the violence of the attack ebbed away.

It is hard to draw any line between compassion and love. If such a division exists, Indra crossed it during this silent vigil. Franklin's loss of manhood had not disgusted her; she knew that something terrible indeed must have happened in his past to bring him to this state. Whatever it was, her own future would not be complete unless she could help him fight it.

Presently Franklin was quiet, though apparently still conscious. He did not resist when she rolled him over so that his face was no longer half-buried in the sand, and he relaxed his frenzied grip upon the tree. But his eyes were empty, and his mouth still moved silently though no words came from it.

'We're going home,' whispered Indra, as if soothing a frightened child. 'Come along – it's all right now.'

She helped him to his feet, and he rose unresistingly. He even assisted her, in a mechanical way, to pack their equipment and to push the catamaran off the beach. He seemed nearly normal again, except that he would not speak and there was a sadness in his eyes that tore at Indra's heart.

They left the island under both sail and power, for Indra was determined to waste no time. Even now it had not occurred to her that she might be in any personal danger, so many miles from any help, with a man who might be mad. Her only concern was to get Franklin back to medical care as quickly as she could.

The light was failing fast; the sun had already touched the horizon and darkness was massing in the east. Beacons on the mainland and the surrounding islands began, one by one, to spring to life. And, more brilliant than any of them, there in the west was Venus, which had somehow caused all this trouble . . .

Presently Franklin spoke, his words forced but perfectly rational.

'I'm very sorry about this, Indra,' he said. 'I'm afraid I spoiled your trip.'

'Don't be silly,' she answered. 'It wasn't your fault. Just take it easy – don't talk unless you want to.' He relapsed into

61

silence, and spoke no more for the rest of the voyage. When Indra reached out to hold his hand again, he stiffened defensively in a way which said, without actually rejecting her, that he would prefer no such contact. She felt hurt, but obeyed his unspoken request. In any event, she was busy enough picking out the beacons as she made the tricky passage between the reefs.

She had not intended to be out as late as this, even though the rising moon was now flooding the sea with light. The wind had freshened, and all too close at hand the breakers along the Wistari Reef were appearing and vanishing in deadly lines of luminous, ghostly white. She kept one eye on them, and the other on the winking beacon that marked the end of the Heron jetty. Not until she could see the jetty itself and make out the details of the island was she able to relax and give her attention once more to Franklin.

He appeared almost normal again when they had berthed the catamaran and walked back to the lab. Indra could not see his expression, for there were no lights here on this part of the beach, and the palms shaded them from the moon. As far as she could tell, his voice was under full control when he bade her good night.

'Thank you for everything, Indra. No one could have done more.'

'Let me take you to Dr Myers right away. You've got to see him.'

'No – there's nothing he can do. I'm quite all right now – it won't happen again.'

'I still think you should see him. I'll take you to your room and then go and call him.'

Franklin shook his head violently.

'That's one thing I don't want you to do. Promise me you won't call him.'

Sorely troubled, Indra debated with her conscience. The wisest thing to do, she was sure, was to make the promise – and then to break it. Yet if she did so, Franklin might never forgive her. In the end, she compromised.

'Will you go and see him yourself, if you won't let me take you?'

Franklin hesitated before answering. It seemed a shame that his parting words with this girl, whom he might have loved, should be a lie. But in the drugged calm that had come upon him now he knew what he must do.

'I'll call him in the morning – and thanks again.' Then he broke away, with a fierce finality, before Indra could question him further.

She watched him disappear into the darkness, along the path that led to the training and administration section. Happiness and anxiety were contending for her soul – happiness because she had found love, anxiety because it was threatened by forces she did not understand. The anxiety resolved itself into a single nagging fear: Should she have insisted, even again his will, that Franklin see Dr Myers at once?

She would have had no doubt of the answer could she have watched Franklin double back through the moonlit forest and make his way, like a man in a waking dream, to the dock from which had begun all his journeys down into the sea.

The rational part of his mind was now merely the passive tool of his emotions, and they were set upon a single goal. He had been hurt too badly for reason to control him now; like an injured animal, he could think of nothing but the abating of his pain. He was seeking the only place where for a little while he had found peace and contentment.

The jetty was deserted as he made the long, lonely walk out to the edge of the reef. Down in the submarine hangar, twenty feet below the water line, he made his final preparations with as much care as he had ever done on his many earlier trips. He felt a fleeting sense of guilt at robbing the bureau of some fairly valuable equipment and still more valuable training time; but it was not his fault that he had no other choice.

Very quietly, the torp slipped out beneath the submerged archway and set course for the open sea. It was the first time that Franklin had ever been out at night; only the fully enclosed subs operated after darkness, for night navigation involved dangers which it was foolhardy for unprotected men to face. That was the least of Franklin's worries as he set the course he remembered so well and headed out into the channel that would lead him to the sea.

Part of the pain, but none of the determination, lifted

from his mind. This was where he belonged; this was where he had found happiness. This was where he would find oblivion.

He was in a world of midnight blue which the pale rays of the moon could do little to illumine. Around him strange shapes moved like phosphorescent ghosts, as the creatures of the reef were attracted or scattered by the sound of his passing. Below him, no more than shadows in a deeper darkness, he could see the coral hills and valleys he had grown to know so well. With a resignation beyond sadness, he bade them all adieu.

There was no point in lingering, now that his destiny was clear before him. He pushed the throttle full down, and the torpedo leaped forward like a horse that had been given the spur. The islands of the Great Barrier Reef were falling swiftly behind him, and he was heading out into the Pacific at a speed which no other creature of the sea could match.

Only once did he glance up at the world he had abandoned. The water was fantastically clear, and a hundred feet above his head he could see the silver track of the moon upon the sea, as few men could ever have witnessed it before. He could even see the hazy, dancing patch of light that was the moon itself, refracted through the water surface yet occasionally freezing, when the moving waves brought a moment of stability, into a perfect, flawless image.

And once a very large shark – the largest he had ever seen – tried to pursue him. The great streamlined shadow, leaving its phosphorescent wake, appeared suddenly almost dead ahead of him, and he made no effort to avoid it. As it swept past he caught a glimpse of the inhuman, staring eye, the slatted gills, and the inevitable retinue of pilot fish and remora. When he glanced back the shark was following him – whether motivated by curiosity, sex, or hunger he neither knew nor cared. It remained in sight for almost a minute before his superior speed left it behind. He had never met a shark that had reacted in this way before; usually they were terrified of the turbine's warning scream. But the laws that ruled the reef during the day were not those that prevailed in the hours of darkness.

He raced on through the luminous night that covered half the world, crouching behind his curved shield for protection against the turbulent waters he was sundering in his haste to reach the open sea. Even now he was navigating with all his old skill and precision; he knew exactly where he was, exactly when he would reach his objective – and exactly how deep were the waters he was now entering. In a few minutes, the sea bed would start slanting sharply down and he must say his last farewell to the reef.

He tilted the nose of the torp imperceptibly towards the depths and at the same time cut his speed to a quarter. The mad, roaring rush of waters ceased; he was sliding gently down a long, invisible slope whose end he would never see.

Slowly the pale and filtered moonlight began to fade as the water thickened above him. Deliberately, he avoided looking at the illuminated depth gauge, avoided all thought of the fathoms that now lay overhead. He could feel the pressure on his body increasing minute by minute, but it was not in the least unpleasant. Indeed, he welcomed it; he gave himself, a willing sacrifice, gladly into the grasp of the great mother of life.

The darkness was now complete. He was alone, driving through a night stranger and more palpable than any to be found upon the land. From time to time he could see, at an unguessable distance below him, tiny explosions of light as the unknown creatures of the open sea went about their mysterious business. Sometimes an entire, ephemeral galaxy would thrust forth and within seconds die; perhaps that other galaxy, he told himself, was of no longer duration, of no greater importance, when seen against the background of eternity.

The dreamy sleep of nitrogen narcosis was now almost upon him; no other human being, using a compressed-air lung alone, could ever have been so deep and returned to tell the tale. He was breathing air at more than ten times normal pressure, and still the torpedo was boring down into the lightless depths. All responsibility, all regrets, all fears had been washed away from his mind by the blissful euphoria that had invaded every level of consciousness.

And yet, at the very end, there was one regret. He felt a mild and wistful sadness, that Indra must now begin again her search for the happiness he might have given her.

Thereafter there was only the sea, and a mindless machine

creeping ever more slowly down to the hundred-fathom line and the far Pacific wastes.

CHAPTER 8

THERE WERE four people in the room, and not one of them was talking now. The chief instructor was biting his lip nervously, Don Burley sat looking stunned, and Indra was trying not to cry. Only Dr Myers seemed fairly well under control, and was silently cursing the fantastic, the still inexplicable bad luck that had brought this situation upon them. He would have sworn that Franklin was well on the road to recovery, well past any serious crisis. And now this!

'There's only one thing to do,' said the chief instructor suddenly. 'And that's to send out all our underwater craft on a general search.'

Don Burley stirred himself, slowly and as if carrying a great weight upon his shoulders.

'It's twelve hours now. In that time he could have covered five hundred miles. And there are only six qualified pilots on the station.'

'I know – it would be like looking for a needle in a haystack. But it's the only thing we can do.'

'Sometimes a few minutes of thought can save a good many hours of random searching,' said Myers. 'After all of a day, a little extra time will make no difference. With your permission, I'd like to have a private talk with Miss Langenburg.'

'Of course – if she agrees.'

Indra nodded dumbly. She was still blaming herself bitterly for what had happened – for not going to the doctor immediately when they had returned to the island. Her intuition had failed her then; now it told her that there was no possibility of any hope, and she could only pray that it was wrong again.

'Now, Indra,' said Myers kindly when the others had left the room, 'if we want to help Franklin we've got to keep our

66

heads, and try to guess what he's done. So stop blaming your-self – this isn't your fault. I'm not sure if it's anyone's fault.'

It might be mine, he added grimly to himself. But who could have guessed? We understand so little about astrophobia, even now ... and heaven knows it's not in my line.

Indra managed a brave smile. Until yesterday, she had thought she was very grown-up and able to take care of herself in any situation. But yesterday was a very, very long time ago.

'Please tell me,' she said, 'what is the matter with Walter. I think it would help me to understand.'

It was a sensible and reasonable request; even before Indra had made it, Myers had come to the same conclusion.

'Very well – but remember, this is confidential, for Walter's own sake. I'm only telling it to you because his is an emergency and you may be able to help him if you know the facts.

'Until a year ago, Walter was a highly qualified spaceman. In fact, he was chief engineer of a liner on the Martian run, which as you know is a very responsible position indeed, and that was certainly merely the beginning of his career.

'Well, there was some kind of emergency in mid-orbit, and the ion drive had to be shut off. Walter went outside in a space suit to fix it – nothing unusual about that, of course. Before he had finished the job, however, his suit failed. No – I don't mean it leaked. What happened was that the pro-pulsion system jammed *on*, and he couldn't shut off the rockets that allowed him to move around in space.

'So there he was, millions of miles from anywhere, build-ing up speed away from his ship. To make matters worse, he'd crashed against some part of the liner when he started, and that had snapped off his radio antenna. So he couldn't talk or receive messages – couldn't call for help or find out what his friends were doing for him. He was completely alone, and in a few minutes he couldn't even see the liner.

'Now, no one who has not been in a situation like that can possibly imagine what it's like. We can try, but we can't really picture being absolutely isolated, with stars all around us, not knowing if we'll ever be rescued. No vertigo that can

67

ever be experienced on Earth can match it – not even sea-sickness at its worst, and that's bad enough.

'It was four hours before Walter was rescued. He was actually quite safe, and probably knew it – but that didn't make any difference. The ship's radar tracked him, but until the drive was repaired it couldn't go after him. When they did get him aboard he was – well, let's say he was in a pretty bad way.

'It took the best psychologists on earth almost a year to straighten him out, and as we've seen, the job wasn't finished properly. And there was one factor that the psychologists could do nothing about.'

Myers paused, wondering how Indra was taking all this, how it would affect her feelings towards Franklin. She seemed to have got over her initial shock; she was not, thank God, the hysterical type it was so difficult to do anything with.

'You see, Walter was married. He had a wife and family on Mars, and was very fond of them. His wife was a second-generation colonist, the children, of course, third-generation ones. They had spent all their lives under Martian gravity – had been conceived and born in it. And so they could never come to Earth, where they would be crushed under three times their normal weight.

'At the same time, Walter could never go back into space. We could patch up his mind so that he would function efficiently here on Earth, but that was the best we could do. He could never again face free fall, the knowledge that there was space all around him, all the way out to the stars. And so he was an exile in his own world, unable ever to see his family again.

'We did our best for him, and I still think it was a good best. This work here could use his skills, but there were also profound psychological reasons why we thought it might suit him, and would enable him to rebuild his life. I think you probably know those reasons as well as I do, Indra – if not better. You are a marine biologist and know the links we have with the sea. We have no such links with space, and so we shall never feel at home there – at least as long as we are men.

'I studied Franklin while he was here; he knew I was

68

doing it, and didn't mind. All the while he was improving, getting to love the work. Don was very pleased with his progress – he was the best pupil he'd ever met. And when I heard – don't ask me how! – that he was going around with you, I was delighted. For he has to rebuild his life all along the line, you know. I hope you don't mind me putting it this way, but when I found he was spending his spare time with you, and even making time to do it, I knew he had stopped looking back.

'And now – this breakdown. I don't mind admitting that I'm completely in the dark. You say that you were looking up at the Space Station, but that doesn't seem enough cause. Walter had a rather bad fear of heights when he came here, but he'd largely got over that. Besides, he must have seen the station dozens of times in the morning or evening. There must have been some other factor we don't know.'

Dr Myers stopped his rapid delivery, then said gently, as if the thought had only just struck him: 'Tell me, Indra – had you been making love?'

'No,' she said without hesitation or embarrassment. 'There was nothing like that.'

It was a little hard to believe, but he knew it was the truth. He could detect – so clear and unmistakable! – the note of regret in her voice.

'I was wondering if he had any guilt feelings about his wife. Whether he knows it or not, you probably remind him of her, which is why he was attracted to you in the first place. Anyway, *that* line of reasoning isn't enough to explain what happened, so let's forget it.

'All we know is that there was an attack, and a very bad one. Giving him that sedative was the best thing you could have done in the circumstances. You're *quite* sure that he never gave any indication of what he intended to do when you got him back to Heron?'

'Quite sure. All he said was, "Don't tell Dr Myers." He said there was nothing you could do.'

That, thought Myers grimly, might well be true, and he did not like the sound of it. There was only one reason why a man might hide from the only person who could help him. That was because he had decided he was now beyond help.

'But he promised,' Indra continued, 'to see you in the morning.'

Myers did not reply. By this time they both knew that that promise had been nothing more than a ruse.

Indra still clung desperately to one last hope.

'Surely,' she said, her voice quivering as if she did not really believe her own words, 'if he'd intended to do – something drastic – he'd have left a message for somebody.'

Myers looked at her sadly, his mind now completely made up.

'His parents are dead,' he replied. 'He said goodbye to his wife long ago. What mesage was there for him to leave?'

Indra knew, with a sickening certainty, that he spoke the truth. She might well be the only person on Earth for whom Franklin felt any affection. And he made his farewell with her . . .

Reluctantly, Myers rose to his feet.

'There's nothing we can do,' he said, 'except to start a general search. There may be a chance that he's just blowing off steam at full throttle, and will creep in shamefaced some time this morning. It's happened before.'

He patted Indra's bowed shoulders, then helped her out of the chair. 'Don't be too upset, my dear. Everyone will do his best.' But in his heart, he knew it was too late. It had been too late hours before, and they were going through the motions of search and rescue because there were times when no one expected logic to be obeyed.

They walked together to the assistant chief instructor's office, where the C I and Burley were waiting for them. Dr Myers threw open the door – and stood paralysed on the threshold. For a moment he thought that he had two more patients – or that he had gone insane himself. Don and the chief instructor, all distinctions of rank forgotten, had their arms around each other's shoulders and were shaking with hysterical laughter. There was no doubt of the hysteria; it was that of relief. And there was equally no doubt about the laughter.

Dr Myers stared at this improbable scene for perhaps five seconds, then glanced swiftly around the room. At once he saw the message form lying on the floor where one of his temporarily disordered colleagues had dropped it. Without asking their permission, he rushed forward and picked it up.

He had to read it several times before it made any sense; then he, too, began to laugh as he had not done for years.

CHAPTER 9

CAPTAIN BERT DARRYL was looking forward to a quiet trip; if there was any justice in this world, he was certainly due for one. Last time there had been that awkward affair with the cops at Mackay; the time before there had been that uncharted rock off Lizard Island; and before *that*, by crikey, there'd been that trigger-happy young fool who had used a nondetachable harpoon on a fifteen-foot tiger and had been towed all over the sea bed.

As far as one could tell by appearances, his customers seemed a reasonable lot this time. Of course, the Sports Agency always guaranteed their reliability as well as their credit – but all the same it was surprising what he sometimes got saddled with. Still, a man had to earn a living, and it cost a lot to keep this old bucket waterproof.

By an odd coincidence, his customers always had the same names – Mr Jones, Mr Robinson, Mr Brown, Mr Smith. Captain Bert thought it was a crazy idea, but that was just another of the agency's little ways. It certainly made life interesting, trying to figure out who they really were. Some of them were so cautious that they wore rubber face masks the whole trip – yes, even under their diving masks. They would be the important boys who were scared of being recognized. Think of the scandal, for instance, if a supreme court judge or chief secretary of the Space Department was found poaching on a World Food reservation! Captain Bert thought of it, and chuckled.

The little five-berth sports cruiser was still forty miles off the outer edge of the reef, feeling her way in from the Pacific. Of course, it was risky operating so near the Capricorns, right in enemy territory as it were. But the biggest fish were here, just because they were the best protected. You had to take a chance if you wanted to keep your clients satisfied ...

Captain Bert had worked out his tactics carefully, as he always did. There were never any patrols out at night, and even if there were, his long-range sonar would spot them and he could run for it. So it would be perfectly safe creeping up during darkness, getting into position just before dawn, and pushing his eager beavers out of the air lock as soon as the sun came up. He would lie doggo on the bottom, keeping in touch through the radios. If they got out of range, they'd still have his low-powered sonar beacon to home on. And if they got too far away to pick up *that*, serve 'em jolly well right. He patted his jacket where the four blood chits reposed safely, absolving him of all responsibility if anything happened to Messrs. Smith, Jones, Robinson, or Brown. There were times when he wondered if it was really any use, considering these weren't their real names, but the agency told him not to worry. Captain Bert was not the worrying type, or he would have given up this job long ago.

At the moment, Messrs. S, J, R, and B were lying on their respective couches, putting the final touches to the equipment they would not need until morning. Smith and Jones had brand-new guns that had obviously never been fired before, and their webbing was fitted with every conceivable underwater gadget. Captain Bert looked at them sardonically; they represented a type he knew very well. They were the boys who were so keen on their equipment that they never did any shooting, either with the guns or their cameras. They would wander happily around the reef, making such a noise that every fish within miles would know exactly what they were up to. Their beautiful guns, which could drill a thousand-pound shark at fifty feet, would probably never be fired. But they wouldn't really mind; they would enjoy themselves.

Now Robinson was a very different matter. His gun was slightly dented, and about five years old. It had seen service, and he obviously knew how to handle it. He was not one of those catalogue-obsessed sportsmen who had to buy the current year's model as soon as it came out, like a woman who couldn't bear to be behind the fashion. Mr Robinson, Captain Bert decided, would be the one who would bring back the biggest catch.

As for Brown – Robinson's partner – he was the only one that Captain Bert hadn't been able to classify. A well-built, strong-featured man in the forties, he was the oldest of the hunters and his face was vaguely familiar. He was probably some official in the upper echelons of the state, who had felt the need to sow a few wild oats. Captain Bert, who was constitutionally unable to work for the World State or any other employer, could understand just how he felt.

There were more than a thousand feet of water below them, and the reef was still miles ahead. But one never took anything for granted in this business, and Captain Bert's eyes were seldom far from the dials and screens of the control board, even while he watched his little crew preparing for their morning's fun. The clear and tiny echo had barely appeared on the sonar scanner before he had fastened on to it.

'Big shark coming, boys,' he announced jovially. There was a general rush to the screen.

'How do you know it's a shark?' someone asked.

'Pretty sure to be. Couldn't be a whale – they can't leave the channel inside the reef.'

'Sure it's not a sub?' said one anxious voice.

'Naow. Look at the size of it. A sub would be ten times as bright on the screen. Don't be a nervous Nelly.'

The questioner subsided, duly abashed. No one said anything for the next five minutes, as the distant echo closed in towards the centre of the screen.

'It'll pass within a quarter of a mile of us,' said Mr Smith. 'What about changing course and seeing if we can make contact?'

'Not a hope. He'll run for it as soon as he picks up our motors. If we stopped still he might come and sniff us over. Anyway, what would be the use? You couldn't get at him. It's night and he's well below the depth where you could operate.'

Their attention was momentarily distracted by a large school of fish – probably tuna, the captain said – which appeared on the southern sector of the screen. When that had gone past, the distinguished-looking Mr Brown said thoughtfully: 'Surely a shark would have changed course by now.'

Captain Bert thought so too, and was beginning to be puzzled. 'Think we'll have a look at it,' he said. 'Won't do any harm.'

He altered course imperceptibly; the strange echo continued on its unvarying way. It was moving quite slowly, and there would be no difficulty in getting within visual distance without risk of collision. At the point of nearest approach, Captain Bert switched on the camera and the UV searchlight – and gulped.

'We're rumbled, boys. It's a cop.'

There were four simultaneous gasps of dismay, then a chorus of 'But you told us . . .' which the captain silenced with a few well-chosen words while he continued to study the screen.

'Something funny here,' he said. 'I was right first time. That's no sub – it's only a torp. So it can't detect us, anyway – they don't carry that kind of gear. But what the hell's it doing out here at night.'

'Let's run for it!' pleaded several anxious voices.

'Shurrup!' shouted Captain Bert. 'Let me think.' He glanced at the depth indicator. 'Crikey,' he muttered, this time in a much more subdued voice. 'We're a hundred fathoms down. Unless that lad's breathing some fancy mixture, he's had it.'

He peered closely at the image on the TV screen; it was hard to be certain, but the figure strapped to the slowly moving torp seemed abnormally still. Yes – there was no doubt of it; he could tell from the attitude of the head. The pilot was certainly unconscious, probably dead.

'This is a bloody nuisance,' announced the skipper, 'but there's nothing else to do. We've got to fetch that guy in.'

Someone started to protest, then thought better of it. Captain Bert was right, of course. The later consequences would have to be dealt with as they arose.

'But how are you going to do it?' asked Smith. 'We can't go outside at this depth.'

'It won't be easy,' admitted the captain. 'It's lucky he's moving so slowly. I think I can flip him over.'

He nosed in towards the torp, making infinitely delicate

adjustments with the controls. Suddenly there was a clang that made everybody jump except the skipper, who knew when it was coming and exactly how loud it would be.

He backed away, and breathed a sigh of relief.

'Made it first time!' he said smugly. The torp had rolled over on its back, with the helpless figure of its rider now dangling beneath it in his harness. But instead of heading down into the depths, it was now climbing towards the distant surface.

They followed it up to the two-hundred-foot mark while Captain Bert gave his detailed instructions. There was still a chance, he told his passengers, that the pilot might be alive. But if he reached the surface, he'd certainly be dead – compression sickness would get him as he dropped from ten atmospheres to one.

'So we've got to haul him in around the hundred-and-fifty-foot level – no higher – and then start staging him in the air lock. Well, who's going to do it? *I* can't leave the controls.'

No one doubted that the captain was giving the single and sufficient reason, and that he would have gone outside without hesitation had there been anyone else aboard who could operate the sub. After a short pause, Smith said: 'I've been three hundred feet down on normal air.'

'So have I,' interjected Jones. 'Not at night, of course,' he added thoughtfully.

They weren't exactly volunteering, but it would do. They listened to the skipper's instructions like men about to go over the top, then put on their equipment and went reluctantly into the air lock.

Fortunately, they were in good training and he was able to bring them up to the full pressure in a couple of minutes. 'OK, boys,' he said. 'I'm opening the door – here you go!'

It would have helped them could they have seen his searchlight, but it had been carefully filtered to remove all visible light. Their hand torches were feeble glow-worms by comparison, as he watched them moving across to the still-ascending torp. Jones went first, while Smith played out the line from the air lock. Both vessels were moving faster than a man could swim, and it was necessary to play Jones like a fish on a line so that as he trailed behind the sub he could work his way across to the torpedo. He was probably not enjoying it, thought the skipper, but he managed to reach the torp on the second try.

After that, the rest was straightforward. Jones cut out the torp's motor, and when the two vessels had come to a halt Smith went to help him. They unstrapped the pilot and carried him back to the sub; his face mask was unflooded, so there was still hope for him. It was not easy to manhandle his helpless body into the tiny air lock, and Smith had to stay outside, feeling horribly lonely, while his partner went ahead.

And thus it was that, thirty minutes later, Walter Franklin woke in a surprising but not totally unfamiliar environment. He was lying in a bunk aboard a small cruiser-class sub, and five men were standing around him. Oddest of all, four of the men had handkerchiefs tied over their faces so that he could only see their eyes . . .

He looked at the fifth man – at his scarred and grizzled countenance and his rakish goatee. The dirty nautical cap was really quite superfluous; no one would have doubted that this was the skipper.

A raging heachache made it hard for Franklin to think straight. He had to make several attempts before he could get out the words: 'Where am I?'

'Never you mind, mate,' replied the bearded character. 'What *we* want to know is what the hell were you doing at a hundred fathoms with a standard compressed-air set. Crikey, he's fainted again!'

The second time Franklin revived, he felt a good deal better, and sufficiently interested in life to want to know what was going on around him. He supposed he should be grateful to these people, whoever they were, but at the moment he felt neither relief nor disappointment at having been rescued.

'What's all this for?' he said, pointing to the conspiratorial handkerchiefs. The skipper, who was now sitting at the controls, turned his head and answered laconically: 'Haven't you worked out where you are yet?'

'No.'

'Mean ter say you don't know who I am?'

'Sorry – I don't.'

76

There was a grunt that might have signified disbelief or disappointment.

'Guess you must be one of the new boys. I'm Bert Darryl, and you're on board the *Sea Lion*. Those two gentlemen behind you risked their necks getting you in.'

Franklin turned in the direction indicated, and looked at the blank triangles of linen.

'Thanks,' he said, and then stopped, unable to think of any further comment. Now he knew where he was, and could guess what had happened.

So this was the famous – or notorious, depending on the point of view – Captain Darryl, whose advertisements you saw in all the sporting and marine journals. Captain Darryl, the organizer of thrilling underwater safaris; the intrepid and skilful hunter – and the equally intrepid and skilful poacher, whose immunity from prosecution had long been a source of cynical comment among the wardens. Captain Darryl – one of the few genuine adventurers of this regimented age, according to some. Captain Darryl, the big phony, according to others . . .

Franklin now understood why the rest of the crew was masked. This was one of the captain's less legitimate enterprises, and Franklin had heard that on these occasions his customers were often from the very highest ranks of society. No one else could afford to pay his fees; it must cost a lot to run the *Sea Lion*, even though Captain Darryl was reputed never to pay cash for anything and to owe money at every port between Sydney and Darwin.

Franklin glanced at the anonymous figures around him, wondering who they might be and whether he knew any of them. Only a half-hearted effort had been made to hide the powerful big-game guns piled on the other bunk. Just where was the captain taking his customers, and what were they after? In the circumstances, he had better keep his eyes shut and learn as little as possible.

Captain Darryl had already come to the same conclusion.

'You realize, mate,' he said over his shoulder as he carefully blocked Franklin's view of the course settings, 'that your presence aboard is just a little bit embarrassing. Still, we couldn't let you drown, even though you deserved it for a silly stunt like that. The point is – what are we going to do with you now?'

'You could put me ashore on Heron. We can't be very far away.' Franklin smiled as he spoke, to show how seriously he intended the suggestion to be taken. It was strange how cheerful and lighthearted he now felt; perhaps it was a merely physical reaction – and perhaps he was really glad at having been given a second chance, a new lease on life.

'What a hope!' snorted the captain. 'These gentlemen have paid for their day's sport, and they don't want you boy scouts spoiling it.'

'They can take off those handkerchiefs, anyway. They don't look very comfortable – and if I recognize someone, I won't give him away.'

Rather reluctantly, the disguises were removed. As he had expected – and hoped – there was no one here whom he knew, either from photographs or direct contact.

'Only one thing for it,' said the captain. 'We'll have to dump you somewhere before we go into action.' He scratched his head as he reviewed his marvellously detailed mental image of the Capricorn Group then came to a decision. 'Anyway, we're stuck with you for tonight, and I guess we'll have to sleep in shifts. If you'd like to make yourself useful, you can get to work in the galley.'

'Aye, aye, sir,' said Franklin.

The dawn was just breaking when he hit the sandy beach, staggered to his feet, and removed his flippers. ('They're my second-best pair, so mind you post them back to me,' Captain Bert had said as he pushed him through the air lock.) Out there beyond the reef, the *Sea Lion* was departing on her dubious business, and the hunters were getting ready for their sortie. Though it was against his principles and his duties, Franklin could not help wishing them luck.

Captain Bert had promised to radio Brisbane in four hours' time, and the message would be passed on to Heron Island immediately. Presumably that four hours would give the captain and his clients the time they needed to make their assault and to get clear of WFO waters.

Franklin walked up the beach, stripped off his wet equipment and clothes, and lay down to watch the sunrise he had never dreamed he would see. He had four hours to wait to wrestle with his thoughts and to face life once more. But he did not need the time, for he had made the decision hours ago.

His life was no longer his to throw away if he chose; not when it had beeen given back to him, at the risk of their own, by men he had never met before and would never see again.

CHAPTER 10

'YOU REALIZE, of course,' said Myers, 'that I'm only the station doctor, not a high-powered psychiatrist. So I'll have to send you back to Professor Stevens and his merry men.'

'Is that really necessary?' asked Franklin.

'I don't think it is, but I can't accept the responsibility. If I was a gambler like Don, I'd take very long odds that you'll never play this trick again. But doctors can't afford to gamble, and anyway I think it would be a good idea to get you off Heron for a few days.'

'I'll finish the course in a couple of weeks. Can't it wait until then?'

'Don't argue with doctors, Walt – you can't win. And if my arithmetic is correct, a month and a half is *not* a couple of weeks. The course can wait for a few days; I don't think Prof Stevens will keep you very long. He'll probably give you a good dressing-down and will send you straight back. Meanwhile, if you're interested in my views, I'd like to get 'em off my chest.'

'Go ahead.'

'First of all, we know *why* you had that attack when you did. Smell is the most evocative of all the senses, and now that you've told me that a spaceship air lock always smells of synthene the whole business makes sense. It was hard luck that you got a whiff of the stuff just when you were looking at the Space Station: the damn thing's nearly hypnotized me sometimes when I've watched it scuttling across the sky like some mad meteor.

'But that isn't the whole explanation, Walter. You had to be, let's say, emotionally sensitized to make you susceptible. Tell me – have you got a photograph of your wife here?'

Franklin seemed more puzzled than disturbed by the unexpected, indeed apparently incongruous, question.

'Yes,' he said. 'Why do you ask?'

'Never mind. May I have a look at it?'

After a good deal of searching, which Myers was quite sure was unnecessary, Franklin produced a leather wallet and handed it over. He did not look at Myers as the doctor studied the woman who was now parted from her husband by laws more inviolable than any that man could make.

She was small and dark, with lustrous brown eyes. A single glance told Myers all that he wanted to know, yet he continued to gaze at the photograph with an unanalysable mixture of compassion and curiosity. How, he wondered, was Franklin's wife meeting her problem? Was she, too, rebuilding her life on that far world to which she was forever bound by genetics and gravity? No, forever was not quite accurate. She could safely journey to the Moon, which had only the gravity of her native world. But there would be no purpose in doing so, for Franklin could never face even the trifling voyage from Earth to Moon.

With a sigh, Dr Myers closed the wallet. Even in the most perfect of social systems, the most peaceful and contented of worlds, there would still be heartbreak and tragedy. And as man extended his powers over the universe, he would inevitably create new evils and new problems to plague him. Yet, apart from its details, there was nothing really novel about this case. All down the ages, men had been separated – often forever – from those they loved by the accident of geography or the malice of their fellows.

'Listen, Walt,' said Myers as he handed back the wallet. 'I know a few things about you that even Prof Stevens doesn't, so here's my contribution.

'Whether you realize it consciously or not, Indra is like your wife. That, of course, is why you were attracted to her in the first place. At the same time, that attraction has set up a conflict in your mind. You don't want to be unfaithful even to someone – please excuse me for speaking so bluntly –

who might as well be dead as far as you are concerned. Well – do you agree with my analysis?'

Franklin took a long time to answer. Then he said at last: 'I think there may be something in that. But what am I to do?'

'This may sound cynical, but there is an old saying which applies in this case. "Cooperate with the inevitable." Once you admit that certain aspects of your life are fixed and have to be accepted, you will stop fighting against them. It won't be a surrender; it will give you the energy you need for the battles that still have to be won.'

'What does Indra really think about me?'

'The silly girl's in love with you, if that's what you want to know. So the least you can do is to make it up to her for all the trouble you've caused.'

'Then do you think I should marry again?'

'The fact that you can ask that question is a good sign, but I can't answer it with a simple "yes" or "no". We've done our best to rebuild your professional life; we can't give you so much help with your emotional one. Obviously, it's highly desirable for you to establish a firm and stable relationship to replace the one you have lost. As for Indra – well, she's a charming and intelligent girl, but no one can say how much of her present feelings are due to sympathy. So don't rush matters; let them take their time. You can't afford to make any mistakes.

'Well, that finishes the sermon – except for one item. Part of the trouble with you, Walter Franklin, is that you've always been too independent and self-reliant. You refused to admit that you had limitations, that you needed help from anyone else. So when you came up against something that was too big for you, you really went to pieces, and you've been hating yourself for it ever since.

'Now that's all over and done with; even if the old Walt Franklin was a bit of a stinker, we can make a better job of the Mark II. Don't you agree?'

Franklin gave a wry smile; he felt emotionally exhausted, yet at the same time most of the remaining shadows had lifted from his mind. Hard though it had been for him to accept help, he had surrendered at last and he felt better for it.

'Thanks for the treatment, Doc,' he said. 'I don't believe the specialists could do any better, and I'm quite sure now that this trip back to Prof Stevens isn't necessary.'

'So am I – but you're going just the same. Now clear out and let me get on with my proper work of putting sticking plaster on coral cuts.'

Franklin was halfway through the door when he paused with a sudden, anxious query.

'I almost forgot – Don particularly wants to take me out tomorrow in the sub. Will that be OK?'

'Oh, sure – Don's big enough to look after you. Just get back in time for the noon plane, that's all I ask.'

As Franklin walked away from the office and two rooms grandly called 'Medical Centre' he felt no resentment at having been ordered off the island. He had received far more tolerance and consideration than he had expected – perhaps more than he deserved. All the mild hostility that had been focused upon him by the less-privileged trainees had vanished at a stroke, but it would be best for him to escape for a few days from an atmosphere that had become embarrassingly sympathetic. In particular, he found it hard to talk without a sense of strain with Don and Indra.

He thought again of Dr Myers' advice, and remembered the jolting leap his heart had given at the words 'The silly girl's in love with you.' Yet it would be unfair, he knew, to take advantage of the present emotional situation; they could only know what they meant to each other when they had both had time for careful and mature thought. Put that way, it seemed a little cold-blooded and calculating. If one was really in love, did one stop to weigh the pros and cons?

He knew the answer to that. As Myers had said, he could not afford any more mistakes. It was far better to take his time and be certain than to risk the happiness of two lives.

The sun had barely lifted above the miles of reef extending to the east when Don Burley hauled Franklin out of bed. Don's attitude towards him had undergone a change which it was not easy to define. He had been shocked and distressed by what had occurred and had tried, in his somewhat boisterous manner, to express sympathy and understanding. At the same time, his *amour-propre* had been hurt; he could not quite believe, even now, that Indra had never been seriously interested in him but only in Franklin, whom he had never thought of as a rival. It was not that he was jealous of Franklin; jealousy was an emotion beyond him. He was worried – as most men are occasionally throughout their lives – by his discovery that he did not understand women as well as he had believed.

Franklin had already packed, and his room looked bleak and bare. Even though he might be gone for only a few days, the accommodation was needed too badly for it to be left vacant just to suit his convenience. It served him right, he told himself philosophically.

Don was in a hurry, which was not unusual, but there was also a conspiratorial air about him, as if he had planned some big surprise for Franklin and was almost childishly anxious that everything should come off as intended. In any other circumstances, Franklin would have suspected some practical joke, but that could hardly be the explanation now.

By this time, the little training sub had become practically an extension of his own body, and he followed the courses Don gave him until he knew, by mental dead reckoning, that they were somewhere out in the thirty mile-wide channel between Wistari Reef and the mainland. For some reason of his own, which he refused to explain, Don had switched off the pilot's main sonar screen, so that Franklin was navigating blind. Don himself could see everything that was in the vicinity by looking at the repeater set at the rear of the cabin, and though Franklin was occasionally tempted to glance back at it he managed to resist the impulse. This was, after all, a legitimate part of his training; one day he might have to navigate a sub that had been blinded by a break-down of its underwater senses.

'You can surface now,' said Don at last. He was trying to be casual, but the undercurrent of excitement in his voice could not be concealed. Franklin blew the tanks, and even without looking at the depth gauge knew when he broke surface by the unmistakable rolling of the sub. It was not a comfortable sensation, and he hoped that they would not stay here for long.

Don gave one more glance at his private sonar screen, then gestured to the hatch overhead.

'Open up,' he said. 'Let's have a look at the scenery.'

'We may ship some water,' protested Franklin. 'It feels pretty rough.'

'With the two of us in that hatch, not much is going to leak past. Here – put on this cape. That'll keep the spray out of the works.'

It seemed a crazy idea, but Don must have a good reason. Overhead, a tiny elliptical patch of sky appeared as the outer seal of the conning tower opened. Don scrambled up the ladder first; then Franklin followed, blinking his eyes against the wind-swept spray.

Yes, Don had known what he was doing. There was little wonder that he had been so anxious to make this trip before Franklin left the island. In his own way, Don was a good psychologist, and Franklin felt an inexpressible gratitude towards him. For this was one of the great moments of his life; he could think of only one other to match it: the moment when he had first seen Earth, in all its heart-stopping beauty, floating against the infinitely distant background of the stars. This scene, also, filled his soul with the same awe, the same sense of being in the presence of cosmic forces.

The whales were moving north, and he was among them. During the night, the leaders must have passed through the Queensland Gate, on the way to the warm seas in which their young could be safely born. A living armada was all around him, ploughing steadfastly through the waves with effortless power. The great dark bodies emerged streaming from the water, then sank with scarcely a ripple back into the sea. As Franklin watched, too fascinated to feel any sense of danger, one of the enormous beasts surfaced less than forty feet away. There was a roaring whistle of air as it emptied its lungs, and he caught a mercifully weakened breath of the fetid air. A ridiculously tiny eye stared at him – an eye that seemed lost in the monstrous, misshapen head. For a moment the two mammals – the biped who had abandoned the sea, the quadruped who had returned to it – regarded each other across the evolutionary gulf that separated them. What did a man look like to a whale? Franklin asked himself, and wondered if there was any way of finding the answer. Then the titanic bulk tilted down into the sea, the great flukes lifted themselves into the air, and the waters flowed back to fill the sudden void.

A distant clap of thunder made him look towards the mainland. Half a mile away, the giants were playing. As he watched, a shape so strange that it was hard to relate it to any of the films and pictures he had seen emerged from the waves with breath-taking slowness, and hung poised for a moment completely out of the water. As a ballet dancer seems at the climax of his leap to defy gravity, so for an instant the whale appeared to hang upon the horizon. Then, with that same unhurried grace, it tumbled back into the sea, and seconds later the crash of the impact came echoing over the waves.

The sheer slowness of that huge leap gave it a dreamlike quality, as if the sense of time had been distorted. Nothing else conveyed so clearly to Franklin the immense size of the beasts that now surrounded him like moving islands. Rather belatedly, he wondered what would happen if one of the whales surfaced beneath the sub, or decided to take too close an interest in it ...

'No need to worry,' Don reassured him. 'They know who we are. Sometimes they'll come and rub against us to remove parasites, and then it gets a bit uncomfortable. As for bumping into us accidentally – they can see where they're going a good deal better than we can.'

As if to refute this statement, a streamlined mountain emerged dripping from the sea and showered water down upon them. The sub rocked crazily, and for a moment Franklin feared it was going to overturn; then it righted itself and he realized that he could, quite literally, reach out and touch the barnacle-encrusted head now lying on the waves. The weirdly shaped mouth opened in a prodigious yawn, the hundreds of strips of whalebone fluttering like a Venetian blind in a breeze.

Had he been alone, Franklin would have been scared stiff, but Don seemed the complete master of the situation. He leaned out of the hatch and yelled in the direction of the whale's invisible ear: 'Move over momma! We're not your baby!'

. The great mouth with its hanging draperies of bone snapped shut, the beady little eye – strangely like a cow's and seemingly not much larger – looked at them with what might have been a hurt expression. Then the sub rocked once more, and the whale was gone.

'It's quite safe, you see,' Don explained. 'They're peaceful, good-natured beasts, except when they have their calves with them. Just like any other cattle.'

'But would you get this close to any of the toothed whales – the sperm whale, for instance?'

'That depends. If it was an old rogue male – a real Moby Dick – I wouldn't care to try it. Same with killer whales; they might think I was good eating, though I could scare them off easily enough by turning on the hooter. I once got into a harem of about a dozen sperm whales, and the ladies didn't seem to mind, even though some of them had calves with them. Nor did the old man, oddly enough. I suppose he knew I wasn't a rival.' He paused thoughtfully, then continued. 'That was the only time I've actually seen whales mating. It was pretty awe-inspiring – gave me such an inferiority complex it put me off my stroke for a week.'

'How many would you say there are in this school?' asked Franklin.

'Oh, about a hundred. The recorders at the gate will give the exact figure. So you can say there are at least five thousand tons of the best meal and oil swimming around us – a couple of million dollars, if it's worth a penny. Doesn't all that cash make you feel good?'

'No,' said Franklin. 'And I'm damn sure it doesn't make any difference to you. Now I know why you like this job, and there's no need to put on an act about it.'

Don made no attempt to answer. They stood together in the cramped hatchway, not feeling the spray upon their faces, sharing the same thoughts and emotions, as the mightiest animals the world had ever seen drove purposefully past them to the north. It was then that Franklin knew, with a final certainty, that his life was firmly set upon its new course. Though much had been taken from him which he would never cease to regret, he had passed the stage of futile grief and solitary brooding. He had lost the freedom of space, but he had won the freedom of the seas.

That was enough for any man.

CHAPTER 11

ATTACHED IS the medical report on Walter Franklin, who has now successfully completed his training and has qualified as third warden with the highest rating ever recorded. In view of certain complaints from senior members of Establishment and Personnel Branch that earlier reports were too technical for comprehension, I am giving this summary in language understandable even to administrative officers.

Despite a number of personality defects, WF's capability rating places him in that small group from which future heads of technical departments must be drawn – a group so desperately small that, as I have frequently pointed out, the very existence of the state is threatened unless we can enlarge it. The accident which eliminated WF from the Space Service, in which he would have undoubtedly had a distinguished career, left him in full possession of all his talents and presented us with an opportunity which it would have been criminal to waste. Not only did it give us a chance of studying what has since become the classic textbook case of astrophobia, but it offered us a striking challenge in rehabilitation. The analogies between sea and space have often been pointed out, and a man used to one can readily adapt to the other. In this case, however, the differences between the two media were equally important; at the simplest level, the fact that the sea is a continuous and sustaining fluid, in which vision is always limited to no more than a few yards, gave WF the sense of security he had lost in space.

The fact that, towards the end of his training, he attempted suicide may at first appear to argue against the correctness of our treatment. This is not the case; the attempt was due to a combination of quite unforeseeable factors (Paragraphs 57–86 of attached report), and its outcome, as often happens, was on improvement in the stability of the subject. The method chosen for the attempt is also highly significant in itself and proves that we had made a correct choice of WF's new vocation. The seriousness of the attempt may also be questioned; had WF been really determined to kill himself, he would have chosen a simpler and less fallible method of doing so.

Now that the subject has re-established – apparently successfully – his emotional life and has shown only trivial symptoms of disturbance, I am confident that we need expect no more trouble. Above all, it is important that we interfere with him as little as possible. His independence and originality of mind, though no longer as exaggerated as they were, are a fundamental part of his personality and will largely determine his future progress.

Only time will show whether all the skill and effort lavished on this case will be repaid in cents and dollars. Even if it is not, those engaged upon it have already received their reward in the rebuilding of a life, which will certainly be useful and may be invaluable.

Ian K. Stevens
Director, Division of Applied Psychiatry,
World Health Organization

PART TWO

The Warden

CHAPTER 12

SECOND WARDEN WALTER FRANKLIN was having his monthly shave when the emergency call came through. It had always seemed a little surprising to him that, after so many years of research, the biochemists had not yet found an inhibitor that would put one's bristles permanently out of action. Still, one should not be ungrateful; only a couple of generations ago, incredible though it seemed, men had been forced to shave themselves every day, using a variety of complicated, expensive, and sometimes lethal instruments.

Franklin did not stop to wipe the layer of cream from his face when he heard the shrill whining of the communicator alarm. He was out of the bathroom, through the kitchen, and into the hall before the sound had died away and the instrument had been able to get its second breath. As he punched the Receive button, the screen lighted up and he was looking into the familiar but now harassed face of the Headquarters operator.

'You're to report for duty at once, Mr Franklin,' she said breathlessly.

'What's the trouble?'

'It's Farms, sir. The fence is down somewhere and one of the herds has broken through. It's eating the spring crop, and we've got to get it out as quickly as we can.'

'Oh, is that all?' said Franklin. 'I'll be over at the dock in ten minutes.'

It was an emergency all right, but not one about which he could feel very excited. Of course, Farms would be yelling its head off as its production quota was being whittled down by thousands of half-ton nibbles. But he was secretly on the side of the whales; if they'd managed to break into the great plankton prairies, then good luck to them.

'What's all the fuss about?' said Indra as she came out of the bedroom, her long, dark hair looking attractive even at this time of the morning as it hung in lustrous tresses over her shoulders. When Franklin told her, she appeared worried.

'It's a bigger emergency than you seem to think,' she said. 'Unless you act quickly, you may have some very sick whales on your hands. The spring overturn was only two weeks ago, and it's the biggest one we've ever had. So your greedy pets will be gorging themselves silly.'

Franklin realized that she was perfectly right. The plankton farms were no affair of his, and formed a completely independent section of the Marine Division. But he knew a great deal about them, since they were an alternative and to some extent rival method of getting food from the sea. The plankton enthusiasts claimed, with a good deal of justice, that crop growing was more efficient than herding, since the whales themselves fed on the plankton and were therefore farther down the food chain. Why waste ten pounds of plankton, they argued, to produce one pound of whale, when you could harvest it directly?

The debate had been in progress for at least twenty years, and so far neither side could claim to have won. Sometimes the argument had been quite acrimonious and had echoed, on an infinitely larger and more sophisticated scale, the rivalry between homesteaders and cattle barons in the days when the American Midwest was being settled. But unfortunately for latter-day mythmakers, competing departments of the Marine Division of the World Food Organization fought each other purely with official minutes and the efficient but unspectacular weapons of bureaucracy. There were no gun fighters prowling the range, and if the fence had gone down it would be due to purely technical troubles, not midnight sabotage . . .

In the sea as on the land, all life depends upon vegetation. And the amount of vegetation in turn depends upon the mineral content of the medium in which it grows – the nitrates, phosphates, and scores of other basic chemicals. In the ocean, there is always a tendency for these vital substances to accumulate in the depths, far below the regions where light penetrates and therefore plants can exist and grow. The upper few hundred feet of the sea is the primary source of its life; everything below that level preys, at second or third hand, on the food formed above.

Every spring, as the warmth of the new year seeps down into the ocean, the waters far below respond to the invisible sun. They expand and rise, lifting to the surface, in untold billions of tons, the salts and minerals they bear. Thus fertilized by food from below and sun from above, the floating plants multiply with explosive violence, and the creatures which browse upon them flourish accordingly. And so spring comes to the meadows of the sea.

This was the cycle that had repeated itself at least a billion times before man appeared on the scene. And now he had changed it. Not content with the upwelling of minerals produced by Nature, he had sunk his atomic generators at strategic spots far down into the sea, where the raw heat they produced would start immense, submerged fountains lifting their chemical treasure towards the fruitful sun. This artificial enhancement of the natural overturn had been one of the most unexpected, as well as the most rewarding, of all the many applications of nuclear energy. By this means alone, the output of food from the sea had been increased by almost ten per cent.

And now the whales were busily doing their best to restore the balance.

The roundup would have to be a combined sea and air operation. There were too few of the subs, and they were far too slow, to do the job unassisted. Three of them – including Franklin's one-man scout – were being flown to the scene of the breakthrough by a cargo plane which would drop them and then cooperate by spotting the movements of the whales from the air, if they had scattered over too large an area for the subs' sonar to pick them up. Two other planes would also try to scare the whales by dropping noise generators near them, but this technique had never worked well in the past and no one really expected much success from it now.

Within twenty minutes of the alarm, Franklin was watching the enormous food-processing plant of Pearl Harbor falling below as the jets of the freighter hauled him up into the sky. Even now, he was still not fond of flying and tried to avoid it when he could. But it no longer worried him, and he could look down on the world beneath without qualms.

A hundred miles east of Hawaii, the sea turned suddenly from blue to gold. The moving fields, rich with the year's first crop, covered the Pacific clear out to the horizon, and showed no sign of ending as the plane raced on towards the rising sun. Here and there the mile-long skimmers of the floating harvesters lay upon the surface like the enigmatic toys of some giant children, while beside them, smaller and more compact, were the pontoons and rafts of the concentration equipment. It was an impressive sight, even in these days of mammoth engineering achievements, but it did not move Franklin. He could not become excited over a billion tons of assorted diatoms and shrimps – not even though he knew that they fed a quarter of the human race.

'Just passing over the Hawaiian Corridor,' said the pilot's voice from the speaker. 'We should see the break in a minute.'

'I can see it now,' said one of the other wardens, leaning past Franklin and pointing out to sea. 'There they are – having the time of their lives.'

It was a spectacle which must be making the poor farmers tear their hair. Franklin suddenly remembered an old nursery rhyme he had not thought of for at least thirty years.

> *Little Boy Blue, come blow your horn,*
> *The sheep's in the meadow, the cow's in the corn.*

There was no doubt that the cows were in the corn, and Little Boy Blue was going to have a busy time getting them out. Far below, myriads of narrow swathes were being carved in the endless yellow sea, as the ravenous, slowly moving mountains ate their way into the rich plankton meadows. A blue line of exposed water marked the track of each whale as it meandered through what must be a cetacean heaven – a heaven from which it was Franklin's job to expel it as promptly as possible.

The three wardens, after a final radio briefing, left the cabin and went down to the hold, where the little subs were already hanging from the davits which would lower them into the sea. There would be no difficulty about this operation; what might not be so easy would be getting them back again, and if the sea became rough they might have to go home under their own power.

It seemed strange to be inside a submarine inside an aeroplane, but Franklin had little time for such thoughts as he

94

went through the routine cockpit drill. Then the speaker on his control panel remarked: 'Hovering at thirty feet; now opening cargo hatches. Stand by, Number One Sub.' Franklin was number two; the great cargo craft was poised so steadily, and the hoists moved down so smoothly that he never felt any impact as the sub dropped into its natural element. Then the three scouts were fanning out along the tracks that had been assigned to them, like mechanized sheep dogs rounding up a flock.

Almost at once, Franklin realized that this operation was not going to be as simple as it looked. The sub was driving through a thick soup that completely eliminated vision and even interfered seriously with sonar. What was still more serious, the hydrojet motors were labouring unhappily as their impellers chewed through the mush. He could not afford to get his propulsion system clogged; the best thing to do would be to dive below the plankton layer and not to surface until it was absolutely necessary.

Three hundred feet down, the water was merely murky and though vision was still impossible he could make good speed. He wondered if the greedily feasting whales above his head knew of his approach and realized that their idyl was coming to an end. On the sonar screen he could see their luminous echoes moving slowly across the ghostly mirror of the air-water surface which his sound beams could not penetrate. It was odd how similar the surface of the sea looked from below both to the naked eye and to the acoustical senses of the sonar.

The characteristically compact little echoes of the two other subs were moving out to the flanks of the scattered herd. Franklin glanced at the chronometer; in less than a minute, the drive was due to begin. He switched on the external microphones and listened to the voices of the sea.

How could anyone have thought that the sea was silent! Even man's limited hearing could detect many of its sounds – the clashing of chitinaus claws, the moan of great boulders made restive by the ocean swell, the high pitched squeak of porpoises, the unmistakable 'flick' of the shark's tail as it suddenly accelerates on a new course. But these were merely the sounds in the audible spectrum; to listen to the full music of the sea one must go both below and above the range of human hearing. This was a simple enough task for the sub's frequency coverters; if he wished, Franklin could tune in to any sounds from almost a million cycles a second down to vibrations as sluggish as the slow opening of an ancient, rusty door.

He set the receiver to the broadest band, and at once his mind began to interpret the multitudinous messages that came pouring into the little cabin from the watery world outside. The man-made noises he dismissed at once; the sounds of his own sub and the more distant whines of his companion vessels were largely eliminated by the special filters designed for that purpose. But he could just detect the distinctive whistles of the three sonar sets – his own almost blanketing the others – and beyond those the faint and far-off BEEP-BEEP-BEEP of the Hawaiian Corridor. The double fence which was supposed to channel the whales safely through the rich sea farm sent out its pulses at five-second intervals, and though the nearest portion of the fence was out of action the more distant parts of the sonic barrier could be clearly heard. The pulses were curiously distorted and drawn-out into a faint continuous echo as each new burst of sound was followed at once by the delayed waves from more and more remote regions of the fence. Franklin could hear each pulse running away into the distance, as sometimes a clap of thunder may be heard racing across the sky.

Against this background, the sounds of the natural world stood out sharp and clear. From all directions, with never a moment's silence, came the shrill shrieks and squealings of the whales as they talked to one another or merely gave vent to their high spirits and enjoyment. Franklin could distinguish between the voices of the males and the females, but he was not one of those experts who could identify individuals and even interpret what they were trying to express.

There is no more eerie sound in all the world than the screaming of a herd of whales, when one moves among it in the depths of the sea. Franklin had only to close his eyes and he could imagine that he was lost in some demon-haunted forest, while ghosts and goblins closed in upon him. Could Hector Berlioz have heard this banshee chorus, he would have known that Nature had already anticipated his 'Dream of the Witches' Sabbath'.

But weirdness lies only in unfamiliarity, and this sound was now part of Franklin's life. It no longer gave him nightmares, as it had sometimes done in his early days. Indeed, the main emotion that it now inspired in him was an affectionate amusement, together with a slight surprise that such enormous animals produced such falsetto screams.

Yet there was a memory that the sound of the sea sometimes evoked. It no longer had power to hurt him, though it could still fill his heart with a wistful sadness. He remembered all the times he had spent in the signals rooms of space ships or space stations, listening to the radio waves coming in as the monitors combed the spectrum in their automatic search. Sometimes there had been, like these same ghostly voices calling in the night, the sound of distant ships or beacons, or the torrents of high-speed code as the colonies talked with Mother Earth. And always one could hear a perpetual murmuring background to man's feeble transmitters, the endless susurration of the stars and galaxies themselves as they drenched the whole universe with radiation.

The chronometer hand came around to zero. It had not scythed away the first second before the sea erupted in a hellish cacophony of sound – a rising and falling ululation that made Franklin reach swiftly for the volume control. The sonic mines had been dropped, and he felt sorry for any whales who were unlucky enough to be near them. Almost at once the pattern of echoes on the screen began to change, as the terrified beasts started to flee in panic towards the west. Franklin watched closely, preparing to head off any part of the herd that looked like it would miss the gap in the fence and turn back into the farms.

The noise generators must have been improved, he decided, since the last time this trick had been tried – or else these whales were more amenable. Only a few stragglers tried to break away, and it was no more than ten minutes' work to round them up on the right path and scare them back with the subs' own sirens. Half an hour after the mines had been dropped the entire herd had been funnelled back through the invisible gap in the fence, and was milling around inside the narrow corridor. There was nothing for the subs to do but to stand by until the engineers had carried out their repairs and the curtain of sound was once more complete.

No one could claim that it was a famous victory. It was just another day's work, a minor battle in an endless campaign. Already the excitement of the chase had died away, and Franklin was wondering how long it would be before the freighter could hoist them out of the ocean and fly them back to Hawaii. This was, after all, supposed to be his day off, and he had promised to take Peter down to Waikiki and start teaching him how to swim.

Even when he is merely standing by, a good warden never lets his attention stray for long from his sonar screen. Every three minutes, without any conscious thought, Franklin switched to the long-range scan and tilted the transmitter down towards the sea bed, just to keep track of what was going on around him. He did not doubt that his colleagues were doing exactly the same, between wondering how long it would be before they were relieved . . .

At the very limit of his range, ten miles away and almost two miles down, a faint echo had crawled on to the edge of the screen. Franklin looked at it with mild interest; then his brows knit in perplexity. It must be an unusually large object to be visible at such a distance – something quite as large as a whale. But no whale could be swimming at such a depth; though sperm whales had been encountered almost a mile down, this was beyond the limits at which they could operate, fabulous divers though they were. A deep-sea shark? Possibly, thought Franklin; it would do no harm to have a closer look at it.

He locked the scanner on to the distant echo and expanded the image as far as the screen magnification would allow. It was too far away to make out any detail, but he could see now that he was looking at a long, thin object – and that it was moving quite rapidly. He stared at it for a moment, then called his colleagues. Unnecessary chatter was discouraged on operations, but here was a minor mystery that intrigued him.

'Sub Two calling,' he said. 'I've a large echo bearing 185 degrees, range 9.7 miles, depth 1.8 miles. Looks like another sub. You know if anyone else is operating around here?'

'Sub One calling Sub Two,' came the first reply. 'That's outside my range. Could be a Research Department sub down there. How big would you say your echo is?'

'About a hundred feet long. Maybe more. It's doing over ten knots.'

'Sub Three calling. There's no research vessel around here. The *Nautilus IV* is laid up for repairs, and the *Cousteau*'s in the Atlantic. Must be a fish you've got hold of.'

'There aren't any fish this size. Have I permission to go after it? I think we ought to check up.'

'Permission granted,' answered Sub One. 'We'll hold the gap here. Keep in touch.'

Franklin swung the sub around to the south, and brought the little vessel up to maximum speed with a smooth rush of power. The echo he was chasing was already too deep for him to reach, but there was always the chance that it might come back to the surface. Even if it did not, he would be able to get a much clearer image when he had shortened his range.

He had travelled only two miles when he saw that the chase was hopeless. There could be no doubt; his quarry had detected either the vibrations of his motor or his sonar and was plunging at full speed straight down to the bottom. He managed to get within four miles, and then the signal was lost in the confused maze of echoes from the ocean bed. His last glimpse of it confirmed his earlier impression of great length and relative thinness, but he was still unable to make out any details of its structure.

'So it got away from you,' said Sub One. 'I thought it would.'

'Then you know what it was?'

'No – nor does anyone else. And if you'll take my advice, you won't talk to any reporters about it. If you do, you'll never live it down.'

Momentarily frozen with astonishment, Franklin stared at the little loudspeaker from which the words had just come. So they had not been pulling his leg, as he had always assumed. He remembered some of the tales he had heard in the bar at Heron Island and wherever wardens gathered together after duty. He had laughed at them then, but now he knew that the tales were true.

That nervous echo skittering hastily out of range had been nothing less than the Great Sea Serpent.

Indra, who was still doing part-time work at the Hawaii Aquarium when her household duties permitted, was not as impressed as her husband had expected. In fact, her first comment was somewhat deflating.

'Yes, but *which* sea serpent? You know there are at least three totally different types.'

'I certainly didn't.'

'Well, first of all there's a giant eel which has been seen on three or four occasions but never properly identified, though its larvae were caught back in the 1940's. It's known to grow up to sixty feet long, and that's enough of a sea serpent for most people. But the really spectacular one is the oarfish – *Regalecus glesne*. That's got a face like a horse, a crest of brilliant red quills like an Indian brave's headdress – and a snakelike body which may be seventy feet long. Since we know that these things exist, how do you expect us to be surprised at anything the sea can produce?'

'What about the third type you mentioned?'

'That's the one we haven't identified or even described. We just call it "X" because people still laugh when you talk about sea serpents. The only thing that we know about it is that it undoubtedly exists, that it's extremely sly, and that it lives in deep water. One day we'll catch it, but when we do it will probably be through pure luck.'

Franklin was very thoughtful for the rest of the evening. He did not like to admit that, despite all the instruments that man now used to probe the sea, despite his own continual patrolling of the depths, the ocean still held many secrets and would retain them for ages yet to come. And he knew that, though he might never see it again, he would be haunted all his life by the memory of that distant, tantalizing echo as it descended swiftly into the abyss that was its home.

CHAPTER 13

THERE ARE many misconceptions about the glamour of a warden's life. Franklin had never shared them, so he was neither surprised nor disappointed that so much of his time was spent on long, uneventful patrols far out at sea. Indeed, he welcomed them. They gave him time to think, yet not time to brood – and it was on these lonely missions in the living heart of the sea that his last fears were shed and his mental scars finally healed.

The warden's year was dominated by the pattern of the whale migration, but that pattern was itself continually changing as new areas of the sea were fenced and fertilized. He might spend summer moving cautiously through the ice, and winter beating back and forth across the equator. Sometimes he would operate from shore stations, sometimes from mobile bases like the *Rorqual,* the *Pequod,* or the *Cachelot.* One season he might be wholly concerned with the great whalebone or baleen whales, who literally strained their food from the sea as they swam, mouth open, through the rich plankton soup. And another season he would have to deal with their very different cousins, the fierce, toothed cetaceans of whom the sperm whales were the most important representatives. These were no gentle herbivores, but pursued and fought their monstrous prey in the lightless deep half a mile from the last rays of the sun.

There would be weeks or even months when a warden would never see a whale. The bureau had many calls on its equipment and personnel, and whales were not its only business. Everyone who had dealings with the sea appeared to come, sooner or later, to the Bureau of Whales with an appeal for help. Sometimes the requests were tragic; several times a year subs were sent on usually fruitless searches for drowned sportsmen or explorers.

At the other extreme, there was a standing joke that a senator had once asked the Sydney office to locate his false teeth, lost when the Bondi surf worked its will upon him. It was said that he had received, with great promptness, the foot-wide jaws of a tiger shark, with an apologetic note saying that these were the only unwanted teeth that an extensive search had been able to find off Bondi Beach.

Some tasks that came the warden's way had a certain glamour, and were eagerly sought after when they arose. A very small and understaffed section of the Bureau of Fisheries was concerned with pearls, and during the slack season wardens were sometimes detached from their normal work and allowed to assist on the pearl beds.

Franklin had one such tour of duty in the Persian Gulf. It was straightforward work, not unlike gardening, and since it involved diving to depths never greater than two hundred feet simple compressed-air equipment was used and the diver employed a torpedo for moving around. The best areas for pearl cultivation had been carefully populated with selected stock, and the main problem was protecting the oysters from their natural enemies – particularly starfish and rays. When they had time to mature, they were collected and carried back to the surface for inspection – one of the few jobs that no one had ever been able to mechanize.

Any pearls discovered belonged, of course, to the Bureau of Fisheries. But it was noticeable that the wives of all the wardens posted to this duty very soon afterward sported pearl necklaces or earrings – and Indra was no exception to this rule.

She had received her necklace the day she gave birth to Peter, and with the arrival of his son it seemed to Franklin that the old chapter of his life had finally closed. It was not true, of course; he could never forget – nor did he wish to – that Irene had given him Roy and Rupert, on a world which was now as remote to him as a planet of the farthest star. But the ache of that irrevocable parting had subsided at last, for no grief can endure forever.

He was glad – though he had once bitterly resented it – that it was impossible to talk to anyone on Mars, or indeed anywhere in space beyond the orbit of the Moon. The six-minute time lag for the round trip, even when the planet was at its nearest, made conversation out of the question, so he could never torture himself by feeling in the presence of Irene and the boys by calling them up on the visiphone. Every Christmas they exchanged recordings and talked over the events of the year; apart from occasional letters, that was the only personal contact they now had, and the only one that Franklin needed.

There was no way of telling how well Irene had adjusted to her virtual widowhood. The boys must have helped, but there were times when Franklin wished that she had married again, for their sakes as well as hers. Yet somehow he had never been able to suggest it, and she had never raised the subject, even when he had made this step himself.

Did she resent Indra? That again was hard to tell. Perhaps some jealousy was inevitable; Indra herself, during the occasional quarrels that punctuated their marriage, made it clear that she sometimes disliked the thought of being only the second woman in Franklin's life.

Such quarrels were rare, and after the birth of Peter they were rarer. A married couple forms a dynamically unstable system until the arrival of the first child converts it from a double to a triple group.

Franklin was as happy now as he had ever hoped to be. His family gave him the emotional security he needed; his work provided the interest and adventure which he had sought in space, only to lose again. There was more life and wonder in the sea than in all the endless empty leagues between the planets, and it was seldom now that his heart ached for the blue beauty of the crescent Earth, the swirling silver mist of the Milky Way, or the tense excitement of landfall on the moons of Mars at the end of a long voyage.

The sea had begun to shape his life and thought, as it must that of all men worthy to master it and learn its secrets. He felt a kinship with all the creatures that moved throughout its length and depth, even when they were enemies which it was his duty to destroy. But above all, he felt a sympathy and an almost mystical reverence, of which he was half ashamed, towards the great beasts whose destinies he ruled.

He believed that most wardens knew that feeling, though they were careful to avoid admitting it in their shoptalk. The nearest they came to it was when they accused each other of being 'whale happy', a somewhat indefinable term which might be summed up as acting more like a whale than a man in a given situation. It was a form of identification without which no warden could be really good at his job, but there were times when it could become too extreme. The classic case – which everyone swore was perfectly true – was that of the senior warden who felt he was suffocating unless he brought his sub up to blow every ten minutes.

Being regarded – and regarding themselves – as the elite of the world's army of underwater experts, the wardens were always called upon when there was some unusual job that no one else cared to perform. Sometimes these jobs were so suicidal that it was necessary to explain to the would-be client that he must find another way out of his difficulties.

But occasionally there was no other way, and risks had to be taken. The bureau still remembered how Chief Warden Kircher, back in '22, had gone up the giant intake pipes through which the cooling water flowed into the fusion power plant supplying half the South American continent. One of the filter grilles had started to come loose, and could be fixed only by a man on the spot. With strong ropes tied around his body to prevent him from being sucked through the wire meshing, Kircher had descended into the roaring darkness. He had done the job and returned safely; but that was the last time he ever went under water.

So far, all Franklin's missions had been fairly conventional ones; he had had to face nothing as hair-raising as Kircher's exploit, and was not sure how he would react if such an occasion arose. Of course, he could always turn down any assignment that involved abnormal risks; his contract was quite specific on that point. But the 'suicide clause', as it was sardonically called, was very much a dead letter. Any warden who invoked it, except under the most extreme circumstances, would incur no displeasure from his superiors, but he would thereafter find it very hard to live with his colleagues.

Franklin's first operation beyond the call of duty did not come his way for almost five years – five busy, crowded, yet in retrospect curiously uneventful, years. But when it came, it more than made up for the delay.

CHAPTER 14

THE CHIEF ACCOUNTANT dropped his tables and charts on the desk, and peered triumphantly at his little audience over the rims of his antiquated spectacles.

'So you see, gentlemen,' he said, 'there's no doubt about it. In this area here' — he stabbed at the map again — 'sperm whale casualties have been abnormally high. It's no longer a question of the usual random variations in the census numbers. During the migrations of the last five years, no less than nine plus or minus two whales have disappeared in this rather small area.

'Now, as you are all aware, the sperm whale has no natural enemies, except for the orcas that occasionally attack small females with calves. But we are quite sure that no killer packs have broken into this area for several years, and at least three adult males have disappeared. In our opinion, that left only one possibility.

'The sea bed here is slightly less than four thousand feet down, which means that a sperm whale can just reach it with a few minutes' time for hunting on the bottom before it has to return for air. Now, ever since it was discovered that Physeter feeds almost exclusively on squids, naturalists have wondered whether a squid can ever win when a whale attacks it. The general opinion was that it couldn't, because the whale is much larger and more powerful.

'But we must remember that even today no one knows how big the giant squid does grow; the Biology Section tells me that tentacles of *Bathyteutis Maximus* have been found up to eighty feet long. Moreover, a squid would only have to keep a whale held down for a matter of a few minutes at this depth, and the animal would drown before it could get back to the surface. So a couple of years ago we formulated the theory that in this area there lives at least one abnormally large squid. We — ahem — christened him Percy.

'Until last week, Percy was only a theory. Then, as you know, Whale S.87693 was found dead on the surface, badly mauled and with its body covered with the typical scars caused by squid claws and suckers. I would like you to look at this photograph.'

He pulled a set of large glossy prints out of his briefcase and passed them around. Each showed a small portion of a whale's body which was mottled with white streaks and perfectly circular rings. A foot ruler lay incongruously in the middle of the picture to give an idea of the scale.

'Those, gentlemen, are sucker marks. They go up to six inches in diameter. I think we can say that Percy is no longer a theory. The question is: What do we do about him? He is costing us at least twenty thousand dollars a year. I should welcome any suggestions.'

There was a brief silence while the little group of officials looked thoughtfully at the photographs. Then the director said: 'I've asked Mr Franklin to come along and give his opinion. What do you say, Walter? Can you deal with Percy?'

'If I can find him, yes. But the bottom's pretty rugged down there, and it might be a long search. I couldn't use a normal sub, of course – there'd be no safety margin at that depth, especially if Percy started putting on the squeeze. Incidentally, what size do you think he is?'

The chief accountant, usually so glib with figures, hesitated for an appreciable instant before replying.

'This isn't *my* estimate,' he said apologetically, 'but the biologists say he may be a hundred and fifty feet long.'

There were some subdued whistles, but the director seemed unimpressed. Long ago he had learned the truth of the old cliché that there were bigger fish in the sea than ever came out of it. He knew also that, in a medium where gravity set no limit to size, a creature could continue to grow almost indefinitely as long as it could avoid death. And of all the inhabitants of the sea, the giant squid was perhaps the safest from attack. Even its one enemy, the sperm whale, could not reach it if it remained below the four-thousand-foot level.

'There are dozens of ways we can kill Percy if we can locate him,' put in the chief biologist. 'Explosives, poison, electrocution – any of them would do. But unless there's no alternative, I think we should avoid killing. He must be one of the biggest animals alive on this planet, and it would be a crime to murder him.'

'*Please*, Dr Roberts!' protested the director. 'May I remind you that this bureau is only concerned with food production – not with research or the conservation of any animals except whales. And I do think that murder is rather a strong term to apply to an overgrown mollusk.'

Dr Roberts seemed quite unabashed by the mild reprimand.

'I agree, sir,' he said cheerfully, 'that production is our main job, and that we must always keep economic factors in mind. At the same time, we're continually cooperating with the Department of Scientific Research and this seems another case where we can work together to our mutual advantage. In fact, we might even make a profit in the long run.'

'Go on,' said the director, a slight twinkle in his eye. He wondered what ingenious plan the scientists who were supposed to be working for him had cooked up with their opposite numbers in Research.

'No giant squid has ever been captured alive, simply because we've never had the tools for the job. It would be an expensive operation, but if we are going to chase Percy anyway, the additional cost should not be very great. So I suggest that we try to bring him back alive.'

No one bothered to ask how. If Dr Roberts said it could be done, that meant he had already worked out a plan of campaign. The directors, as usual, bypassed the minor technical details involved in hauling up several tons of fighting squid from a depth of a mile, and went straight to the important point.

'Will Research pay for any of this? And what will you do with Percy when you've caught him?'

'Unofficially, Research will provide the additional equipment if we make the subs and pilots available. We'll also need that floating dock we borrowed from Maintenance last year; it's big enough to hold two whales, so it can certainly hold one squid. There'll be some additional expenditure here – extra aeration plant for the water, electrified mesh to stop Percy climbing out, and so on. In fact, I suggest that we use the dock as a lab while we're studying him.'

'And after that?'

'Why, we sell him.'

'The demand for hundred-and-fifty-foot squids as household pets would seem to be rather small.'

Like an actor throwing away his best line, Dr Roberts casually produced his trump card.

'If we can deliver Percy alive and in good condition, Marineland will pay fifty-thousand dollars for him. That was Professor Milton's first informal offer when I spoke to him this morning. I've no doubt that we can get more than that; I've even been wondering if we could arrange things on a royalty basis. After all, a giant squid would be the biggest attraction Marineland ever had.'

'Research was bad enough,' grumbled the director. 'Now it looks as if you're trying to get us involved in the entertainment business. Still, as far as I'm concerned it sounds fairly plausible. If Accounts can convince me that the project is not too expensive, and if no other snags turn up, we'll go ahead with it. That is, of course, if Mr Franklin and his colleagues think it can be done. They're the people who'll have to do the work.'

'If Dr Roberts has any practical plan, I'll be glad to discuss it with him. It's certainly a very interesting project.'

That, thought Franklin, was the understatement of the year. But he was not the sort of man who ever waxed too enthusiastic over any enterprise, having long ago decided that this always resulted in eventual disappointment. If 'Operation Percy' came off, it would be the most exciting job he had ever had in his five years as a warden. But it was too good to be true; something would turn up to cancel the whole project.

It did not. Less than a month later, he was dropping down to the sea bed in a specially modified deep-water scout. Two hundred feet behind him, Don Burley was following in a second machine. It was the first time they had worked together since those far-off days on Heron Island, but when Franklin had been asked to choose his partner he had automatically thought of Don. This was the chance of a lifetime, and Don would never forgive him if he selected anyone else.

Franklin sometimes wondered if Don resented his own rapid rise in the service. Five years ago, Don had been a first warden; Franklin, a completely inexperienced trainee. Now they were both first wardens, and before long Franklin would probably be promoted again. He did not altogether welcome this, for, though he was ambitious enough, he knew that the higher he rose in the bureau the less time he would spend at sea. Perhaps Don knew what he was doing; it was very hard to picture him settling down in an office . . .

'Better try your lights,' said Don's voice from the speaker. 'Doc Roberts wants me to get a photograph of you.'

'Right,' Franklin replied. 'Here goes.'

'My – you *do* look pretty! If I was another squid, I'm sure I'd find you irresistible. Swing broadside a minute. Thanks. Talk about a Christmas tree! It's the first time I've ever seen one making ten knots at six hundred fathoms.'

Franklin grinned and switched off the illuminations. This idea of Dr Roberts' was simple enough, but it remained to be seen if it would work. In the lightless abyss, many creatures carry constellations of luminous organs which they can switch on or off at will, and the giant squid, with its enormous eyes, is particularly sensitive to such lights. It uses them not only to lure its prey into its clutches, but also to attract its mates. If squids were as intelligent as they were supposed to be, thought Franklin, Percy would soon see through his disguise. It would be ironic, however, if a deep-diving sperm whale was deceived and he had an unwanted fight on his hands.

The rocky bottom was now only five hundred feet below, every detail of it clearly traced on the short-range sonar scanner. It looked like an unpromising place for a search; there might be countless caves here in which Percy could hide beyond all hope of detection. On the other hand, the whales had detected him – to their cost. And anything that Physeter can do, Franklin, told himself, my sub can do just as well.

'We're in luck,' said Don. 'The water's as clear as I've ever seen it down here. As long as we don't stir up any mud, we'll be able to see a couple of hundred feet.'

That was important; Franklin's luminous lures would be useless if the water was too turbid for them to be visible. He switched on the external TV camera, and quickly located the faint glow of Don's starboard light, two hundred feet away. Yes, this was extremely good luck; it should simplify their task enormously.

Franklin tuned in to the nearest beacon and fixed his position with the utmost accuracy. To make doubly sure, he got Don to do the same, and they split the difference between them. Then, cruising slowly on parallel courses, they began their careful search of the sea bed.

It was unusual to find bare rock at such a depth, for the ocean bed is normally covered with a layer of mud and sediment hundreds or even thousands of feet thick. There must, Franklin decided, be powerful currents scouring this area clear – but there was certainly no current now, as his drift meter assured him. It was probably seasonal, and associated with the ten-thousand-foot-deeper cleft of the Miller Canyon, only five miles away.

Every few seconds, Franklin switched on his pattern of coloured lights, then watched the screen eagerly to see if there was any response. Before long he had half a dozen fantastic deep-sea fish following him – nightmare creatures, two or three feet long, with enormous jaws and ridiculously attenuated feelers and tendrils trailing from their bodies. The lure of his lights apparently overcame their fear of his engine vibration, which was an encouraging sign. Though his speed quickly left them behind, they were continually replaced by new monsters, no two of which appeared to be exactly the same.

Franklin paid relatively little attention to the TV screen; the longer-range senses of the sonar, warning him of what lay in the thousand feet ahead of him, were more important. Not only had he to keep a look out for his quarry, but he had to avoid rocks and hillocks which might suddenly rear up in the track of the sub. He was doing only ten knots, which was slow enough, but it required all his concentration. Sometimes he felt as if he was flying at treetop height over hilly country in a thick fog.

They travelled five uneventful miles, then made a hairpin turn and came back on a parallel course. If they were doing nothing else, thought Franklin, at least they were producing a survey of this area in more detail than it had ever been mapped before. Both he and Don were operating with their recorders on, so that the profile of the sea bed beneath them was being automatically mapped.

'Whoever said this was an exciting life?' said Don when they made their fourth turn. 'I've not even seen a baby octopus. Maybe we're scaring the squids away.'

'Roberts said they're not very sensitive to vibrations, so I don't think that's likely. And somehow I feel that Percy isn't the sort who's easily scared.'

'*If* he exists,' said Don sceptically.

'Don't forget those six-inch sucker marks. What do you think made them – mice?'

'Hey!' said Don. Have a look at that echo on bearing 250, range 750 feet. Looks like a rock, but I thought it moved then.'

Another false alarm, Franklin told himself. No – the echo did seem a bit fuzzy. By God, it *was* moving!

'Cut speed to half a knot,' he ordered. 'Drop back behind me – I'll creep up slowly and switch on my lights.'

'It's a weird-looking echo. Keeps changing size all the time.'

'That sounds like our boy. Here we go.'

The sub was now moving across an endless, slightly tilted plain, still accompanied by its inquisitive retinue of finned dragons. On the TV screen all objects were lost in the haze at a distance of about a hundred and fifty feet; the full power of the ultraviolet projectors could probe the water no farther than this. Franklin switched off his headlights and all external illumination, and continued his cautious approach using the sonar screen alone.

At five hundred feet the echo began to show its unmistakable structure; at four hundred feet there was no longer any doubt; at three hundred feet Franklin's escort of fish suddenly fled at high speed as if aware that this was no healthy spot. At two hundred feet he turned on his visual lures, but he waited a few seconds before switching on the searchlights and TV.

A forest was walking across the sea bed – a forest of writhing, serpentine trunks. The great squid rose for a moment as if impaled by the searchlights; probably it could see them, though they were invisible to human eyes. Then it gathered up its tentacles with incredible swiftness, folding itself into a compact, streamlined mass – and shot straight towards the sub under the full power of its own jet propulsion.

I swerved at the last minute, and Franklin caught a glimpse of a huge and lidless eye that must have been at least a foot in diameter. A second later there was a violent blow on the hull, followed by a scraping sound as of great claws being dragged across metal. Franklin remembered the scars he had so often seen on the blubbery hides of sperm whales, and was glad of the thickness of steel that protected him. He could hear the wiring of his external illumination being ripped away; no matter – it had served its purpose.

It was impossible to tell what the squid was doing; from time to time the sub rocked violently, but Franklin made no effort to escape. Unless things got a little too rough, he proposed to stay here and take it.

'Can you see what he's doing?' he asked Don, rather plaintively.

'Yes – he's got his eight arms wrapped around you, and the two tentacles are waving hopefully at me. And he's going through the most beautiful colour changes you can imagine – I can't begin to describe them. I wish I knew whether he's really trying to eat you – or whether he's just being affectionate.'

'Whichever it is, it's not very comfortable. Hurry up and take your photos so that I can get out of here.'

'Right – give me another couple of minutes so I can get a movie sequence as well. Then I'll try to plant my harpoon.'

It seemed a long two minutes, but at last Don had finished. Percy still showed none of the shyness which Dr Roberts had rather confidently predicted, though by this time he could hardly have imagined that Franklin's sub was another squid.

Don planted his dart with neatness and precision in the thickest part of Percy's mantle, where it would lodge securely but would do no damage. At the sudden sting, the great mollusk abruptly released its grip, and Franklin took the opportunity for going full speed ahead. He felt the horny palps grating over the stern of the sub; then he was free and rising swiftly up towards the distant sky. He felt rather pleased that he had managed to escape without using any of the battery of weapons that had been provided for this very purpose.

Don followed him at once, and they circled five hundred feet above the sea bed – far beyond visual range. On the sonar screen the rocky bottom was a sharply defined plane, but now at its centre pulsed a tiny, brilliant star. The little beacon – less than six inches long and barely an inch wide – that had been anchored in Percy was already doing its job. It would continue to operate for more than a week before its batteries failed.

'We've tagged him!' cried Don gleefully. 'Now he can't hide.'

'As long as he doesn't get rid of that dart,' said Franklin cautiously. 'If he works it out, we'll have to start looking for him all over again.'

'*I* aimed it,' pointed out Don severely. 'Bet you ten to one it stays put.'

'If I've learned one thing in this game,' said Franklin, 'it's not to accept your bets.' He brought the drive up to maximum cruising power, and pointed the sub's nose to the surface, still more than half a mile away. 'Let's not keep Doc Roberts waiting – the poor man will be crazy with impatience. Besides, I want to see those pictures myself. It's the first time I've ever played a starring role with a giant squid.'

And this, he reminded himself, was only the curtain raiser. The main feature had still to begin.

CHAPTER 15

'How nice it is,' said Franklin, as he relaxed lazily in the contour-form chair on the porch, 'to have a wife who's not scared stiff of the job I'm doing.'

'There are times when I am,' admitted Indra. 'I don't like these deep-water operations. If anything goes wrong down there, you don't have a chance.'

'You can drown just as easily in ten feet of water as ten thousand.'

'That's silly, and you know it. Besides, no warden has ever been killed by drowning, as far as I've ever heard. The things that happen to them are never as nice and simple as that.'

'I'm sorry I started this conversation,' said Franklin ruefully, glancing around to see if Peter was safely out of earshot. 'Anyway, you're not worried about Operation Percy, are you?'

'No, I don't think so. I'm as anxious as everybody else to see you catch him – and I'm still more interested to see if Dr Roberts can keep him alive.' She rose to her feet and walked over to the bookshelf recessed into the wall. Ploughing through the usual pile of papers and magazines that had accumulated there, she finally unearthed the volume for which she was looking.

'Listen to this,' she continued, 'and remember that it was written almost two hundred years ago.' She began to read in her best lecture-room voice, while Franklin listened at first with mild reluctance, and then with complete absorption.

'In the distance, a great white mass lazily rose, and rising higher and higher, and distentangling itself from the azure, at last gleamed before our prow like a snow-slide, new slid from the hills. Thus glistening for a moment, as slowly it subsided, and sank. Then once more arose, and slightly gleamed. It seemed not a whale; and yet is this Moby Dick? thought Daggoo. Again the phantom went down, but on reappearing once more, like a stiletto-like cry that startled every man from his nod, the negro yelled out – "There! there again! there she breaches! Right ahead! The White Whale! The White Whale!"

'The four boats were soon on the water; Ahab's in advance, and all swiftly pulling towards their prey. Soon it went down, and while, with oars suspended, we were awaiting its appearance, lo! in the same spot where it sank, once more it slowly rose. Almost forgetting for the moment all thoughts of Moby Dick, we now gazed at the most wondrous phenomenon which the secret seas have hitherto revealed to mankind. A vast pulpy mass, furlongs in length and breadth, of a glancing cream-colour, lay floating on the water, innumerable long arms radiating from its centre, and curling and twisting like a nest of anacondas, as if blindly to catch at any hapless object within reach. No perceptible face or front did it have; no conceivable token of either sensation or instinct; but undulated there on the billows, an unearthly, formless, chance-like apparition of life.

'As with a low sucking sound it slowly disappeared again, Starbuck still gazing at the agitated waters where it had sunk, with a wild voice exclaimed – "Almost rather had I seen Moby Dick and fought him, than to have seen thee, thou white ghost!"

' "What was it, Sir?" said Flask.

' "The great live squid, which, they say, few whale-ships ever beheld, and returned to their ports to tell of it."

'But Ahab said nothing; turning his boat, he sailed back to the vessel; the rest as silently following.'

Indra paused, closed the book, and waited for her husband's response. Franklin stirred himself in the too-comfortable couch and said thoughtfully: 'I'd forgotten that bit – if I ever read as far. It rings true to life, but what was a squid doing on the surface?'

'It was probably dying. They sometimes surface at night, but never in the daytime, and Melville says this was on "one transparent blue morning".'

'Anyway, what's a furlong? I'd like to know if Melville's squid was as big as Percy. The photos make him a hundred and thirty feet from his flukes to the tip of his feelers.'

'So he beats the largest blue whale ever recorded.'

'Yes, by a couple of feet. But of course he doesn't weigh a tenth as much.'

Franklin heaved himself from his couch and went in search of a dictionary. Presently Indra heard indignant noises coming from the living-room, and called out: 'What's the matter?'

'It says here that a furlong is an obsolete measure of length equal to an eighth of a mile. Melville was talking through his hat.'

'He's usually very accurate, at least as far as whales are concerned. But "furlong" is obviously ridiculous – I'm surprised no one's spotted it before. He must have meant fathoms, or else the printer got it wrong.'

Slightly mollified, Franklin put down the dictionary and came back to the porch. He was just in time to see Don Burley arrive, sweep Indra off her feet, plant a large but brotherly kiss on her forehead, and dump her back in her chair.

'Come along, Walt!' he said. 'Got your things packed? I'll give you a lift to the airport.'

'Where's Peter hiding?' said Franklin. 'Peter! Come and say goodbye – Daddy's off to work.'

A four-year-old bundle of uncontrollable energy came flying into the room, almost capsizing his father as he jumped into his arms.

'Daddy's going to bring me back a 'quid?' he asked.

'Hey – how did you know about all this?'

'It was on the news this morning, while you were still asleep,' explained Indra. 'They showed a few seconds of Don's film, too.'

'I was afraid of that. Now we'll have to work with a crowd of cameramen and reporters looking over our shoulders. That means that something's sure to go wrong.'

'They can't follow us down to the bottom, anyway,' said Burley.

'I hope you're right – but don't forget we're not the only people with deep-sea subs.'

'I don't know how you put up with him,' Don protested to Indra. 'Does he *always* look on the black side of things?'

'Not always,' smiled Indra, as she unravelled Peter from his father. 'He's cheerful at least twice a week.'

Her smile faded as she watched the sleek sportster go whispering down the hill. She was very fond of Don, who was practically a member of the family, and there were times when she worried about him. It seemed a pity that he had never married and settled down; the nomadic, promiscuous life he led could hardly be very satisfying. Since they had known him, he had spent almost all his time on or under the sea, apart from hectic leaves when he had used their home as a base – at their invitation but often to their embarrassment when there were unexpected lady guests to entertain at breakfast.

Their own life, by many standards, had been nomadic enough, but at least they had always had a place they could call home. That apartment in Brisbane, where her brief but happy career as a lecturer at the University of Queensland had ended with the birth of Peter; that bungalow in Fiji, with the roof that had a mobile leak which the builders could never find; the married quarters at the South Georgian whaling station (she could still smell the mountains of offal, and see the gulls wheeling over the flensing yards); and finally, this house looking out across the sea to the other islands of Hawaii. Four homes in five years might seem excessive to many people, but for a warden's wife Indra knew she had done well.

She had few regrets for the career that had been temporarily interrupted. When Peter was old enough, she told herself, she would go back to her research; even now she read all the literature and kept in touch with current work. Only a few months ago the *Journal of Selachians* had published her letter 'On the possible evolution of the Goblin Shark (*Scapanorhynchus owstoni*)', and she had since been involved in an enjoyable controversy with all five of the scientists qualified to discuss the subject.

Even if nothing came of these dreams, it was pleasant to have them and to know you might make the best of both worlds. So Indra Franklin, housewife and ichthyologist, told herself as she went back into the kitchen to prepare lunch for her ever-hungry son.

The floating dock had been modified in many ways that would have baffled its original designers. A thick steel mesh, supported on sturdy insulators, extended its entire length, and above this mesh was a canvas awning to cut out the sunlight which would injure Percy's sensitive eyes and skin. The only illumination inside the dock came from a battery of amber-tinted bulbs; at the moment, however, the great doors at either end of the huge concrete box were open, letting in both sunlight and water.

The two subs, barely awash, lay tied up beside the crowded catwalk as Dr Roberts gave his final instructions.

'I'll try not to bother you too much when you're down there,' he said, 'but for heaven's sake tell me what's going on.'

'We'll be too busy to give a running commentary,' answered Don with a grin, 'but we'll do our best. And if anything goes wrong, trust us to yell right away. All set, Walt?'

'OK,' said Franklin, climbing down into the hatch. 'See you in five hours, with Percy – I hope.'

They wasted no time in diving to the sea bed; less than ten minutes later there was four thousand feet of water overhead, and the familiar rocky terrain was imaged on TV and sonar screen. But there was no sign of the pulsing star that should have indicated the presence of Percy.

'Hope the beacon hasn't packed up,' said Franklin as he reported this news to the hopefully waiting scientists. 'If it has, it may take us days to locate him again.'

'Do you suppose he's left the area? I wouldn't blame him,' added Don.

Dr Roberts' voice, still confident and assured, came down to them from the distant world of sun and light almost a mile above.

'He's probably hiding in a cleft, or shielded by rock. I suggest you rise five hundred feet so that you're well clear of all the sea-bed irregularities, and start a high-speed search. That beacon has a range of more than a mile, so you'll pick him up pretty quickly.'

An hour later even the doctor sounded less confident, and from the comments that leaked down to them over the sonar communicator it appeared that the reporters and TV networks were getting impatient.

'There's only one place he can be,' said Roberts at last. 'If he's there at all, and the beacon's still working, he must have gone down into the Miller Canyon.'

'That's fifteen thousand feet deep,' protested Don. 'These subs are only cleared for twelve.'

'I know – I know. But he won't have gone to the bottom. He's probably hunting somewhere down the slope. You'll see him easily if he's there.'

'Right,' replied Franklin, not very optimistically. 'Well go and have a look but if he's more than twelve thousand feet down, he'll have to stay there.'

On the sonar screen, the canyon was clearly visible as a sudden gap in the luminous image of the sea bed. It came rapidly closer as the two subs raced towards it at forty knots

— the fastest creatures, Franklin mused, anywhere beneath the surface of the sea. He had once flown low towards the Grand Canyon, and seen the land below suddenly whipped away as the enormous cavity gaped beneath him. And now, though he must rely for vision solely on the pattern of echoes brought back by his probing sound waves, he felt exactly that same sensation as he swept across the edge of this still mightier chasm in the ocean floor.

He had scarcely finished the thought when Don's voice, high-pitched with excitement, came yelling from the speaker.

'There he is! A thousand feet down!'

'No need to break my eardrums,' grumbled Franklin. 'I can see him.'

The precipitous slope of the canyon wall was etched like an almost vertical line down the centre of the sonar screen. Creeping along the face of that wall was the tiny, twinkling star for which they had been searching. The patient beacon had betrayed Percy to his hunters.

They reported the situation to Dr Roberts; Franklin could picture the jubilation and excitement up above, some hints of which trickled down through the open microphone. Presently Dr Roberts, a little breathless, asked: 'Do you think you can still carry out our plan?'

'I'll try,' he answered. 'It won't be easy with this cliff face right beside us, and I hope there aren't any caves Percy can crawl into. You ready, Don?'

'All set to follow you down.'

'I think I can reach him without using the motors. Here we go.'

Franklin flooded the nose tanks, and went down in a long, steep glide – a silent glide, he hoped. By this time, Percy would have learned caution and would probably run for it as soon as he knew that they were around.

The squid was cruising along the face of the canyon, and Franklin marvelled that it could find any food in such a forbidding and apparently lifeless spot. Every time it expelled a jet of water from the tube of its siphon it moved forward in a distinct jerk; it seemed unaware that it was no longer alone, since it had not changed course since Franklin had first observed it.

'Two hundred feet – I'm going to switch on my lights again,' he told Don.

'He won't see you – visibility's only about eighty today.'

'Yes, but I'm still closing in – he's spotted me! Here he comes!'

Franklin had not really expected that the trick would work a second time on an animal as intelligent as Percy. But almost at once he felt the sudden thud, followed by the rasping of horny claws as the great tentacles closed around the sub. Though he knew that he was perfectly safe, and that no animal could harm walls that had been built to withstand pressures of a thousand tons on every square foot, that grating, slithering sound was one calculated to give him nightmares.

Then, quite suddenly, there was silence. He heard Don exclaim, 'Christ, that stuff acts quickly! He's out cold.' Almost at once Dr Roberts interjected anxiously: 'Don't give him too much! And keep him moving so that he'll still breathe!'

Don was too busy to answer. Having carried out his role as decoy, Franklin could do nothing but watch as his partner manoeuvred dexterously around the great mollusk. The anaesthetic bomb had paralysed it completely; it was slowly sinking, its tentacles stretched limply upwards. Pieces of fish, some of them over a foot across, were floating away from the cruel beak as the monster disgorged its last meal.

'Can you get underneath?' Don asked hurriedly. 'He's sinking too fast for me.'

Franklin threw on the drive and went around in a tight curve. There was a soft thump, as of a snowdrift falling from a roof, and he knew that five or ten tons of gelatinous body were now draped over the sub.

'Fine – hold him there – I'm getting into position.'

Franklin was now blind, but the occasional clanks and whirs coming from the water outside told him what was happening. Presently Don said triumphantly: 'All set! We're ready to go.'

The weight lifted from the sub, and Franklin could see again. Percy had been neatly gaffed. A band of thick, elastic webbing had been fastened around his body at the narrowest part, just behind the flukes. From this harness a cable extended to Don's sub, invisible in the haze a hundred feet away. Percy was being towed through the water in his normal direction of motion – backwards. Had he been conscious and actively resisting, he could have escaped easily enough, but in his present state the collar he was wearing enabled Don to handle him without difficulty. The fun would begin when he started to revive . . .

Franklin gave a brief eyewitness description of the scene for the benefit of his patiently waiting colleagues a mile above. It was probably being broadcast, and he hoped that Indra and Peter were listening. Then he settled down to keep an eye on Percy as the long haul back to the surface began.

They could not move at more than two knots, lest the collar lose its none-too-secure grip on the great mass of jelly it was towing. In any event, the trip back to the surface had to take at least three hours, to give Percy a fair chance of adjusting to the pressure difference. Since an airbreathing – and therefore more vulnerable – animal like a sperm whale could endure almost the same pressure change in ten or twenty minutes, this caution was probably excessive. But Dr Roberts was taking no chances with his unprecedented catch.

They had been climbing slowly for nearly an hour, and had reached the three-thousand-foot level, when Percy showed signs of life. The two long arms, terminating in their great sucker-covered palps, began to writhe purposefully; the monstrous eyes, into which Franklin had been staring half hypnotized from a distance of no more than five feet, began to light once more with intelligence. Quite unaware that he was speaking in a breathless whisper, he swiftly reported these symptoms to Dr Roberts.

The doctor's first reaction was a hearty sigh of relief: 'Good!' he said. 'I was afraid we might have killed him. Can you see if he's breathing properly? Is the siphon contracting?'

Franklin dropped a few feet so that he could get a better view of the fleshy tube projecting from the squid's mantle. It was opening and closing in an unsteady rhythm which seemed to be getting stronger and more regular at every beat.

'Splendid!' said Dr Roberts. 'He's in fine shape. As soon as he starts to wriggle too hard, give him one of the small bombs. But leave it until the last possible moment.'

Franklin wondered how that moment was to be decided. Percy was now beginning to glow a beautiful blue; even with the searchlights switched off he was clearly visible. Blue, he remembered Dr Roberts saying, was a sign of excitement in squids. In that case, it was high time he did something.

'Better let go that bomb. I think he's getting lively,' he told Don.

'Right – here it is.'

A glass bubble floated across Franklin's screen and swiftly vanished from sight.

'The damn thing never broke!' he cried. 'Let go another one!'

'OK – here's number two. I hope this works; I've only got five left.'

But once again the narcotic bomb failed. This time Franklin never saw the sphere; he only knew that instead of relaxing into slumber once more Percy was becoming more active second by second. The eight short tentacles – short, that is, compared with the almost hundred-foot reach of the pair carrying the grasping palps – were now beginning to twine briskly together. He recalled Melville's phrase: 'Like a nest of anacondas.' No; somehow that did not seem to fit. It was more like a miser – a submarine Shylock – twisting, his fingers together as he gloated over his wealth. In any event, it was a disconcerting sight when those fingers were a foot in diameter and were operating only two yards away . . .

'You'll just have to keep on trying,' he told Don. 'Unless we stop him soon, he'll get away.'

An instant later he breathed a sigh of relief as he saw broken shards of glass drifting by. They would have been quite invisible, surrounded as they were by water, had they not been fluorescing brilliantly under the light of his ultra-violet searchlight. But for the moment he was too relieved to wonder why he had been able to see something as prov-erbially elusive as a piece of broken glass in water; he only knew that Percy had suddenly relaxed again and no longer appeared to be working himself into a rage.

'What happened?' said Dr Roberts plaintively from above.

'These confounded knockout drops of yours. Two of them didn't work. That leaves me with just four – and at the present rate of failure, I'll be lucky if even one goes off.'

'I don't understand it. The mechanism worked perfectly every time we tested it in the lab.'

'Did you test it at a hundred atmospheres pressure?'

'Er – no. It didn't seem necessary.'

Don's 'Huh!' seemed to say all that was needful about biologists who tried to dabble with engineering, and there was silence on all channels for the next few minutes of slow ascent. Then Dr Roberts, sounding a little diffident, came back to the subject.

'Since we can't rely on the bombs,' he said, 'you'd better come up more quickly. He'll revive again in about thirty minutes.'

'Right – I'll double speed. I only hope this collar doesn't slip off.'

The next twenty minutes were perfectly uneventful; then everything started to happen at once.

'He's coming around again,' said Franklin. 'I think the higher speed has waked him up.'

'I was afraid of that,' Dr Roberts answered. 'Hold on as long as you can, and then let go a bomb. We can only pray that *one* of them will work.'

A new voice suddenly cut into the circuit.

'Captain here. Lookout has just spotted some sperm whales about two miles away. They seem to be heading toward us; I suggest you have a look at them – we've got no horizontal search sonar on this ship.'

Franklin switched quickly over to the long-range scanner and picked up the echoes at once.

'Nothing to worry about,' he said. 'If they come too close, we can scare them away.' He glanced back at the TV screen and saw that Percy was now getting very restive.

'Let go your bomb,' he told Don, 'and keep your fingers crossed.'

'I'm not betting on *this*,' Don answered. 'Anything happen?'

'No; another dud. Try again.'

'That leaves three. Here goes.'

'Sorry – I can see that one. It isn't cracked.'

'Two left. Now there's only one.'

'That's a dud too. What had we better do, Doc? Risk the last one? I'm afraid Percy will slip off in a minute.'

'There's nothing else we can do,' replied Dr Roberts, his voice now clearly showing the strain. 'Go ahead, Don.'

Almost at once Franklin gave a cry of satisfaction.

'We've made it!' he shouted. 'He's knocked cold again! How long do you think it will keep him under this time?'

'We can't rely on more than twenty minutes, so plan your ascent accordingly. We're right above you – and remember what I said about taking at least ten minutes over that last two hundred feet. I don't want any pressure damage after all the trouble we've been to.'

'Just a minute,' put in Don. 'I've been looking at those whales. They've put on speed and they're coming straight toward us. I think they've detected Percy – or the beacon we put in him.'

'So what?' said Franklin. 'We can frighten them with – oh.'

'Yes – I thought you'd forgotten that. These aren't patrol subs, Walt. No sirens on them. And you can't scare sperm whales just by revving your engines.'

That was true enough, though it would not have been fifty years ago, when the great beasts had been hunted almost to extinction. But a dozen generations had lived and died since then; now they recognized the subs as harmless, and certainly no obstacle to the meal they were anticipating. There was a real danger that the helpless Percy be eaten before he could be safely caged.

'I think we'll make it,' said Franklin, as he anxiously calculated the speed of the approaching whales. This was a hazard that no one could have anticipated; it was typical of the way in which underwater operations developed unexpected snags and complications.

'I'm going straight up to the two-hundred-foot level,' Don told him. 'We'll wait there just as long as it's safe, and then run for the ship. What do you think of that, Doc?'

'It's the only thing to do. But remember that those whales can make fifteen knots if they have to.'

'Yes, but they can't keep it up for long, even if they see their dinner slipping away. Here we go.'

The subs increased their rate of ascent, while the water brightened around them and the enormous pressure slowly relaxed. At last they were back in the narrow zone where an unprotected man could safely dive. The mother ship was less than a hundred yards away, but this final stage in the climb back to the surface was the most critical of all. In this last two hundred feet, the pressure would drop swiftly from eight atmospheres to only one – as great a change in ratio as had occurred in the previous quarter of a mile. There were no enclosed air spaces in Percy which might cause him to explode if the ascent was too swift, but no one could be certain what other internal damage might occur.

'Whales only half a mile away,' reported Franklin. 'Who said they couldn't keep up that speed? They'll be here in two minutes.'

'You'll have to hold them off somehow,' said Dr Roberts, a note of desperation in his voice.

'Any suggestions?' asked Franklin, a little sarcastically.

'Suppose you pretend to attack; that might make them break off.'

This, Franklin told himself, was not his idea of fun. But there seemed no alternative; with a last glance at Percy, who was now beginning to stir again, he started off at half-speed to meet the advancing whales.

There were three echoes dead ahead of him – not very large ones, but he did not let that encourage him. Even if those were the relatively diminutive females, each one was as big as ten elephants and they were coming towards him at a combined speed of forty miles an hour. He was making all the noise he could, but so far it seemed to be having no effect.

Then he heard Don shouting: 'Percy's waking up fast! I can feel him starting to move.'

'Come straight in,' ordered Dr Roberts. 'We've got the doors open.'

'And get ready to close the back door as soon as I've slipped the cable. I'm going straight through – I don't want to share your swimming pool with Percy when he finds what's happened to him.'

Franklin heard all this chattering with only half an ear. Those three approaching echoes were ominously close. Were they going to call his bluff? Sperm whales were among the most pugnacious animals in the sea, as different from their vegetarian cousins as wild buffaloes from a herd of prize Guernseys. It was a sperm whale that had rammed and sunk the *Essex* and thus inspired the closing chapter of *Moby Dick*; he had no desire to figure in a submarine sequel.

Yet he held stubbornly to his course, though now the racing echoes were less than fifteen seconds away. Then he saw that they were beginning to separate; even if they were not scared, the whales had become confused. Probably the noise of his motors had made them lose contact with their target. He cut his speed to zero, and the three whales began to circle him inquisitively, at a range of about a hundred feet. Sometimes he caught a shadowy glimpse of them on the TV screen. As he had thought, they were young females, and he felt a little sorry to have robbed them of what should have been their rightful food.

He had broken the momentum of their charge; now it was up to Don to finish his side of the mission. From the brief and occasionally lurid comments from the loudspeaker, it was obvious that this was no easy task. Percy was not yet fully conscious, but he knew that something was wrong and he was beginning to object.

The men on the floating dock had the best view of the final stages. Don surfaced about fifty yards away – and the sea behind him became covered with an undulating mass of jelly, twisting and rolling on the waves. At the greatest speed he dared to risk, Don headed for the open end of the dock. One of Percy's tentacles made a halfhearted grab at the entrance, as if in a somnambulistic effort to avoid captivity, but the speed at which he was being hurried through the water broke his grip. As soon as he was safely inside, the massive steel gates began to close like horizontally operating jaws, and Don jettisoned the towrope fastened around the squid's flukes. He wasted no time in leaving from the other exit, and the second set of lock gates started to close even before he was through. The caging of Percy had taken less than a quarter of a minute.

When Franklin surfaced, in company with three disappointed but not hostile sperm whales, it was some time before he could attract any attention. The entire personnel of the dock were busy staring, with awe, triumph, scientific curiosity, and even downright disbelief, at the monstrous captive now swiftly reviving in his great concrete tank. The water was being thoroughly aerated by the streams of bubbles from a score of pipes, and the last traces of the drugs that had paralysed him were being flushed out of Percy's system. Beneath the dim amber light that was now the sole illumination inside the dock, the giant squid began to investigate its prison.

First it swam slowly from end to end of the rectangular concrete box, exploring the sides with its tentacles. Then the two immense palps started to climb into the air, waving towards the breathless watchers gathered round the edge of the dock. They touched the electrified netting – and flicked away with a speed that almost eluded the eye. Twice again Percy repeated the experiment before he had convinced himself that there was no way out in this direction, all the while staring up at the puny spectators with a gaze that seemed to betoken an intelligence every wit as great as theirs.

By the time Don and Franklin came aboard, the squid appeared to have settled down in captivity, and was showing a mild interest in a number of fish that had been dropped into its tank. As the two wardens joined Dr Roberts behind the wire meshing, they had their first clear and complete view of the monster they had hauled up from the ocean depths.

Their eyes ran along the hundred and more feet of flexible sinewy strength, the countless claw-ringed suckers, the slowly pulsing jet, and the huge staring eyes of the most superbly equipped beast of prey the world had ever seen. Then Don summed up the thoughts that they were both feeling.

'He's all yours, Doc. I hope you know how to handle him.'

Dr Roberts smiled confidently enough. He was a very happy man, though a small worry was beginning to invade his mind. He had no doubt at all that he could handle Percy, and he was perfectly right. But he was not so sure that he could handle the director when the bills came in for the research equipment he was going to order – and for the mountains of fish that Percy was going to eat.

CHAPTER 16

THE SECRETARY of the Department of Scientific Research had listened to him attentively enough – and not merely with attention, Franklin told himself, but with a flattering interest. When he had finished the sales talk which had taken such long and careful preparation, he felt a sudden and unexpected emotional letdown. He knew that he had done his best; what happened now was largely out of his hands.

'There are a few points I would like to clear up,' said the secretary. 'The first is a rather obvious one. Why didn't you go to the Marine Division's own research department instead of coming all the way up to World Secretariat level and contacting DSR?'

It was, Franklin admitted, a rather obvious point – and a somewhat delicate one. But he knew that it would be raised, and he had come prepared.

'Naturally, Mr Farlan,' he answered, 'I did my best to get support in the division. There was a good deal of interest, especially after we'd captured that squid. But Operation Percy turned out to be much more expensive than anyone had calculated, and there were a lot of awkward questions about it. The whole affair ended with several of our scientists transferring to other divisions.'

'I know,' interjected the secretary with a smile. 'We've got some of them.'

'So any research that isn't of direct practical importance is now frowned on in the division, which is one reason why I came to you. And, frankly, it hasn't the authority to do the sort of thing I propose. The cost of running even two deep-sea subs is considerable, and would have to be approved at higher than divisional level.'

'But if it was approved, you are confident that the staff could be made available?'

'Yes, at the right time of the year. Now that the fence is practically one hundred per cent reliable – there's been no major breakdown for three years – we wardens have a fairly slack time except at the annual roundups and slaughterings. That's why it seemed a good idea—'

'To utilize the wasted talents of the wardens?'

'Well, that's putting it a little bluntly. I don't want to give the idea that there is any inefficiency in the bureau.'

'I wouldn't dream of suggesting such a thing,' smiled the secretary. 'The other point is a more personal one. Why are you so keen on this project? You have obviously spent a lot of time and trouble on it– and, if I may say so, risked the disapproval of your superiors by coming directly to me.'

That question was not so easy to answer, even to someone you knew well, still less to a stranger. Would this man, who had risen so high in the service of the state, understand the fascination of a mysterious echo on a sonar screen, glimpsed only once, and that years ago? Yes, he would, for he was at least partly a scientist.

'As a chief warden,' explained Franklin, 'I probably won't be on sea duty much longer. I'm thirty-eight, and getting old for this kind of work. And I've an inquisitive type of mind; perhaps I should have been a scientist myself. This is a problem I'd like to see settled, though I know the odds against it are pretty high.'

'I can appreciate that. This chart of confirmed sightings covers about half the world's oceans.'

'Yes, I know it looks hopeless, but with the new sonar sets we can scan a volume three times as great as we used to, and an echo that size is easy to pick up. It's only a matter of time before somebody detects it.'

'And you want to be that somebody. Well, that's reasonable enough. When I got your original letter I had a talk with my marine biology people, and got about three different opinions – none of them very encouraging. Some of those who admit that these echoes have been seen say that they are probably ghosts due to faults in the sonar sets or returns from discontinuities of some kind in the water.'

Franklin snorted. 'Anyone who's seen them would know better than that. After all, we're familiar with all the ordinary sonar ghosts and false returns. We have to be.'

'Yes, that's what I feel. Some more of my people think that the – let us say – conventional sea serpents have already been accounted for by squids, oarfish, and eels, and that what your patrols have been seeing is either one of these or else a large deep-sea shark.'

Franklin shook his head. 'I know what all those echoes look like. This is quite different.'

'The third objection is a theoretical one. There simply isn't enough food in the extreme ocean depths to support any very large and active forms of life.'

'No one can be sure of that. Only in the last century scientists were saying that there could be no life at all on the ocean bed. We know what nonsense *that* turned out to be.'

'Well, you've made a good case. I'll see what can be done.'

'Thank you very much, Mr Farlan. Perhaps it would be best if no one in the bureau knew that I'd come to see you.'

'We won't tell them, but they'll guess.' The secretary rose to his feet, and Franklin assumed that the interview was over. He was wrong.

'Before you go, Mr Franklin,' said the secretary, 'you might be able to clear up one little matter that's been worrying me for a good many years.'

'What's that, sir?'

'I've never understood what a presumably well-trained warden would be doing in the middle of the night off the Great Barrier Reef, breathing compressed air five hundred feet down.'

There was a long silence while the two men, their relationship suddenly altered, stared at each other across the room. Franklin searched his memory, but the other's face evoked no echoes; that was so long ago, and he had met so many people during the intervening years.

'Were you one of the men who pulled me in?' he asked. 'If so, I've a lot to thank you for.' He paused for a moment, then added, 'You see, that wasn't an accident.'

'I rather thought so; that explains everything. But before we change the subject, just what happened to Bert Darryl? I've never been able to find the true story.'

'Oh, eventually he ran out of credit; he could never make the *Sea Lion* pay its way. The last time I ever saw him was in Melbourne; he was heartbroken because customs duties had been abolished and there was no way an honest smuggler could make a living. Finally he tried to collect the insurance on the *Sea Lion*; he had a convincing fire and had to abandon ship off Cairns. She went to the bottom, but the appraisers went after her, and started asking some very awkward questions when they found that all the valuable fittings had been removed before the fire. I don't know how the captain got out of that mess.

'That was about the end of the old rascal. He took to the bottle in earnest, and one night up in Darwin he decided to go for a swim off the jetty. But he'd forgotten that it was low tide – and in Darwin the tide drops thirty feet. So he broke his neck, and a lot of people besides his creditors were genuinely sorry.'

'Poor old Bert. The world will be a dull place when there aren't any more people like him.'

That was rather a heretical remark, thought Franklin, coming from the lips of so senior a member of the World Secretariat. But it pleased him greatly, and not merely because he agreed with it. He knew now that he had unexpectedly acquired an influential friend, and that the chances of his project going forward had been immeasurably improved.

He did not expect anything to happen in a hurry, so was not disappointed as the weeks passed in silence. In any event, he was kept busy; the slack season was still three months away, and meanwhile a whole series of minor but annoying crises crowded upon him.

And there was one that was neither minor nor anything, if indeed it could be called a crisis at all. Anne Franklin arrived wide-eyed and wide-mouthed into the world, and Indra began to have her first serious doubts of continuing her academic career.

Franklin, to his great disappointment, was not home when his daughter was born. He had been in charge of a small task force of six subs, carrying out an offensive sweep off the Pribilof Islands in an attempt to cut down the number of killer whales. It was not the first mission of its kind, but it was the most successful, thanks to the use of improved techniques. The characteristic calls of seals and the smaller whales had been recorded and played back into the sea, while the subs had waited silently for the killers to appear.

They had done so in hundreds, and the slaughter had been immense. By the time the little fleet returned to Base, more than a thousand orcas had been killed. It had been hard and sometimes dangerous work, and despite its importance Franklin had found this scientific butchery extremely depressing. He could not help admiring the beauty, speed, and ferocity of the hunters he was himself hunting, and towards the end of the mission he was almost glad when the rate of kill began to fall off. It seemed that the orcas were learning by bitter experience, and the bureau's statisticians would have to decide whether or not it would be economically worth while repeating the operation next season.

Franklin had barely had time to thaw out from this mission and to fondle Anne gingerly, without extracting any signs of recognition from her, when he was shot off to South Georgia. His problem there was to discover why the whales, who had previously swum into the slaughtering pens without any qualms, had suddenly become suspicious and shown a great reluctance to enter the electrified sluices. As it turned out, he did nothing at all to solve the mystery; while he was still looking for psychological factors, a bright young plant inspector discovered that some of the bloody waste from the processing plants was accidentally leaking back into the sea. It was not surprising that the whales, though their sense of smell was not as strongly developed as in other marine animals had become alarmed as the moving barriers tried to guide them to the place where so many of their relatives had met their doom.

As a chief warden, already being groomed for higher things, Franklin was now a kind of mobile trouble shooter who might be sent anywhere in the world on the bureau's business. Apart from the effect on his home life, he welcomed this state of affairs. Once a man had learned the mechanics of a warden's trade, straightforward patrolling and herding had little future in it. People like Don Burley got all the excitement and pleasure they needed from it, but then Don was neither ambitious nor much of an intellectual heavyweight. Franklin told himself this without any sense of superiority; it was a simple statement of fact which Don would be the first to admit.

He was in England, giving evidence as an expert witness before the Whaling Commission – the bureau's state-appointed watchdog – when he received a plaintive call from Dr Lundquist, who had taken over when Dr Roberts had left the Bureau of Whales to accept a much more lucrative appointment at the Marineland aquarium.

'I've just had three crates of gear delivered from the Department of Scientific Research. It's nothing we ever ordered, but your name is on it. What's it all about?'

Franklin thought quickly. It *would* arrive when he was away, and if the director came across it before he could prepare the ground there would be fireworks.

'It's too long a story to give now,' Franklin answered. 'I've got to go before the committee in ten minutes. Just push it out of the way somewhere until I get back – I'll explain everything then.'

'I hope it's all right – it's most unusual.'

'Nothing to worry about – see you the day after tomorrow. If Don Burley comes to Base, let him have a look at the stuff. But I'll fix all the paper work when I get back.'

That, he told himself, would be the worst part of the whole job. Getting equipment that had never been officially requisitioned on to the bureau's inventory without too many questions was going to be at least as difficult as locating the Great Sea Serpent . . .

He need not have worried. His new and influential ally, the secretary of the Department of Scientific Research, had already anticipated most of his problems. The equipment was to be on loan to the bureau, and was to be returned as soon as it had done its job. What was more, the director had been given the impression that the whole thing was a DSR project; he might have his doubts, but Franklin was officially covered.

'Since you seem to know all about it, Walter,' he said in the lab when the gear was finally unpacked, 'you'd better explain what it's supposed to do.'

'It's an automatic recorder, much more sophisticated than the ones we have at the gates for counting the whales as they go through. Essentially, it's a long-range sonar scanner that explores a volume of space fifteen miles in radius, clear down to the bottom of the sea. It rejects all fixed echoes, and will only record moving objects. And it can also be set to ignore all objects of less than any desired size. In other words, we can use it to count the number of whales more than, say, fifty feet long, and take no notice of the others. It does this once every six minutes – two hundred and forty times a day – so it will give a virtually continuous census of any desired region.'

'Quite ingenious. I suppose DSR wants us to moor the thing somewhere and service it?'

'Yes – and to collect the recordings every week. They should be very useful to us as well. Er – there are three of the things, by the way.'

'Trust DSR to do it in style! I wish we had as much money to throw around. Let me know how the things work – if they do.'

It was as simple as that, and there had been no mention at all of sea serpents.

Nor was there any sign of them for more than two months. Every week, whatever patrol sub happened to be in the neighbourhood would bring back the records from the three instruments, moored half a mile below sea level at the spots Franklin had chosen after a careful study of all the known sightings. With an eagerness which slowly subsided to a stubborn determination, he examined the hundreds of feet of old-fashioned sixteen-millimetre film – still unsurpassed in its own field as a recording medium. He looked at thousands of echoes as he projected the film, condensing into minutes the comings and goings of giant sea creatures through many days and nights.

Usually the pictures were blank, for he had set the discriminator to reject all echoes from objects less than seventy feet in length. That, he calculated, should eliminate all but the very largest whales – and the quarry he was seeking. When the herds were on the move, however, the film would be dotted with echoes which would jump across the screen at fantastically exaggerated speeds as he projected the images. He was watching the life of the sea accelerated almost ten thousand times.

After two months of fruitless watching, he began to wonder if he had chosen the wrong places for all three recorders, and was making plans to move them. When the next rolls of film came back, he told himself he would do just that, and he had already decided on the new locations.

But this time he found what he had been looking for. It was on the edge of the screen, and had been caught by only four sweeps of the scanner. Two days ago that unforgotten, curiously linear echo had appeared on the recorder; now he had evidence, but he still lacked proof.

He moved the other two recorders into the area, arranging the three instruments in a great triangle fifteen miles on a side, so that their fields overlapped. Then it was a question of waiting with what patience he could until another week had passed.

The wait was worth it; at the end of that time he had all the ammunition he needed for his campaign. The proof was there, clear and undeniable.

A very large animal, too long and thin to be any of the known creatures of the sea, lived at the astonishing depth of twenty thousand feet and came halfway to the surface twice a day, presumably to feed. From its intermittent appearance on the screens of the recorders, Franklin was able to get a fairly good idea of its habits and movements. Unless it suddenly left the area and he lost track of it, there should be no great difficulty in repeating the success of Operation Percy.

He should have remembered that in the sea nothing is ever twice the same.

CHAPTER 17

'YOU KNOW, DEAR,' said Indra, 'I'm rather glad this is going to be one of your last missions.'

'If you think I'm getting too old—'

'Oh, it's not only that. When you're on headquarters duty we'll be able to start leading a normal social life. I'll be able to invite people to dinner without having to apologize because you've suddenly been called out to round up a sick whale. And it will be better for the children; I won't have to keep explaining to them who the strange man is they sometimes meet around the house.'

'Well, it's not *that* bad, is it, Pete?' laughed Franklin, tousling his son's dark, unruly hair.

'When are you going to take me down in a sub, Daddy?' asked Peter, for approximately the hundredth time.

'One of these days, when you're big enough not to get in the way.'

'But if you wait until I am big, I *will* get in the way.'

'There's logic for you!' said Indra. 'I told you my child was a genius.'

'He may have got his hair from you,' said Franklin, 'But it doesn't follow that you're responsible for what lies beneath it.' He turned to Don, who was making ridiculous noises for Anne's benefit. She seemed unable to decide whether to laugh or to burst into tears, but was obviously giving the problem her urgent attention. 'When are you going to settle down to the joys of domesticity? You can't be an honorary uncle all your life.'

For once, Don looked a little embarrassed.

'As a matter of fact,' he said slowly, 'I'm thinking about it. I've met someone at last who looks as if she might be willing.'

'Congratulations! I thought you and Marie were seeing a lot of each other.'

Don looked still more embarrassed.

'Well – ah – it isn't Marie. I was just trying to say goodbye to *her*.'

'Oh,' said Franklin, considerably deflated. 'Who is it?'

'I don't think you know her. She's named June – June Curtis. She isn't in the bureau at all, which is an advantage in some ways. I've not quite made up my mind yet, but I'll probably ask her next week.'

'There's only one thing to do,' said Indra firmly. 'As soon as you come back from this hunt, bring her around to dinner and I'll tell you what we think of her.'

'And I'll tell her what we think of *you*,' put in Franklin. 'We can't be fairer than that, can we?'

He remembered Indra's words – 'this is going to be one of your last missions' – as the little depth ship slanted swiftly down into the eternal night. It was not strictly true, of course; even though he had now been promoted to a permanent shore position, he would still occasionally go to sea. But the opportunities would become fewer and fewer; this was his swan song as a warden, and he did not know whether to be sorry or glad.

For seven years he had roamed the oceans – one year of his life to each of the seas – and in that time he had grown to know the creatures of the deep as no man could ever have done in any earlier age. He had watched the sea in all its moods; he had coasted over mirror-flat waters, and had felt the surge of mighty waves lifting his vessel when it was a hundred feet below the storm-tossed surface. He had looked upon beauty and horror and birth and death in all their multitudinous forms, as he moved through a liquid world so teeming with life that by comparison the land was an empty desert.

No man could ever exhaust the wonder of the sea, but Franklin knew that the time had come for him to take up new tasks. He looked at the sonar screen for the accompanying cigar of light which was Don's ship, and thought affectionately of their common characteristics and of the differences which now must take them further apart. Who would have imagined, he told himself, that they would become such good friends, that far-off day when they had met warily as instructor and pupil?

That had been only seven years ago, but already it was hard for him to remember the sort of person he had been in those days. He felt an abiding gratitude for the psychologists who had not only rebuilt his mind but had found him the work that could rebuild his life.

His thoughts completed the next, inevitable step. Memory tried to recreate Irene and the boys – good heavens, Rupert would be twelve years old now! – around whom his whole existence had once revolved, but who now were strangers drifting further and further apart year by year. The last photograph he had of them was already more than a year old; the last letter from Irene had been posted on Mars six months ago, and he reminded himself guiltily that he had not yet answered it.

All the grief had gone long ago; he felt no pain at being an exile in his own world, no ache to see once more the faces of friends he had known in the days when he counted all space his empire. There was only a wistful sadness, not even wholly unpleasant, and a mild regret for the inconsistency of sorrow.

Don's voice broke into his reverie, which had never taken his attention away from his crowded instrument panel.

'We're just passing my record, Walt. Ten thousand's the deepest I've ever been.'

'And we're only halfway there. Still, what difference does it make if you've got the right ship? It just takes a bit longer to go down, and a bit longer to come up. These subs would still have a safety factor of five at the bottom of the Philippine Trench.'

'That's true enough, but you can't convince me there's no psychological difference. Don't *you* feel two miles of water on your shoulders?'

It was most unlike Don to be so imaginative; usually it was Franklin who made such remarks and was promptly laughed at. If Don was getting moody, it would be best to give him some of his own medicine.

'Tell me when you've got to start boiling,' said Franklin. 'If the water gets up to your chin, we'll turn back.'

He had to admit that the feeble joke helped his own morale. The knowledge that the pressure around him was rising steadily to five tons per square inch did have a definite effect on his mind – an effect he had never experienced in shallow-water operations where disaster could be just as instantaneous, just as total. He had complete confidence in his equipment and knew that curious feeling of depression which seemed to have taken most of the zest out of the project into which he had put so much effort.

Five thousand feet lower down, that zest returned with all its old vigour. They both saw the echo simultaneously, and for a moment were shouting at cross purposes until they remembered their signals discipline. When silence had been restored, Franklin gave his orders.

'Cut your motor to quarter speed,' he said. 'We know the

beast's very sensitive and we don't want to scare it until the last minute.'

'Can't we flood the bow tanks and glide down?'

'Take too long – he's still three thousand feet below. And cut your sonar to minimum power; I don't want him picking up our pulses.'

The animal was moving in a curiously erratic path at a constant depth, sometimes making little darts to right or left as if in search of food. It was following the slopes of an unusually steep submarine mountain, which rose abruptly some four thousand feet from the sea bed. Not for the first time, Franklin thought what a pity it was that the world's most stupendous scenery was all sunk beyond sight in the ocean depths. Nothing on the land could compare with the hundred-mile-wide canyons of the North Atlantic, or the monstrous potholes that gave the Pacific the deepest soundings on earth.

They sank slowly below the summit of the submerged mountain – a mountain whose topmost peak was three miles below sea level. Only a little way beneath them now that mysteriously elongated echo seemed to be undulating through the water with a sinuous motion which reminded Franklin irresistibly of a snake. It would, he thought, be ironic if the Great Sea Serpent turned out to be exactly that. But that was impossible, for there were no water-breathing snakes.

Neither man spoke during the slow and cautious approach to their goal. They both realized that this was one of the great moments of their lives, and wished to savour it to the full. Until now, Don had been mildly sceptical, believing that whatever they found would be no more than some already-known species of animal. But as the echo on the screen expanded, so its strangeness grew. This was something wholly new.

The mountain was now looming above them; they were skirting the foot of a cliff more than two thousand feet high, and their quarry was less than half a mile ahead. Franklin felt his hand itching to throw on the ultraviolet searchlights which in an instant might solve the oldest mystery of the sea, and bring him enduring fame. How important to him was that? he asked himself, as the seconds ticked by. That it was important, he did not attempt to hide from himself. In all his career, he might never have another opportunity like this . . .

Suddenly, without the slightest warning, the sub trembled as if struck by a hammer. At the same moment Don cried out: 'My God – what was that?'

'Some damn fool is letting off explosives,' Franklin replied, rage and frustration completely banishing fear. 'Wasn't everyone notified of our dive?'

'That's no explosion. I've felt it before – it's an earthquake.'

No other word could so swiftly have conjured up once more all that terror of the ultimate depths which Franklin had felt brushing briefly against his mind during their descent. At once the immeasurable weight of the waters crushed down upon them like a physical burden; his sturdy craft seemed the frailest of cockleshells, already doomed by forces which all man's science could no longer hold at bay.

He knew that earthquakes were common in the deep Pacific, where the weights of rock and water were forever poised in precarious equilibrium. Once or twice on patrols he had felt distant shocks – but this time, he felt certain, he was near the epicentre.

'Make full speed for the surface,' he ordered. 'That may be just the beginning.'

'But we only need another five minutes,' Don protested. 'Let's chance it, Walt.'

Franklin was sorely tempted. That single shock might be the only one; the strain on the tortured strata miles below might have been relieved. He glanced at the echo they had been chasing; it was moving much faster now, as if it, too, had been frightened by this display of Natures' slumbering power.

'We'll risk it,' Franklin decided. 'But if there's another one we'll go straight up.'

'Fair enough,' answered Don. 'I'll bet you ten to one—'

He never completed the sentence. This time the hammer blow was no more violent, but it was sustained. The entire ocean seemed to be in travail as the shock waves, travelling at almost a mile a second, were reflected back and forth between surface and sea bed. Franklin shouted the one word

'Up!' and tilted the sub as steeply as he dared towards the distant sky.

But the sky was gone. The sharply defined plane which marked the water-air interface on the sonar screen had vanished, replaced by a meaningless jumble of hazy echoes. For a moment Franklin assumed that the set had been put out of action by the shocks; then his mind interpreted the incredible, the terrifying picture that was taking shape upon the screen.

'Don,' he yelled, 'run for the open sea – the mountain's falling!'

The billions of tons of rock that had been towering above them were sliding down into the deep. The whole face of the mountain had split away and was descending in a waterfall of stone, moving with a deceptive slowness and an utterly irresistible power. It was an avalanche in slow motion, but Franklin knew that within seconds the waters through which the sub was driving would be torn with falling debris.

He was moving at full speed, yet he seemed motionless. Even without the amplifiers, he could hear through the hull the rumble and roar of grinding rock. More than half the sonar image was now obliterated, either by solid fragments or by the immense clouds of mud and silt that were now beginning to fill the sea. He was becoming blind; there was nothing he could do but hold his course and pray.

With a muffled thud, something crashed against the hull and the sub groaned from end to end. For a moment Franklin thought he had lost control; then he managed to fight the vessel back to an even keel. No sooner had he done this than he realized he was in the grip of a powerful current, presumably due to water displaced by the collapsing mountain. He welcomed it, for it was sweeping him to the safety of the open sea, and for the first time he dared to hope.

Where was Don? It was impossible to see his echo in the shifting chaos of the sonar screen. Franklin switched his communication set to high power and started calling through the moving darkness. There was no reply; probably Don was too busy to answer, even if he had received the signal.

The pounding shock waves had ceased; with them had

gone the worst of Franklin's fears. There was no danger now of the hull being cracked by pressure, and by this time, surely, he was clear of the slowly toppling mountain. The current that had been aiding his engines had now lost its strength, proving that he was far away from its source. On the sonar screen, the luminous haze that had blocked all vision was fading minute by minute as the silt and debris subsided.

Slowly the wrecked face of the mountain emerged from the mist of conflicting echoes. The pattern on the screen began to stabilize itself, and presently Franklin could see the great scar left by the avalanche. The sea bed itself was still hidden in a vast fog of mud; it might be hours before it would be visible again and the damage wrought by Nature's paroxysm could be ascertained.

Franklin watched and waited as the screen cleared. With each sweep of the scanner, the sparkle of interference faded; the water was still turbid, but no longer full of suspended matter. He could see for a mile – then two – then three.

And in all that space there was no sign of the sharp and brilliant echoes that would mark Don's ship. Hope faded as his radius of vision grew and the screen remained empty. Again and again he called into the lonely silence, while grief and helplessness strove for the mastery of his soul.

He exploded the signal grenades that would alert all the hydrophones in the Pacific and send help racing to him by sea and air. But even as he began his slowly descending spiral search, he knew that it was in vain.

Don Burley had lost his last bet.

PART THREE

The Bureaucrat

CHAPTER 18

THE GREAT MERCATOR chart that covered the whole of one wall was a most unusual one. All the land areas were completely blank; as far as this map maker was concerned, the continents had never been explored. But the sea was crammed with detail, and scattered over its face were countless spots of coloured light, projected by some mechanism inside the wall. Those spots moved slowly from hour to hour, recording as they did so, for skilled eyes to read, the migration of all the main schools of whales that roamed the seas.

Franklin had seen the master chart scores of times during the last fourteen years – but never from this vantage point. For he was looking at it now from the director's chair.

'There's no need for me to warn you, Walter,' said his ex-chief, 'that you are taking over the bureau at a very tricky time. Sometime in the next five years we're going to have a showdown with the farms. Unless we can improve our efficiency, plankton-derived proteins will soon be substantially cheaper than any we can deliver.

'And that's only one of our problems. The staff position is getting more difficult every year – and this sort of thing isn't going to help.'

He pushed a folder across to Franklin, who smiled wryly when he saw what it contained. The advertisement was familiar enough; it had appeared in all the major magazines during the past week, and must have cost the Space Department a small fortune.

An underwater scene of improbable clarity and colour was spread across two pages. Vast scaly monsters, more huge and hideous than any that had lived on Earth since the Jurassic period, were battling each other in the crystalline depths. Franklin knew, from the photographs he had seen, that they were very accurately painted, and he did not grudge the illustrator his artistic licence in the matter of underwater clarity.

The text was dignified and avoided sensationalism; the painting was sensational enough and needed no embellishment. The Space Department, he read, urgently needed young men as wardens and food production experts for the exploitation of the seas of Venus. The work, it was added, was probably the most exciting and rewarding to be found anywhere in the solar system; pay was good and the qualifications were not as high as those needed for space pilot or astrogator. After the short list of physical and educational requirements, the advertisement ended with the words which the Venus Commission had been plugging for the last six months, and which Franklin had grown heartily tired of seeing: HELP TO BUILD A SECOND EARTH.

'Meanwhile,' said the ex-director, 'our problem is to keep the first one going, when the bright youngsters who might be joining us are running away to Venus. And between you and me, I shouldn't be surprised if the Space Department had been after some of our men.'

'They wouldn't do a thing like that!'

'Wouldn't they now? Anyway, there's a transfer application in from First Warden McRae; if you can't talk him out of it, try to find what made him want to leave.'

Life was certainly going to be difficult, Franklin thought. Joe McRae was an old friend; could he impose on that friendship now that he was Joe's boss?

'Another of your little problems is going to be keeping the scientists under control. Lundquist is worse than Roberts ever was; he's got about six crazy schemes going, and at least Roberts only had one brainstorm at a time. He spends half his time over on Heron Island. It might be a good idea to fly over and have a look at him. That was something I never had a chance to get around to.'

Franklin was still listening politely as his predecessor continued, with obvious relish, to point out the many disadvantages of his new post. Most of them he already knew, and his mind was now far away. He was thinking how pleasant it would be to begin his directorate with an official visit to Heron Island, which he had not seen for nearly five years, and which had so many memories of his first days in the bureau.

Dr Lundquist was flattered by the new director's visit, being innocent enough to hope that it might lead to increased support for his activities. He would not have been so enthusiastic had he guessed that the opposite was more likely to be the case. No one could have been more sympathetic than Franklin to scientific research, but now that he had to approve the bills himself he found that his point of view was subtly altered. Whatever Lundquist was doing would have to be of direct value to the bureau. Otherwise it was out – unless the Department of Scientific Research could be talked into taking it over.

Lundquist was a small, intense little man whose rapid and somewhat jerky movements reminded Franklin of a sparrow. He was an enthusiast of a type seldom met these days, and he combined a sound scientific background with an unfettered imagination. How unfettered, Franklin was soon to discover.

Yet at first sight it seemed that most of the work going on at the lab was of a fairly routine nature. Franklin spent a dull half-hour while two young scientists explained the methods they were developing to keep whales free of the many parasites that plagued them, and then escaped by the skin of his teeth from a lecture on cetacean obstetrics. He listened with more interest to the latest work on artificial insemination, having in the past helped with some of the early – and often hilariously unsuccessful – experiments along this line. He sniffed cautiously at some synthetic ambergris, and agreed that it seemed just like the real thing. And he listened to the recorded heartbeat of a whale before and after the cardiac operation that had saved his life, and pretended that he could hear the difference.

Everything here was perfectly in order, and just as he had expected. Then Lundquist steered him out of the lab and down to the big pool, saying as he did so: 'I think you'll find this more interesting. It's only in the experimental stage, of course, but it has possibilities.'

The scientist looked at his watch and muttered to himself, 'Two minutes to go; she's usually in sight by now.' He glanced out beyond the reef, then said with satisfaction, 'Ah – there she is!'

A long black mound was moving in towards the island, and a moment later Franklin saw the typical stubby spout of vapour which identified the humpback whale. Almost at once he saw a second, much smaller spout, and realized that he was watching a female and her calf. Without hesitation, both animals came in through the narrow channel that had been blasted through the coral years ago so that small boats could come up to the lab. They turned left into a large tidal pool that had been here on Franklin's last visit, and remained there waiting patiently like well-trained dogs.

Two lab technicians, wearing oilskins, were trundling something that looked like a fire extinguisher to the edge of the pool. Lundquist and Franklin hurried to join them, and it was soon obvious why the oilskins were necessary on this bright and cloudless day. Every time the whales spouted there was a miniature rainstorm, and Franklin was glad to borrow protection from the descending and nauseous spray.

Even a warden seldom saw a live whale at such close quarters, and under such ideal conditions. The mother was about fifty feet long, and, like all humpbacks, very massively built. She was no beauty, Franklin decided, and the large, irregular warts along the leading edges of her flippers did nothing to add to her appearance. The little calf was about twenty feet in length, and did not appear to be too happy in its confined quarters, for it was anxiously circling its stolid mother.

One of the scientists gave a curious, high-pitched, shout, and at once the whale rolled over on her side, bringing half of her pleated belly out of the water. She did not seem to mind when a large rubber cup was placed over the now-exposed teat; indeed, she was obviously cooperating, for the meter on the collecting tank was recording an astonishing rate of flow.

'You know, of course,' explained Lundquist, 'that the cows eject their milk under pressure, so that the calves can feed when the teats are submerged without getting water in their mouths. But when the calves are *very* young, the mother rolls over like this so that the baby can feed above water. It makes things a lot simpler for us.'

The obedient whale, without any instructions that Franklin could detect, had now circled round in her pen and was rolling over on the other side, so that her second teat could be milked. He looked at the meter; it now registered just under fifty gallons, and was still rising. The calf was obviously getting worried, or perhaps it had become excited by the milk that had accidentally spilled into the water. It made several attempts to bunt its mechanical rival out of the way, and had to be discouraged by a few sharp smacks.

Franklin was impressed, but not surprised. He knew that this was not the first time that whales had been milked, though he did not know that it could now be done with such neatness and dispatch. But where was it leading? Knowing Dr Lundquist, he could guess.

'Now,' said the scientist, obviously hoping that the demonstration had made its desired impact, 'we can get at least five hundred pounds of milk a day from a cow without interfering with the calf's growth. And if we start breeding for milk as the farmers have done on land, we should be able to get a ton a day without any trouble. You think that's a lot? I regard it as quite a modest target. After all, prize cattle have given over a hundred pounds of milk a day – and a whale weighs a good deal more than twenty times as much as a cow!'

Franklin did his best to interrupt the statistics.

'That's all very well,' he said. 'I don't doubt your figures. And equally I don't doubt that you can process the milk to remove that oily taste – yes, I've tried it, thanks. But how the devil are you going to round up all the cows in a herd – especially a herd that migrates ten thousand miles a year?'

'Oh, we've worked all that out. It's partly a matter of training, and we've learned a lot getting Susan here to obey our underwater recordings. Have you ever been to a dairy farm and watched how the cows walk into the autolactor at milking time and walk out again – without a human being coming within miles of the place? And believe me, whales are a lot smarter and more easily trained than cows! I've sketched out the rough designs for a milk tanker that can deal with four whales at once, and could follow the herd as it migrates. In any case, now that we can control the plankton yield we can stop migration if we want to, and keep the whales in the tropics without them getting hungry. The whole thing's quite practical, I assure you.'

Despite himself, Franklin was fascinated by the idea. It had been suggested, in some form or other, for many years, but Dr Lundquist seemed to have been the first to do anything about it.

The mother whale and her still somewhat indignant calf had now set out to sea, and were soon spouting and diving noisily beyond the edge of the reef. As Franklin watched them go, he wondered if in a few years' time he would see hundreds of the great beasts lined up obediently as they swam to the mobile milking plants, each delivering a ton of what was known to be one of the richest foods on earth. But it might remain only a dream; there would be countless practical problems to be faced, and what had been achieved on the laboratory scale with a single animal might prove out of the question in the sea.

'What I'd like you to do,' he said to Lundquist, 'is to let me have a report showing what an – er – whale dairy would require in terms of equipment and personnel. Try to give costs wherever you can. And then estimate how much milk it could deliver, and what the processing plants would pay for that. Then we'll have something definite to work on. At the moment it's an interesting experiment, but no one can say if it has any practical application.'

Lundquist seemed slightly disappointed at Franklin's lack of enthusiasm, but rapidly warmed up again as they walked away from the pool. If Franklin had thought that a little project like setting up a whale dairy had exhausted Lundquist's powers of extrapolation, he was going to learn better.

'The next proposal I want to talk about,' began the scientist, 'is still entirely in the planning stage. I know that one of our most serious problems is staff shortage, and I've been trying to think of ways in which we can improve efficiency by releasing men from routine jobs.'

'Surely that process had gone about as far as it can, short of making everything completely automatic? Anyway, it's less than a year since the last team of efficiency experts went over us.' (And, added Franklin to himself, the bureau isn't quite back to normal yet.)

'My approach to the problem,' explained Lundquist, 'is a little unconventional, and as an ex-warden yourself I think you'll be particularly interested in it. As you know, it normally takes two or even three subs to round up a large school of whales; if a single sub tries it, they'll scatter in all directions. Now this has often seemed to me a shocking waste of man power and equipment, since all the thinking could be done by a single warden. He only needs his partners to make the right noises in the right places – something a machine could do just as well.'

'If you're thinking of automatic slave subs,' said Franklin, 'it's been tried – and it didn't work. A warden can't handle two ships at once, let alone three.'

'I know all about *that* experiment,' answered Lundquist. 'It could have been a success if they'd tackled it properly. But my idea is much more revolutionary. Tell me – does the name "sheep dog" mean anything to you?'

Franklin wrinkled his brow. 'I think so,' he replied. 'Weren't they dogs that the old-time shepherds used to protect their flocks, a few hundred years ago?'

'It happened until less than a hundred years ago. And "protect" is an understatement with a vengeance. I've been looking at film records of sheep dogs in action, and no one who hadn't seen them would believe some of the things they could do. Those dogs were so intelligent and so well-trained that they could make a flock of sheep do anything the shepherd wanted merely at a word of command from him. They could split a flock into sections, single out one solitary sheep from its fellows, or keep a flock motionless in one spot as long as their master ordered.

'Do you see what I am driving at? We've been training dogs for centuries, so such a performance doesn't seem miraculous to us. What I am suggesting is that we repeat the pattern in the sea. We know that a good many marine mammals – seals and porpoises, for instance – are at least as intelligent as dogs, but except in circuses and places like Marineland there's been no attempt to train them. You've seen the tricks our porpoises here can do, and you know how affectionate and friendly they are. When you've watched these old films of sheep-dog trials, you'll agree that anything a dog could do a hundred years ago we can teach a porpoise to do today.'

'Just a minute,' said Franklin, a little overwhelmed. 'Let me get this straight. Are you proposing that every warden should have a couple of – er – hounds working with him when he rounds up a school of whales?'

'For certain operations, yes. Of course, the technique would have limitations; no marine animal has the speed and range of a sub, and the hounds, as you've called them, couldn't always get to the places where they were needed. But I've done some studies and I think it would be possible to double the effectiveness of our wardens in this way, by eliminating the times when they had to work in pairs or trios.'

'But,' protested Franklin, 'what notice would whales take of porpoises? They'd ignore them completely.'

'Oh, I wasn't suggesting that we should use porpoises; that was merely an example. You're quite right – the whales wouldn't even notice them. We'll have to use an animal that's fairly large, at least as intelligent as the porpoise, and which whales will pay a great deal of attention to indeed. There's only one animal that fills the bill, and I'd like your authority to catch one and train it.'

'Go on,' said Franklin, with such a note of resignation in his voice that even Lundquist, who had little sense of humour, was forced to smile.

'What I want to do,' he continued, 'is to catch a couple of killer whales and train them to work with one of our wardens.'

Franklin thought of the thirty-foot torpedoes of ravening power he had so often chased and slaughtered in the frozen polar seas. It was hard to picture one of these ferocious beasts tamed to man's bidding; then he remembered the chasm betweeen the sheep dog and the wolf, and how that had long ago been bridged. Yes, it could be done again – if it was worthwhile.

When in doubt, ask for a report, one of his superiors had once told him. Well, he was going to bring back at least two from Heron Island, and they would both make very thought-provoking reading. But Lundquist's schemes, exciting though they were, belong to the future; Franklin had to run the bureau as it was here and now. He would prefer to avoid drastic changes for a few years, until he had learned his way about. Besides, even if Lundquist's idea could be proved practical, it would be a long, stiff battle selling them to the people who approved the funds. 'I want to buy fifty milking machines for whales, please.' Yes, Franklin could picture the reaction in certain conservative quarters. And as for training killer whales – why, they would think he had gone completely crazy.

He watched the island fall away as the plane lifted him towards home (strange, after all his travels, that he should be living again in the country of his birth). It was almost fifteen years since he had first made this journey with poor old Don; how glad Don would have been, could he have seen this final fruit of his careful training! And Professor Stevens, too – Franklin had always been a little scared of him, but now he could have looked him in the face, had he still been alive. With a twinge of remorse, he realized that he had never properly thanked the psychologist for all that he had done.

Fifteen years from a neurotic trainee to director of the bureau; that wasn't bad going. And what now, Walter? Franklin asked himself. He felt no need of any further achievement; perhaps his ambition was now satisfied. He would be quite content to guide the bureau into a placid and uneventful future.

It was lucky for his peace of mind that he had no idea how futile that hope was going to be.

CHAPTER 19

THE PHOTOGRAPHER had finished, but the young man who had been Franklin's shadow for the last two days still seemed to have an unlimited supply of notebooks and questions. Was it worth all this trouble to have your undistinguished features – probably superimposed on a montage of whales – displayed upon every bookstand in the world? Franklin doubted it, but he had no choice in the matter. He remembered the saying: 'Public servants have no private lives.' Like all aphorisms, it was only half true. No one had ever heard of the last director of the bureau, and he might have led an equally inconspicuous existence if the Marine Division's Public Relations Department had not decreed otherwise.

'Quite a number of your people, Mr Franklin,' said the young man from *Earth Magazine*, 'have told me about your interest in the so-called Great Sea Serpent, and the mission in which First Warden Burley was killed. Have there been any further developments in this field?'

Franklin sighed; he had been afraid that this would come up sooner or later, and he hoped that it wouldn't be overplayed in the resulting article. He walked over to his private file cabinet, and pulled out a thick folder of notes and photographs.

'Here are all the sightings, Bob,' he said. 'You might like to have a glance through them – I've kept the record up to date. One day I hope we'll have the answer; you can say it's still a hobby of mine, but it's one I've had no chance of doing anything about for the last eight years. It's up to the Department of Scientific Research now – not the Bureau of Whales. We've other jobs to do.'

He could have added a good deal more, but decided against it. If Secretary Farlan had not been transferred from DSR soon after the tragic failure of their mission, they might have had a second chance. But in the inquiries and recriminations that had followed the disaster, the opportunity had been lost, possibly for years. Perhaps in every man's life there must be some cherished failure, some unfinished business which outweighed many successes.

'Then there's only one other question I want to ask,' continued the reporter. 'What about the future of the bureau? Have you any interesting long-term plans you'd care to talk about?'

This was another tricky one. Franklin had learned long ago that men in his position must cooperate with the press, and in the last two days his busy interrogator had practically become one of the family. But there were some things that sounded a little too farfetched, and he had contrived to keep Dr Lundquist out of the way when Bob had flown over to Heron Island. True, he had seen the prototype milking machine and been duly impressed by it, but he had been told nothing about the two young killer whales being maintained, at great trouble and expense, in the enclosure off the eastern edge of the reef.

'Well, Bob,' he began slowly, 'by this time you probably know the statistics better than I do. We hope to increase the size of our herds by ten per cent over the next five years. If this milking scheme comes off – and it's still purely experimental – we'll start putting back on the sperm whales and will build up the humpbacks. At the moment we are providing twelve and a half per cent of the total food requirements of the human race, and that's quite a responsibility. I hope to see it fifteen per cent while I'm still in office.'

'So that everyone in the world will have whale steak at least once a week, eh?'

'Put it that way if you like. But people are eating whale all day without knowing it – every time they use cooking fat or spread margarine on a piece of bread. We could double our output and we'd get no credit for it, since our products are almost always disguised in something else.'

'The Art Department is going to put that right; when the story appears, we'll have a picture of the average household's groceries for a week, with a clock face on each item showing what percentage of it comes from whales.'

'That'll be fine. Er – by the way – have you decided what you're going to call me?'

The reporter grinned.

'That's up to my editor,' he answered. 'But I'll tell him to avoid the word "whaleboy" like the plague. It's too hackneyed, anyway.'

'Well, I'll believe you when we see the article. Every journalist promises he won't call us that, but it seems they can never resist the temptation. Incidentally, when do you expect the story to appear?'

'Unless some news story crowds it off, in about four weeks. You'll get the proofs, of course, before that – probably by the end of next week.'

Franklin saw him off through the outer office, half sorry to lose an entertaining companion who, even if he asked awkward questions, more than made up for it by the stories he could tell about most of the famous men on the planet. Now, he supposed, he belonged to that group himself, for at least a hundred million people would read the current 'Men of Earth' series.

The story appeared, as promised, four weeks later. It was accurate, well-written, and contained one mistake so trivial that Franklin himself had failed to notice it when he checked the proofs. The photographic coverage was excellent and contained an astonishing study of a baby whale suckling its mother, a shot obviously obtained at enoromus risk and after months of patient stalking. The fact that it was actually taken in the pool at Heron Island without the photographer even getting his feet wet was an irrelevance not allowed to distract the reader.

Apart from the shocking pun beneath the cover picture ('Prince of Whales', indeed!), Franklin was delighted with it; so was everyone else in the bureau, the Marine Division, and even the World Food Organization itself. No one could have guessed that within a few weeks it was to involve the Bureau of Whales in the greatest crisis of its entire history.

It was not lack of foresight; sometimes the future can be charted in advance, and plans made to meet it. But there are also times in human affairs when events that seem to have no possible connexion — to be as remote as if they occurred on different planets — may react upon each other with shattering violence.

The Bureau of Whales was an organization which had taken half a century to build up, and which now employed twenty thousand men and possessed equipment valued at over two billion dollars. It was a typical unit of the scientific world state, with all the power and prestige which that implied.

And now it was to be shaken to its foundations by the gentle words of a man who had lived half a thousand years before the birth of Christ.

Franklin was in London when the first hint of trouble

came. It was not unusual for officers of the World Food Organization to bypass his immediate superiors in the Marine Division and to contact him directly. What was unusual, however, was for the secretary of the WFO himself to interfere with the everyday working of the bureau, causing Franklin to cancel all his engagements and to find himself, still a little dazed, flying halfway around the world to a small town in Ceylon of which he had never heard before and whose name he could not even pronounce.

Fortunately, it had been a hot summer in London and the extra ten degrees at Colombo was not unduly oppressive. Franklin was met at the airport by the local WFO representative, looking very cool and comfortable in the sarong which had now been adopted by even the most conservative of westerners. He shook hands with the usual array of minor officials, was relieved to see that there were no reporters around who might tell him more about this mission than he knew himself, and swiftly transferred to the cross-country plane which would take him on the last hundred miles of his journey.

'Now,' he said, when he had recovered his breath and the miles of neatly laid-out automatic tea planations were flashing past beneath him, 'you'd better start briefing me. Why is it so important to rush me to Anna – whatever you call the place?'

'Anuradhapura. Hasn't the secretary told you?'

'We had just five minutes at London Airport. So you might as well start from scratch.'

'Well, this is something that has been building up for several years. We've warned Headquarters, but they've never taken us seriously. Now your interview in *Earth* has brought matters to a head; the Mahanayake Thero of Anuradhapura – he's the most influential man in the East, and you're going to hear a lot more about him – read it and promptly asked us to grant him facilities for a tour of the bureau. We can't refuse, of course, but we know perfectly well what he intends to do. He'll take a team of cameramen with him and will collect enough material to launch an all-out propaganda campaign against the bureau. Then, when it's had time to sink in, he'll demand a referendum. And if that goes against us, we *will* be in trouble.'

The pieces of the jigsaw fell into place; the pattern was at last clear. For a moment Franklin felt annoyed that he had been diverted across the world to deal with so absurd a challenge. Then he realized that the men who had sent him here did not consider it absurd; they must know, better than he did, the strength of the forces that were being marshalled. It was never wise to underestimate the power of religion, even a religion as pacific and tolerant as Buddhism.

The position was one which, even a hundred years ago, would have seemed unthinkable, but the catastrophic political and social changes of the last century had all combined to give it a certain inevitability. With the failure or weakening of its three great rivals, Buddhism was now the only religion that still possessed any real power over the minds of men.

Christianity, which had never fully recovered from the shattering blow given it by Darwin and Freud, had finally unexpectedly succumbed before the archaeological discoveries of the late twentieth century. The Hindu religion, with its fantastic pantheon of gods and goddesses, had failed to survive in an age of scientific rationalism. And the Mohammedan faith, weakened by the same forces, had suffered additional loss of prestige when the rising Star of David had outshone the pale crescent of the Prophet.

These beliefs still survived, and would linger on for generations yet, but all their power was gone. Only the teachings of the Buddha had maintained and even increased their influence, as they filled the vacuum left by the other faiths. Being a philosophy and not a religion, and relying on no revelations vulnerable to the archaeologists' hammer, Buddhism had been largely unaffected by the shocks that had destroyed the other giants. It had been purged and purified by internal reformations, but its basic structure was unchanged.

One of the fundamentals of Buddhism, as Franklin knew well enough, was respect for all other living creatures. It was a law that few Buddhists had ever obeyed to the letter, excusing themselves with the sophistry that it was quite in order to eat the flesh of an animal that someone else had killed. In recent years, however, attempts had been made to enforce this rule more rigorously, and there had been endless debates between vegetarians and meat eaters covering the whole spectrum of crankiness. That these arguments could have any practical effect on the work of the World Food Organization was something that Franklin had never seriously considered.

'Tell me,' he asked, as the fertile hills rolled swiftly past beneath him, 'what sort of man is this Thero you're taking me to see?'

'Thero is the title; you can translate it by archbishop if you like. His real name is Alexander Boyce, and he was born in Scotland sixty years ago.'

'Scotland?'

'Yes – he was the first westerner ever to reach the top of the Buddhist hierarchy, and he had to overcome a lot of opposition to do it. A bhikku – er, monk – friend of mine once complained that the Maha Thero was a typical elder of the kirk, born a few hundred years too late – so he'd reformed Buddhism instead of the church of Scotland.'

'How did he get to Ceylon in the first place?'

'Believe it or not, he came out as a junior technician in a film company. He was about twenty then. The story is that he went to film the statue of the Dying Buddha at the cave temple of Dambulla, and became converted. After that it took him twenty years to rise to the top, and he's been responsible for most of the reforms that have taken place since then. Religions get corrupt after a couple of thousand years and need a spring-cleaning. The Maha Thero did that job for Buddhism in Ceylon by getting rid of the Hindu gods that had crept into the temples.'

'And now he's looking around for fresh worlds to conquer?'

'It rather seems like it. He pretends to have nothing to do with politics, but he's thrown out a couple of governments just by raising his finger, and he's got a huge following in the East. His "Voice of Buddha" programmes are listened to by several hundred million people, and it's estimated that at least a billion are sympathetic towards him even if they won't go all the way with his views. So you'll understand why we are taking this seriously.'

Now that he had penetrated the disguise of an unfamiliar name, Franklin remembered that the Venerable

Alexander Boyce had been the subject of a cover story in *Earth Magazine* two or three years ago. So they had something in common; he wished now that he had read that article, but at the time it had been of no interest to him and he could not even recall the Thero's appearance.

'He's a deceptively quiet little man, very easy to get on with,' was the reply to his question. 'You'll find him reasonable and friendly, but once he's made up his mind he grinds through all opposition like a glacier. He's not a fanatic, if that's what you are thinking. If you can prove to him that any course of action is essential, he won't stand in the way even though he may not like what you're doing. He's not happy about our local drive for increased meat production, but he realizes that everybody can't be a vegetarian. We compromised with him by not building our new slaughter-house in either of the sacred cities, as we'd intended to do originally.'

'Then why should he suddenly have taken an interest in the Bureau of Whales?'

'He's probably decided to make a stand somewhere. And besides – don't you think whales are in a different class from other animals?' The remark was made half apologetically, as if in the expectation of denial or even ridicule.

Franklin did not answer; it was a question he had been trying to decide for twenty years, and the scene now passing below absolved him from the necessity.

He was flying over what had once been the greatest city in the world – a city against which Rome and Athens in their prime had been no more than villages – a city unchallenged in size or population until the heydays of London and New York, two thousand years later. A ring of huge artificial lakes, some of them miles across, surrounded the ancient home of the Singhalese kings. Even from the air, the modern town of Anuradhapura showed startling contrasts of old and new. Dotted here and there among the colourful, gossamer buildings of the twenty-first century were the immense, bell-shaped domes of the great dagobas. The mightiest of all – the Abhayagiri Dagoba – was pointed out to Franklin as the plane flew low over it. The brickwork of the dome had long ago been overgrown with grass and even small trees, so that the great temple now appeared no more than a curiously symmetrical hill surmounted by a broken spire. It was a hill exceeded in size by one only of the pyramids that the Pharaohs had built beside the Nile.

By the time that Franklin had reached the local Food Production office, conferred with the superintendent, donated a few platitudes to a reporter who had somehow discovered his presence, and eaten a leisurely meal, he felt that he knew how to handle the situation. It was, after all, merely another public-relations problem; there had been a very similar one about three weeks ago, when a sensational and quite inaccurate newspaper story about methods of whale slaughtering had brought a dozen Societies for the Prevention of Cruelty down upon his head. A fact-finding commission had disposed of the charges very quickly, and no permanent damage had been done to anybody except the reporter concerned.

He did not feel quite so confident, a few hours later, as he stood looking up at the soaring, gilded spire of the Ruanveliseya Dagoba. The immense white dome had been so skilfully restored that it seemed inconceivable that almost twenty-two centuries had passed since its foundations were laid. Competely surrounding the paved courtyard of the temple was a line of life-sized elephants, forming a wall more than a quarter of a mile long. Art and faith had united here to produce one of the world's masterpieces of architecture, and the sense of antiquity was overwhelming. How many of the creations of modern man, wondered Franklin, would be so perfectly preserved in the year 4000?

The great flagstones in the courtyard were burning hot, and he was glad that he had retained his stockings when he left his shoes at the gate. At the base of the dome, which rose like a shining mountain towards the cloudless blue sky, was a single-storied modern building whose clean lines and white plastic walls harmonized well with the work of architects who had died a hundred years before the beginning of the Christian era.

A saffron-robed bhikku led Franklin into the Thero's neat and comfortably air-conditioned office. It might have been that of any busy administrator, anywhere in the world, and the sense of strangeness, which had made him feel ill at ease ever since he had entered the courtyard of the temple, began to fade.

The Maha Thero rose to greet him; he was a small man, his head barely reaching the level of Franklin's shoulders. His gleaming, shaven scalp somehow depersonalized him, making it hard to judge what he was thinking and harder still to fit him into any familiar categories. At first sight, Franklin was not impressed; then he remembered how many small men had been movers and shakers of the world.

Even after forty years, the Mahanayake Thero had not lost the accent of his birth. At first it seemed incongruous, if not slightly comic, in these surroundings, but within a few minutes Franklin was completely unaware of it.

'It's very good of you to come all this way to see me, Mr Franklin,' said the Thero affably as he shook hands. 'I must admit that I hardly expected my request to be dealt with quite so promptly. It hasn't inconvenienced you, I trust?'

'No,' replied Franklin manfully. 'In fact,' he added with rather more truth, 'this visit is a novel experience, and I'm grateful for the opportunity of making it.'

'Excellent!' said the Thero, apparently with genuine pleasure. 'I feel just the same way about my trip down to your South Georgia base, though I don't suppose I'll enjoy the weather there.'

Franklin remembered his instructions – 'Head him off if you possibly can, but don't try to put any fast ones across on him.' Well, he had been given an opening here.

'There's one point I wanted to raise with you, Your Reverence,' he answered, hoping he had chosen the correct honorific. 'It's midwinter in South Georgia, and the base is virtually closed down until late spring. It won't be operating again for about five months.'

'How foolish of me – I should have remembered. But I've never been to the Antarctic and I've always wanted to; I suppose I was trying to give myself an excuse. Well – it will have to be one of the northern bases. Which do you suggest – Greenland or Iceland? Just tell me which is more convenient. We don't want to cause any trouble.'

It was that last phrase which defeated Franklin before the battle had fairly begun. He knew now that he was dealing with an adversary who could be neither fooled nor deflected from his course. He would simply have to go along with the Thero, dragging his heels as hard as he could, and hoping for the best.

CHAPTER 20

THE WIDE bay was dotted with feathery plumes of mist as the great herd milled around in uncertain circles, not alarmed by the voices that had called it to this spot between the mountains, but merely undecided as to their meaning. All their lives the whales had obeyed the orders that came, sometimes in the form of water-borne vibrations, sometimes in electric shocks, from the small creatures whom they recognized as masters. Those orders, they had come to learn, had never harmed them; often, indeed, they had led them to fertile pastures which they would never have found unaided, for they were in regions of the sea which all their experience and the memories of a million years told them should be barren. And sometimes the small masters had protected them from the killers, turning aside the ravening packs before they could tear their living victims into fragments.

They had no enemies and no fears. For generations now they had roamed the peaceful oceans of the world, growing fatter and sleeker and more contented than all their ancestors back to the beginning of time. In fifty years they had grown, on an average, ten per cent longer and thirty per cent heavier, thanks to the careful stewardship of the masters. Even now the lord of all their race, the hundred-and-fifty-one-foot blue whale B69322, universally known as Leviathan, was sporting in the Gulf Stream with his mate and newborn calf. Leviathan could never have reached his present size in any earlier age; though such matters were beyond proof, he was probably the largest animal that had ever existed in the entire history of Earth.

Order was emerging out of chaos as the directing fields started to guide the herd along invisible channels. Presently the electric barriers gave way to concrete ones; the whales were swimming along four parallel canals, too narrow for more than one to pass at a time. Automatic senses weighed and measured them, rejecting all those below a certain size and diverting them back into the sea – doubtless a little puzzled, and quite unaware how seriously their numbers had been depleted.

The whales that had passed the test swam on trustfully along the the two remaining channels until presently they came to a large lagoon. Some tasks could not be left entirely to machines; there were human inspectors here to see that no mistakes had been made, to check the condition of the animals, and to log the numbers of the doomed beasts as they left the lagoon on their last, short swim into the killing pens.

'B52111 coming up,' said Franklin to the Thero as they stood together in the observation chamber. 'Seventy-foot female, known to have had five calves – past the best age for breeding.' Behind him, he knew the cameras were silently recording the scene as their ivory-skulled, saffron-robed operators handled them with a professional skill which had surprised him until he learned that they had all been trained in Hollywood.

The whale never had any warning; it probably never even felt the gentle touch of the flexible copper fingers as they brushed its body. One moment it was swimming quietly along the pen; a second later it was a lifeless hulk, continuing to move forwards under its own momentum. The fifty-thousand-ampere current, passing through the heart like a stroke of lightning, had not been allowed time for a final convulsion.

At the end of the killing pen, the wide conveyor belt took the weight of the immense body and carried it up a short slope until it was completely clear of the water. Then it began to move slowly forwards along an endless series of spinning rollers which seemed to stretch halfway to the horizon.

'This is the longest conveyor of its kind in the world,' Franklin explained with justifiable pride. 'It may have as many as ten whales – say a thousand tons – on it at one time. Although it involves us in considerable expense, and greatly restricts our choice of site, we always have the processing plant at least half a mile from the pens, so there is no danger of the whales being frightened by the smell of blood. I think you'll agree that not only is the slaughtering instantaneous but the animals show no alarm whatsoever right up to the end.'

'Perfectly true,' said the Thero. 'It all seems very humane. Still, if the whales did get frightened it would be very difficult to handle them, wouldn't it? I wonder if you would go to all this trouble merely to spare their feelings?'

It was a shrewd question, and like a good many he had been asked in the last few days Franklin was not quite sure how to answer it.

'I suppose,' he said slowly, 'that would depend on whether we could get the money. It would be up to the World Assembly, in the final analysis. The finance committees would have to decide how kind we could afford to be. It's a theoretical question, anyway.'

'Of course – but other questions aren't so theoretical,' answered the Venerable Boyce, looking thoughtfully at the eighty tons of flesh and bone moving into the distance. 'Shall we get back to the car? I want to see what happens at the other end.'

And I, thought Franklin grimly, will be very interested to see how you and your colleagues take it. Most visitors who went through the processing yards emerged rather pale and shaken, and quite a few had been known to faint. It was a standard joke in the bureau that this lesson in food production removed the appetites of all who watched it for several hours after the experience.

The stench hit them while they were still a hundred yards away. Out of the corner of his eye, Franklin could see that the young bhikku carrying the sound recorder was already showing signs of distress, but the Maha Thero seemed completely unaffected. He was still calm and dispassionate five minutes later as he stared down into the reeking inferno where the great carcasses were torn asunder into mountains of meat and bone and guts.

'Just think of it,' said Franklin, 'for almost two hundred years this job was done by men, often working on board a pitching deck in filthy weather. It's not pretty to watch even now, but can you imagine being down there hacking away with a knife nearly as big as yourself?'

'I think I could,' answered the Thero, 'but I'd prefer not to.' He turned to his cameraman and gave some brief instructions, then watched intently as the next whale arrived on the conveyer belt.

The great body had already been scanned by photo-electric eyes and its dimensions fed in the computer controlling the operations. Even when one knew how it was done, it was uncanny to watch the precision with which the knives and saws moved out on their extensible arms, made their carefully planned pattern of cuts, and then retreated again. Huge grabs seized the foot-thick blanket of blubber and stripped it off as a man peels a banana, leaving the naked, bleeding carcass to move on along the conveyer to the first stage of its dismemberment.

The whale travelled as fast as a man could comfortably walk, and disintegrated before the eyes of the watchers as they kept pace with it. Slabs of meat as large as elephants were torn away and went sliding down side chutes; circular saws whirred through the scaffolding of ribs in a cloud of bone dust; the interlinked plastic bags of the intestines, stuffed with perhaps a ton of shrimps and plankton from the whale's last meal, were dragged away in noisome heaps.

It had taken less than two minutes to reduce a lord of the sea to a bloody shambles which no one but an expert could have recognized. Not even the bones were wasted; at the end of the conveyer belt, the disarticulated skeleton fell into a pit where it would be ground into fertilizer.

'This is the end of the line,' said Franklin, 'but as far as the processing side is concerned it's only the beginning. The oil has to be extracted from the blubber you saw peeled off in stage one; the meat has to be cut down into more manageable portions and sterilized – we use a high-intensity neutron source for that – and about ten other basic products have to be sorted out and packed for shipment. I'll be glad to show you around any part of the factory you'd like to see. It won't be quite so gruesome as the operations we've just been watching.'

The Thero stood for a moment in thoughtful silence, studying the notes he had been making in his incredibly tiny hand-writing. Then he looked back along the blood-stained quarter-mile of moving belt, towards the next whale arriving from the killing pen.

'There's one sequence I'm not sure we managed to film properly,' he said, coming to a sudden decision. 'If you don't mind, I'd like to go back to the beginning and start again.'

Franklin caught the recorder as the young monk dropped it. 'Never mind, son,' he said reassuringly, 'the first time is always the worst. When you've been here a few days, you'll be quite puzzled when newcomers complain of the stink.'

That was hard to believe, but the permanent staff had assured him that it was perfectly true. He only hoped that the Venerable Boyce was not so thoroughgoing that he would have a chance of putting it to the proof.

'And now, Your Reverence,' said Franklin, as the plane lifted above the snow-covered mountains and began the homeward flight to London and Ceylon, 'do you mind if I ask how you intend to use all the material you've gathered?'

During the two days they had been together, priest and administrator had established a degree of friendship and mutual respect that Franklin, for his part, still found as surprising as it was pleasant. He considered – as who does not? – that he was good at summing men up, but there were depths in the Mahanayake Thero beyond his powers of analysis. It did not matter; he now knew instinctively that he was in the presence not only of power but also of – there was no escaping from that trite and jejune word – goodness. He had even begun to wonder, with a mounting awe that at any moment might deepen into certainty, if the man who was now his companion would go down into history as a saint.

'I have nothing to hide,' said the Thero gently, 'and, as you know, deceit is contrary to the teachings of the Buddha. Our position is quite simple. We believe that all creatures have a right to life, and it therefore follows that what you are doing is wrong. Accordingly, we would like to see it stopped.'

That was what Franklin had expected, but it was the first time he had obtained a definite statement. He felt a slight sense of disappointment; surely someone as intelligent as the

Thero must realize that such a move was totally impracticable, since it would involve cutting off one eighth of the total food supply of the world. And for that matter, why stop at whales? What about cows, sheep, pigs – all the animals that man kept in luxury and then slaughtered at his convenience?

'I know what you are thinking,' said the Thero, before he could voice his objections. 'We are fully aware of the problems involved, and realize that it will be necessary to move slowly. But a start must be made somewhere, and the Bureau of Whales gives us the most dramatic presentation of our case.'

'Thank you,' answered Franklin dryly. 'But is that altogether fair? What you've seen here happens in every slaughterhouse on the planet. The fact that the scale of operations is different hardly alters the case.'

'I quite agree. But we are practical men, not fanatics. We know perfectly well that alternative food sources will have to be found before the world's meat supplies can be cut off.'

Franklin shook his head in vigorous disagreement.

'I'm sorry,' he said, 'but even if you could solve the supply problem, you're not going to turn the entire population of the planet into vegetarians – unless you are anxious to encourage emigration to Mars and Venus. I'd shoot myself if I thought I could never eat a lamb chop or a well-done steak again. So your plans are bound to fail on two counts: human psychology and the sheer facts of food production.'

The Maha Thero looked a little hurt.

'My dear Director,' he said, 'surely you don't think we would overlook something as obvious as that? But let me finish putting our point of view before I explain how we propose to implement it. I'll be interested in studying your reactions, because you represent the maximum – ah – consumer resistance we are likely to meet.'

'Very well,' smiled Franklin. 'See if you can convert me out of my job.'

'Since the beginning of history,' said the Thero, 'man has assumed that the other animals exist only for his benefit. He has wiped out whole species, sometimes through sheer greed, sometimes because they destroyed his crops or interfered with his other activities. I won't deny that he often had justification, and frequently no alternative. But down the ages man has blackened his soul with his crimes against the animal kingdom – some of the very worst, incidentally, being in your particular profession, only sixty or seventy years ago. I've read of cases where harpooned whales died after hours of such frightful torment that not a scrap of their meat could be used – it was poisoned with the toxins produced by the animal's death agonies.'

'Very exceptional,' interjected Franklin. 'And anyway we've put a stop to that.'

'True, but it's all part of the debt we have to discharge.'

'Svend Foyn wouldn't have agreed with you. When he invented the explosive harpoon, back in the 1870's, he made an entry in his diary thanking God for having done all the work.'

'An interesting point of view,' answered the Thero dryly. 'I wish I'd had a chance of arguing it with him. You know, there is a simple test which divides the human race into two classes. If a man is walking along the street and sees a beetle crawling just where he is going to place his foot – well, he can break his stride and miss it or he can crush it into pulp. Which would *you* do, Mr Franklin?'

'It would depend on the beetle. If I knew it was poisonous, or a pest, I'd kill it. Otherwise I'd let it go. That, surely, is what any reasonable man would do.'

'Then we are not reasonable. We believe that killing is only justified to save the life of a higher creature – and it is surprising how seldom that situation arises. But let me get back to my argument; we seem to have lost our way.

'About a hundred years ago an Irish poet named Lord Dunsany wrote a play called *The Use of Man*, which you'll be seeing on one of our TV programmes before long. In it a man dreams that he's magically transported out of the solar system to appear before a tribunal of animals – and if he cannot find two to speak on his behalf, the human race is doomed. Only the dog will come forward to fawn over his master; all the others remember their old grievances and maintain that they would have been better off if man had never existed. The sentence of annihilation is about to be pronounced when another sponsor arrives in the nick of time, and humanity is saved. The only other creature who has any use for man is – the mosquito.

'Now you may think that this is merely an amusing jest; so, I am sure, did Dunsany – who happened to be a keen hunter. But poets often speak hidden truth of which they themselves are unaware, and I believe that this almost forgotten play contains an allegory of profound importance to the human race.

'Within a century or so, Franklin, we will literally be going outside the solar system. Sooner or later we will meet types of intelligent life much higher than our own, yet in forms completely alien. And when that times comes, the treatment man receives from his superiors may well depend upon the way he has behaved towards the other creatures of his own world.'

The words were spoken so quietly, yet with such conviction, that they struck a sudden chill into Franklin's soul. For the first time he felt that there might be something in the other's point of view – something, that is, besides mere humanitarianism. (But could humanitarianism ever be 'mere'?) He had never liked the final climax of his work, for he had long ago developed a great affection for his monstrous charges, but he had always regarded it as a regrettable necessity.

'I grant that your points are well made,' he admitted, 'but whether we like them or not, we have to accept the realities of life. I don't know who coined the phrase "Nature red in tooth and claw," but that's the way she is. And if the world has to choose between food and ethics, I know which will win.'

The Thero gave that secret, gentle smile which, consciously or otherwise, seemed to echo the benign gaze that so many generations of artists had made the hallmark of the Buddha.

'But that is just the point, my dear Franklin,' he answered. 'There is no longer any need for a choice. Ours is the first generation in the world's history that can break the ancient cycle, and eat what it pleases without spilling the blood of innocent creatures. I am sincerely grateful to you for helping to show me how.'

'Me!' exploded Franklin.

'Exactly,' said the Thero, the extent of his smile now far exceeding the canons of Buddhist art. 'And now, if you will excuse me, I think I'll go to sleep.'

CHAPTER 21

'So THIS,' grumbled Franklin, 'is my reward for twenty years of devoted public service – to be regarded even by my own family as a blood-stained butcher.'

'But all that was true, wasn't it?' said Anne, pointing to the TV screen, which a few seconds ago had been dripping with gore.

'Of course it was. But it was also very cleverly edited propaganda. I could make out just as good a case for our side.'

'Are you sure of that?' asked Indra. 'The division will certainly want you to, but it may not be easy.'

Franklin snorted indignantly.

'Why, those statistics are all nonsense! The very idea of switching our entire herds to milking instead of slaughtering is just crazy. If we converted all our resources to whalemilk production we couldn't make up a quarter of the loss of fats and protein involved in closing down the processing plants.'

'Now, Walter,' said Indra placidly, 'there's no need to break a blood vessel trying to keep calm. What's really upset you is the suggestion that the plankton farms should be extended to make up the deficit.'

'Well, you're the biologist. Is it practical to turn that pea soup into prime ribs of beef or T-bone steaks?'

'It's obviously *possible*. It was a very clever move, having the chef of the Waldorf tasting both the genuine and the synthetic product, and being unable to tell the difference. There's no doubt you're going to have a lovely fight on your hands – the farm people will jump right in on the Thero's side of the fence, and the whole Marine Division will be split wide open.'

'He probably planned that,' said Franklin with reluctant admiration. 'He's diabolically well-informed. I wish now I hadn't said so much about the possibilities of milk production during that interview – and they did overplay it a bit in the final article. I'm sure that's what started the whole business.'

'That's another thing I was going to mention. Where did he get the figures on which he based his statistics? As far as I know, they have never been published anywhere outside the bureau.'

'You're right,' conceded Franklin. 'I should have thought of that before. First thing tomorrow morning I'm going out to Heron Island to have a little talk with Dr Lundquist.'

'Will you take me, Daddy?' pleaded Anne.

'Not this time, young lady. I wouldn't like an innocent daughter of mine to hear some of the things I may have to say.'

'Dr Lundquist is out in the lagoon, sir,' said the chief lab assistant. 'There's no way of contacting him until he decides to come up.'

'Oh, isn't there? I could go down and tap him on the shoulder.'

'I don't think that would be at all wise, sir. Attila and Genghis Khan aren't very fond of strangers.'

'Good God – is he swimming with *them*!'

'Oh yes – they're quite fond of him, and they've got very friendly with the wardens who work with them. But anyone else might be eaten rather quickly.'

Quite a lot seemed to be going on, thought Franklin, that he knew very little about. He decided to walk to the lagoon; unless it was extremely hot, or one had something to carry, it was never worthwhile to take a car for such short distances.

He had changed his mind by the time he reached the new eastern jetty. Either Heron Island was getting bigger or he was beginning to feel his years. He sat down on the keel of an upturned dinghy, and looked out to sea. The tide was in, but the sharp dividing line marking the edge of the reef was clearly visible, and in the fenced-off enclosure the spouts of the two killer whales appeared as intermittent plumes of mist. There was a small boat out there, with somebody in it, but it was too far away for him to tell whether it was Dr Lundquist or one of his assistants.

He waited for a few minutes, then telephoned for a boat to carry him out to the reef. In slightly more time than it would have taken him to swim there, he arrived at the enclosure and had his first good look at Attila and Genghis Khan.

The two killer whales were a little under thirty feet long, and as his boat approached them they simultaneously reared out of the water and stared at him with their huge, intelligent eyes. The unusual attitude, and the pure white of the bodies now presented to him, gave Franklin the uncanny impression that he was face to face not with animals but with beings who might be higher in the order of creation than himself. He knew that the truth was far otherwise, and reminded himself that he was looking at the most ruthless killer in the sea.

No, that was not quite correct. The *second* most ruthless killer in the sea . . .

The whales dropped back into the water, apparently satisfied with their scrutiny. It was then that Franklin made out Lundquist, working about thirty feet down with a small torpedo loaded with instruments. Probably the commotion had disturbed him, because he came quickly to the surface and lay treading water, with his face mask pushed back, as he recognized his visitor.

'Good morning, Mr Franklin. I wasn't expecting you today. What do you think of my pupils?'

'Very impressive. How well are they learning their lessons?'

'There's no doubt about it – they're brilliant. Even cleverer than porpoises, and surprisingly affectionate when they get to know you. I can teach them to do anything now. If I wanted to commit the perfect murder, I could tell them that you were a seal on an ice floe, and they'd have the boat over in two seconds.'

'In that case, I'd prefer to continue our conversation back on land. Have you finished whatever you're doing?'

'It's never finished, but that doesn't matter. I'll ride the torp back – no need to lift all this gear into the boat.'

The scientist swung his tiny metal fish around towards the island, and promptly set off at a speed which the dinghy could not hope to match. At once the two killers streaked after him, their huge dorsal fins leaving a creamy wake in the water. It seemed a dangerous game of tag to play, but before Franklin could discover what would happen when the killers caught the torpedo, Lundquist had crossed the shallow but clearly marked mesh around the enclosure, and the two whales broke their rush in a flurry of spray.

Franklin was very thoughtful on the way back to land. He had known Lundquist for years, but now he felt that this was the first time he had ever really seen him. There had never been any doubt concerning his originality – indeed, his brilliance – but he also appeared to possess unsuspected courage and initiative. None of which, Franklin determined grimly, would help him unless he had a satisfactory answer to certain questions.

Dressed in his everyday clothes, and back in the familiar laboratory surroundings, Lundquist was the man Franklin had always known. 'Now, John,' he began, 'I suppose you've seen this television propaganda against the bureau?'

'Of course. But is it *against* us?'

'It's certainly against our main activity, but we won't argue that point. What I want to know is this: Have you been in touch with the Maha Thero?'

'Oh yes. He contacted me immediately after that article appeared in *Earth Magazine*.'

'And you passed on confidential information to him?'

Lundquist looked sincerely hurt.

'I resent that, Mr Franklin. The only information I gave him was an advance proof of my paper on whalemilk production, which comes out in the *Cetological Review* next month. You approved it for publication yourself.'

The accusations that Franklin was going to make collapsed around his ears, and he felt suddenly rather ashamed of himself.

'I'm sorry, John,' he said. 'I take that back. All this has made me a bit jumpy and I just want to sort out the facts before HQ starts chasing me. But don't you think you should have told me about this inquiry?'

'Frankly, I don't see why. We get all sorts of queries every day and I saw no reason to suppose that this was not just another routine one. Of course, I was pleased that somebody was taking a particular interest in my special project, and I gave them all the help I could.'

'Very well,' said Franklin resignedly. 'Let's forget the post-mortem. But answer for me this question: As a scientist, do you really believe that we can afford to stop whale slaughtering and switch over to milk and synthetics?'

'Given ten years, we can do it if we have to. There's no technical objection that I can see. Of course I can't guarantee the figures on the plankton-farming side, but you can bet your life that the Thero had accurate sources of information there as well.'

'But you realize what this will mean! If it starts with whales, sooner or later it will go right down the line through all the domestic animals.'

'And why not? The prospect rather appeals to me. If science and religion can combine to take some of the cruelty out of Nature, isn't that a good thing?'

'You sound like a crypto-Buddhist – and I'm tired of pointing out that there's no cruelty in what we are doing. Meanwhile, if the Thero asks any more questions, kindly refer him to me.'

'Very good, Mr Franklin,' Lundquist replied rather stiffly. There was an awkward pause, providentially broken by the arrival of a messenger.

'Headquarters wants to speak to you, Mr Franklin. It's urgent.'

'I bet it is,' muttered Franklin. Then he caught sight of Lundquist's still somewhat hostile expression, and could not suppress a smile.

'If you can train orcas to be wardens, John,' he said, 'you'd better start looking around for a suitable mammal – preferably amphibious – to be the next director.'

On a planet of instantaneous and universal communications, ideas spread from pole to pole more rapidly than they could once have done by word of mouth in a single village. The skilfully edited and presented programme which had spoiled the appetites of a mere twenty million people on its first appearance had a far larger audience on its second. Soon there were few other topics of conversation;

one of the disadvantages of life in a peaceful and well-organized world state was that with the disappearance of wars and crises very little was left of what was once called 'news'. Indeed, the complaint had often been made that since the ending of national sovereignty, history had also been abolished. So the argument raged in club and kitchen, in World Assembly and lonely space freighter, with no competition from any other quarter.

The World Food Organization maintained a dignified silence, but behind the scenes there was furious activity. Matters were not helped by the brisk lobbying of the farm group, which it had taken no great foresight on Indra's part to predict. Franklin was particularly annoyed by the efforts of the rival department to profit from his difficulties, and made several protests to the Director of Plankton Farms when the infighting became a little too rough. 'Damn it all, Ted,' he had snarled over the viewphone on one occasion, 'you're just as big a butcher as I am. Every ton of raw plankton you process contains half a billion shrimps with as much right to life, liberty, and the pursuit of happiness as my whales. So don't try to stand in a white sheet. Sooner or later the Thero will work down to you – this is only the thin edge of the wedge.'

'Maybe you're right, Walter,' the culprit had admitted cheerfully enough, 'but I think the farms will last out my time. It's not easy to make people sentimental over shrimps – they don't have cute little ten-ton babies to nurse.'

That was perfectly true; it was very hard to draw the line between maudlin sentimentality and rational humanitarianism. Franklin remembered a recent cartoon showing the Thero raising his arms in protest while a shrieking cabbage was brutally dragged from the ground. The artist had taken no sides; he had merely summed up the viewpoint of those who considered that a great deal of fuss was being made about nothing. Perhaps this whole affair would blow over in a few weeks when people became bored and started arguing about something else – but he doubted it. That first television programme had shown that the Thero was an expert in moulding public opinion; he could be relied upon not to let his campaign lose momentum.

It took less than a month for the Thero to obtain the ten

per cent vote needed under the constitution to set up a commission of inquiry. The fact that one tenth of the human race was sufficiently interested in the matter to request that all the facts be laid before it did not mean that they agreed with the Thero; mere curiosity and the pleasure of seeing a department of the state fighting a defensive rear-guard action was quite enough to account for the vote. In itself, a commission of inquiry meant very little. What would matter would be the final referendum on the commission's report, and it would be months before that could be arranged.

One of the unexpected results of the twentieth century's electronic revolution was that for the first time in history it was possible to have a truly democratic government – in the sense that every citizen could express his views on matters of policy. What the Athenians, with indifferent success, had tried to do with a few thousand score of free men could now be achieved in a global society of five billions. Automatic sampling devices originally devised for the rating of television programmes had turned out to have a far wider significance, by making it a relatively simple and inexpensive matter to discover exactly what the public really thought on any subject.

Naturally, there had to be safeguards, and such a system would have been disastrous before the days of universal education – before, in fact, the beginning of the twenty-first century. Even now, it was possible for some emotionally laden issue to force a vote that was really against the best interests of the community, and no government could function unless it held the final right to decide matters of policy during its terms of office. Even if the world demanded some course of action by a ninety-nine per cent vote, the state could ignore the expressed will of the people – but it would have to account for its behaviour at the next election.

Franklin did not relish the privilege of being a key witness at the commission's hearings, but he knew that there was no way in which he could escape this ordeal. Much of his time was now spent in collecting data to refute the arguments of those who wished to put an end to whale slaughtering, and it proved to be a more difficult task than he had imagined. One could not present a neat, clear-cut case by saying that processed whale meat cost so much per pound by the time it reached the consumer's table whereas synthetic meats derived from plankton or algae would cost more. Nobody knew – there were far too many variables. The biggest unknown of all was the cost of running the proposed sea dairies, if it was decided to breed whales purely for milk and not for slaughter.

The data was insufficient. It would be honest to say so, but there was pressure on him to state outright that the suspension of whale slaughtering would never be a practical or economic possibility. His own loyalty to the bureau, not to mention the security of his present position, prompted him in the same direction.

But it was not merely a matter of economics; there were emotional factors which disturbed Franklin's judgement and made it impossible for him to make up his mind. The days he had spent with the Maha Thero, and his brief glimpse of a civilization and a way of thought far older than his own, had affected him more deeply than he had realized. Like most men of his highly materialistic era, he was intoxicated with the scientific and sociological triumphs which had irradiated the opening decades of the twenty-first century. He prided himself on his sceptical rationalism, and his total freedom from superstition. The fundamental question of philosophy had never bothered him greatly; he knew that they existed, but they seemed the concern of other people.

And now, whether he liked it or not, he had been challenged from a quarter so unexpected that he was almost defenceless. He had always considered himself a humane man, but now he had been reminded that humanity might not be enough. As he struggled with his thoughts, he became progressively more and more irritable with the world around him, and matters finally became so bad that Indra had to take action.

'Walter,' she said firmly, when Anne had gone tearfully to bed after a row in which there was a good deal of blame on both sides, 'it will save a lot of trouble if you face the facts and stop trying to fool yourself.'

'What the devil do you mean?'

'You've been angry with everybody this last week – with just one exception. You've lost your temper with Lundquist – though that was partly my fault – with the press, with just about every other bureau in the division, with the children, and any moment you're going to lose it with me. But there's one person you're not angry with – and that's the Maha Thero, who's the cause of all the trouble.'

'Why should I be? He's crazy, of course, but he's a saint – or as near it as I ever care to meet.'

'I'm not arguing about that. I'm merely saying that you really agreed with him, but you won't admit it.'

Franklin started to explode. 'That's utterly ridiculous!' he began. Then his indignation petered out. It *was* ridiculous; but it was also perfectly true.

He felt a great calm come upon him; he was no longer angry with the world and with himself. His childish resentment of the fact that *he* should be the man involved in a dilemma not of his making suddenly evaporated. There was no reason why he should be ashamed of the fact that he had grown to love the great beasts he guarded; if their slaughter could be avoided, he should welcome it, whatever the consequences to the bureau.

The parting smile of the Thero suddenly floated up into his memory. Had that extraordinary man foreseen that he would win him around to his point of view? If his gentle persuasiveness – which he had not hesitated to combine with the shock tactics of that bloodstained television programme – could work with Franklin himself, then the battle was already half over.

CHAPTER 22

LIFE WAS a good deal simpler in the old days, thought Indra with a sigh. It was true that Peter and Anne were both at school or college most of the time, but somehow that had given her none of the additional leisure she had expected. There was so much entertaining and visiting to do, now that Walter had moved into the upper echelons of the state. Though perhaps that was exaggerating a little; the director of the Bureau of Whales was still a long way – at least six steps – down from the rarefied heights in which the president and his advisers dwelt.

But there were some things that cut right across official rank. No one could deny that there was a glamour about Walt's job and an interest in his activities that had made him known to a far wider circle than the other directors of the Marine Division, even before the *Earth Magazine* article or the present controversy over whale slaughtering. How many people could name the director of Plankton Farms or of Fresh-Water Food Production? Not one to every hundred that had heard of Walter. It was a fact that made her proud, even though at the same time it exposed Walter to a good deal of interdepartmental jealousy.

Now, however, it seemed likely to expose him to worse than that. So far, no one in the bureau, still less any of the higher officials of the Marine Division or the World Food Organization imagined for one moment that Walter had any private doubts or that he was not wholeheartedly in support of the *status quo*.

Her attempts to read the current *Nature* were interrupted by the private-line viewphone. It had been installed, despite her bitter protests, the day that Walter had become director. The public service, it seemed, was not good enough; now the office could get hold of Walter whenever it liked, unless he took precautions to frustrate it.

'Oh, good morning, Mrs Franklin,' said the operator, who was now practically a friend of the family. 'Is the director in?'

'I'm afraid not,' said Indra with satisfaction. 'He hasn't had a day off for about a month, and he's out sailing in the bay with Peter. If you want to catch him, you'll have to send a plane out; J.94's radio has broken down again.'

'*Both* sets? That's odd. Still, it's not urgent. When he comes in, will you give him this memo?'

There was a barely audible click, and a sheet of paper drifted down into the extra large-sized memorandum basket. Indra read it, gave the operator an absent-minded farewell, and at once called Franklin on his perfectly serviceable radio.

The creak of the rigging, the soft rush of water past the smooth hull – even the occasional cry of a sea bird – these sounds came clearly from the speaker and transported her at once out into Moreton Bay.

'I thought you'd like to know, Walter,' she said, 'the Policy Board is having its special meeting next Wednesday, here in Brisbane. That gives you three days to decide what you're going to tell them.'

There was a slight pause during which she could hear her husband moving about the boat; then Franklin answered: 'Thanks, dear. I know what I've got to say – I just don't know how to say it. But there's something I've thought of that you can do to help. You know all the wardens' wives – suppose you call up as many as you can, and try to find what their husbands feel about this business. Can you do that without making it look too obvious? It's not so easy for me, nowadays, to find what the men in the field are thinking. They're too liable to tell me what they imagine I want to know.'

There was a wistful note in Franklin's voice which Indra had been hearing more and more frequently these days, though she knew her husband well enough to be quite sure that he had no real regrets for having taken on his present responsibilities.

'That's a good idea,' she said. 'There are at least a dozen people I should have called up weeks ago, and this will give me an excuse. It probably means that we'll have to have another party though.'

'I don't mind that, as long as I'm still director and can afford to pay for it. But if I revert to a warden's pay in a month or so, we'll have to cut out the entertaining.'

'You don't really think—'

'Oh, it won't be as bad as that. But they may shift me to some nice safe job, though I can't imagine what use I am now outside the bureau. GET OUT OF THE WAY, YOU BLASTED FOOL – CAN'T YOU SEE WHERE YOU'RE GO-ING. Sorry, dear – too many weekend sailors around. We'll be back in ninety minutes, unless some idiot rams us. Pete says he wants honey for tea. Bye now.'

Indra looked thoughtfully at the radio as the sounds of the distant boat ceased abruptly. She half wished that she had accompanied Walter and Pete on their cruise out into the bay, but she had faced the fact that her son now needed his father's company rather than hers. There were times when she grudged this, realizing that in a few months they would both lose the boy whose mind and body they had formed, but who was now slipping from their grasp.

It was inevitable, of course; the ties that bound father and son together must now drive them apart. She doubted if Peter realized why he was so determined to get into space; after all, it was a common enough ambition among boys of his age. But he was one of the youngest ever to obtain a triplanetary scholarship, and it was easy to understand why. He was determined to conquer the element that had defeated his father.

But enough of this daydreaming, she told herself. She got out her file of visiphone numbers, and began to tick off the names of all the wardens' wives who would be at home.

The Policy Board normally met twice a year, and very seldom had much policy to discuss, since more of the bureau's work was satisfactorily taken care of by the committees dealing with finance, production, staff, and technical development. Franklin served on all of these, though only as an ordinary member, since the chairman was always someone from the Marine Division or the World Secretariat. He sometimes came back from the meetings depressed and discouraged; what was very unusual was for him to come back in a bad temper as well.

Indra knew that something had gone wrong the moment he entered the house. 'Let me know the worst,' she said resignedly as her exhausted husband flopped into the most comfortable chair in sight. 'Do you have to find a new job?'

She was only half joking, and Franklin managed a wan smile. 'It's not as bad as that,' he answered, 'but there's more in this business than I thought. Old Burrows had got it all worked out before he took the chair; someone in the Secretariat had briefed him pretty thoroughly. What it comes to is this: Unless it can be proved that food production from whale milk and synthetics will be *drastically* cheaper than the present method, whale slaughtering will continue. Even a ten per cent saving isn't regarded as good enough to justify a switch-over. As Burrows put it, we're concerned with cost accounting, not abtruse philosophical principles like justice to animals.

'That's reasonable enough, I suppose, and certainly I wouldn't try to fight it. The trouble started during the break for coffee, when Burrows got me into a corner and asked me what the wardens thought about the whole business. So I told him that eighty per cent of them would like to see slaughtering stopped, even if it meant a rise in food costs. I don't know why he asked me this particular question, unless news of our little survey has leaked out.

'Anyway, it upset him a bit and I could see him trying to get around to something. Then he put it bluntly that I'd be a key witness when the inquiry started, and that the Marine Division wouldn't like me to plead the Thero's case in open court with a few million people watching. "Suppose I'm asked for my personal opinion?" I said. "No one's worked harder than me to increase the whale-meat and oil production, but as soon as it's possible I'd like to see the bureau become a purely conservation service." He asked if this was my considered viewpoint and I told him it was.

'Then things got a bit personal, though still in a friendly sort of way, and we agreed that there was a distinct cleavage of opinion between the people who handled whales as whales and those who saw them only as statistics on food-production charts. After that Burrows went off and made some phone calls, and kept us all waiting around for half an hour while he talked to a few people up in the Secretariat. He finally came back with what were virtually my orders, though he was careful not to put it that way. It comes to this: I've got to be an obedient little ventriloquist's dummy at the inquiry.'

'But suppose the other side asks you outright for your personal views?'

'Our counsel will try to head them off, and if he fails I'm not supposed to have any personal views.'

'And what's the point of all this?'

'That's what I asked Burrows, and I finally managed to get it out of him. There are political issues involved. The Secretariat is afraid that the Maha Thero will get too powerful if he wins this case, so it's going to be fought whatever its merits.'

'Now I understand,' said Indra slowly. 'Do you think that the Thero is after political power?'

'For it's own sake – no. But he may be trying to gain influence to put across his religious ideas, and that's what the Secretariat's afraid of.'

'And what are you going to do about it?'

'I don't know,' Franklin answered. 'I really don't know.'

He was still undecided when the hearings began and the Maha Thero made his first personal appearance before a world-wide audience. He was not, Franklin could not help thinking as he looked at the small, yellow-robed figure with its gleaming skull, very impressive at first sight. Indeed, there was something almost comic about him – until he began to speak, and one knew without any doubt that one was in the presence both of power and conviction.

'I would like to make one thing perfectly clear,' said the Maha Thero, addressing not only the chairman of the commission but also the unseen millions who were watching this first hearing. 'It is not true that we are trying to enforce vegetarianism on the world, as some of our opponents have tried to maintain. The Buddha himself did not abstain from eating meat, when it was given to him; nor do we, for a guest should accept gratefully whatever his host offers.

'Our attitude is based on something deeper and more fundamental than food prejudices, which are usually only a matter of conditioning. What is more, we believe that most reasonable men, whether their religious beliefs are the same as ours or not, will eventually accept our point of view.

'It can be summed up very simply, though it is the result of twenty-six centuries of thought. We consider that it is wrong to inflict injury or death on any living creature, but we are not so foolish as to imagine that it can be avoided altogether. Thus we recognize, for example, the need to kill microbes and insect pests, much though we may regret the necessity.

'But as soon as such killing is no longer essential, it should cease. We believe that this point has now arrived as far as many of the higher animals are concerned. The production of all types of synthetic protein from purely vegetable sources is now an economic possibility – or it will be if the effort is made to achieve it. Within a generation, we can shed the burden of guilt which, however lightly or heavily it has weighed on individual consciences, must at some time or other have haunted all thinking men as they look at the world of life which shares their planet.

'Yet this is not an attitude which we seek to enforce on anyone against his will. Good actions lose any merit if they are imposed by force. We will be content to let the facts we will present speak for themselves, so that the world may make its own choice.'

It was, thought Franklin, a simple, straightforward speech, quite devoid of any of the fanaticism which would have fatally prejudiced the case in this rational age. And yet the whole matter was one that went beyond reason; in a purely logical world, this controversy could never have arisen, for no one would have doubted man's right to use the animal kingdom as he felt fit. Logic, however, could be easily discredited here; it could be used too readily to make out a convincing case for cannibalism.

The Thero had not mentioned, anywhere in his argument, one point which had made a considerable impact on Franklin. He had not raised the possibility that man might someday come into contact with alien life forms that might judge him by his conduct towards the rest of the animal kingdom. Did he think that this was so far-fetched an idea that the general public would be unable to take it seriously, and would thus grow to regard his whole campaign as a joke? Or had he realized that it was an argument that might particularly appeal to an ex-astronaut? There was no way of guessing; in either event it proved that the Thero was a shrewd judge both of private and public reactions.

Franklin switched off the receiver; the scenes it was showing now were quite familiar to him, since he had helped the Thero to film them. The Marine Division, he thought wryly, would now be regretting the facilities it had offered His Reverence, but there was nothing else it could have done in the circumstances.

In two days he would be appearing to give his evidence; already he felt more like a criminal on trial than a witness. And in truth he was on trial – or, to be more accurate, his conscience was. It was strange to think that having once tried to kill himself, he now objected to killing other creatures. There was some connexion here, but it was too complicated for him to unravel – and even if he did, it would not help him to solve his dilemma.

Yet the solution was on the way, and from a totally unexpected direction.

CHAPTER 23

FRANKLIN WAS boarding the plane that would take him to the hearings when the 'Sub-Smash' signal came through. He stood in the doorway, reading the scarlet-tabbed message that had been rushed out to him, and at that moment all his other problems ceased to exist.

The SOS was from the Bureau of Mines, the largest of all the sections of the Marine Division. Its title was a slightly misleading one, for it did not run a single mine in the strict sense of the word. Twenty or thirty years ago there had indeed been mines on the ocean beds, but now the sea itself was an inexhaustible treasure chest. Almost every one of the natural elements could be extracted directly and economically from the millions of tons of dissolved matter in each cubic mile of sea water. With the perfection of selective ion-exchange filters, the nightmare of metal shortages had been banished forever.

The Bureau of Mines was also responsible for the hundreds of oil wells that now dotted the sea beds, pumping up the precious fluid that was the basic material for half the chemical plants on earth – and which earlier generations, with criminal shortsightedness, had actually burned for fuel. There were plenty of accidents that could befall the bureau's world-wide empire; only last year Franklin had lent it a whaling sub in an unsuccessful attempt to salvage a tank of gold concentrate. But this was far more serious, as he discovered after he had put through a few priority calls.

Thirty minutes later he was airborne, though not in the direction he had expected to be going. And it was almost an hour after he had taken off before all the orders had been given and he at last had a chance of calling Indra.

She was surprised at the unexpected call, but her surprise quickly turned to alarm. 'Listen, dear,' Franklin began. 'I'm not going to Berne after all. Mines has had a serious accident and has appealed for our help. One of their big subs is trapped on the bottom – it was drilling a well and hit a high-pressure gas pocket. The derrick was blown over and toppled on the sub so that it can't get away. There's a load of VIP's aboard, including a senator and the director of Mines. I don't know how we're going to pull them out, but we'll do our best. I'll call you again when I've got time.'

'Will you have to go down yourself?' asked Indra anxiously.

'Probably. Now don't look so upset! I've been doing it for years!'

'I'm *not* upset,' retorted Indra, and Franklin knew better than to contradict her. 'Goodbye, darling,' he continued, 'give my love to Anne, and don't worry.'

Indra watched the image fade. It had already vanished when she realized that Walter had not looked so happy for weeks. Perhaps that was not the right word to use when mens' lives were at stake; it would be truer to say that he looked full of life and enthusiasm. She smiled, knowing full well the reason why.

Now Walter could get away from the problems of his office, and could lose himself again, if only for a while, in the clear-cut and elemental simplicities of the sea.

'There she is,' said the pilot of the sub, pointing to the image forming at the edge of the sonar screen. 'On hard rock eleven hundred feet down. In a couple of minutes we'll be able to make out the details.'

'How's the water clarity – can we use TV?'

'I doubt it. That gas geyser is still spouting – there it is – that fuzzy echo. It's stirred up all the mud for miles around.'

Franklin stared at the screen, comparing the image forming there with the plans and sketches on the desk. The smooth ovoid of the big shallow-water sub was partly obscured by the wreckage of the drills and derrick – a thousand or more tons of steel pinning it to the ocean bed. It was not surprising that, though it had blown its buoyancy tanks and turned its jets on to full power, the vessel had been unable to move more than a foot or two.

'It's a nice mess,' said Franklin thoughtfully. 'How long will it take for the big tugs to get here?'

'At least four days. *Hercules* can lift five thousand tons, but she's down at Singapore. And she's too big to be flown here; she'll have to come under her own steam. You're the only people with subs small enough to be airlifted.

That was true enough, thought Franklin, but it also meant that they were not big enough to do any heavy work. The only hope was that they could operate cutting torches and carve up the derrick until the trapped sub was able to escape.

Another of the bureau's scouts was already at work; someone, Franklin told himself, had earned a citation for the speed with which the torches had been fitted to a vessel not designed to carry them. He doubted if even the Space Department, for all its fabled efficiency, could have acted any more swiftly than this.

'Captain Jacobsen calling,' said the loudspeaker. 'Glad to have you with us, Mr Franklin. Your boys are doing a good job, but it looks as if it will take time.'

'How are things inside?'

'Not so bad. The only thing that worries me is the hull between bulkheads three and four. It took the impact there, and there's some distortion.'

'Can you close off the section if a leak develops?'

'Not very well,' said Jacobsen dryly. 'It happens to be the middle of the control room. If we have to evacuate that, we'll be completely helpless.'

'What about your passengers?'

'Er – they're fine,' replied the captain, in a tone suggesting that he was giving some of them the benefit of a good deal of doubt. 'Senator Chamberlain would like a word with you.'

'Hello, Franklin,' began the senator. 'Didn't expect to meet you again under these circumstances. How long do you think it will take to get us out?'

The senator had a good memory, or else he had been well briefed. Franklin had met him on not more than three occasions – the last time in Canberra, at a session of the Committee for the Conservation of Natural Resources. As a witness, Franklin had been before the CCNR for about ten minutes, and he would not have expected its busy chairman to remember the fact.

'I can't make any promises, Senator,' he answered cautiously. 'It may take some time to clear away all this rubbish. But we'll manage all right – no need to worry about that.'

As the sub drew closer, he was not so sure. The derrick was over two hundred feet long, and it would be a slow business nibbling it away in sections that the little scoutsubs could handle.

For the next ten minutes there was a three-cornered conference between Franklin, Captain Jacobsen, and Chief Warden Barlow, skipper of the second scout-sub. At the end of that time they had agreed that the best plan was to continue to cut away the derrick; even taking the most pessimistic view, they should be able to finish the job at least two days before the *Hercules* could arrive. Unless, of course, there were any unexpected snags; the only possible danger seemed to be the one that Captain Jacobsen had mentioned. Like all large undersea vessels, his ship carried an air-purifying plant which would keep the atmosphere breathable for weeks, but if the hull failed in the region of the control room all the sub's essential services would be disrupted. The occupants might retreat behind the pressure bulkheads, but that would give them only a temporary reprieve, because the air would start to become foul immediately. Moreover, with part of the sub flooded, it would be extremely difficult even for the *Hercules* to lift her.

Before he joined Barlow in the attack on the derrick, Franklin called Base on the long-range transmitter and ordered all the additional equipment that might conceivably be needed. He asked for two more subs to be flown out at once, and started the workshops mass producing buoyancy tanks by the simple process of screwing air couplings on to old oil drums. If enough of these could be hitched to the derrick, it might be lifted without any help from the submarine salvage vessel.

There was one other piece of equipment which he hesitated for some time before ordering. Then he muttered to himself: 'Better get too much than too little,' and sent off the requisition, even though he knew that the Stores Department would probably think him crazy.

The work of cutting through the girders of the smashed derrick was tedious, but not difficult. The two subs worked together, one burning through the steel while the other pulled away the detached section as soon as it came loose. Soon Franklin became completely unconscious of time; all that existed was the short length of metal which he was dealing with at that particular moment. Messages and instructions continually came and went, but another part of his mind dealt with them. Hands and brain were functioning as two separate entities.

The water, which had been completely turbid when they arrived, was now clearing rapidly. The roaring geyser of gas that was bursting from the sea bed barely a hundred yards away must have sucked in fresh water to sweep away the mud it had originally disturbed. Whatever the explanation, it made the task of salvage very much simpler, since the subs' external eyes could function again

Franklin was almost taken aback when the reinforcements arrived. It seemed impossible that he had been here for more than six hours; he felt neither tired nor hungry. The two subs brought with them, like a long procession of tin cans, the first batch of the buoyancy tanks he had ordered.

Now the plan of campaign was altered. One by one the oil drums were clipped to the derrick, air hoses were coupled to them, and the water inside them was blown out until they strained upwards like captive balloons. Each had a lifting power of two or three tons; by the time a hundred had been attached, Franklin calculated, the trapped sub might be able to escape without any further help.

The remote handling equipment on the outside of the scoutsub, so seldom used in normal operations, now seemed an extension of his own arms. It had been at least four years since he had manipulated the ingenious metal fingers that enabled a man to work in places where his unprotected body could never go – and he remembered, from ten years earlier still, the first time he had attempted to tie a knot and the hopeless tangle he had made of it. That was one of the skills he had hardly ever used; who would have imagined that it would be vital now that he had left the sea and was no longer a warden?

They were starting to pump out the second batch of oil drums when Captain Jacobsen called.

'I'm afraid I've got bad news, Franklin,' he said, his voice heavy with apprehension. 'There's water coming in, and the leak's increasing. At the present rate, we'll have to abandon the control room in a couple of hours.'

This was the news that Franklin had feared. It transformed a straightforward salvage job into a race against time – a race hopelessly handicapped, since it would take at least a day to cut away the rest of the derrick.

'What's your internal air pressure?' he asked Captain Jacobsen.

'I've already pushed it up to five atmospheres. It's not safe to put it up any farther.'

'Take it up to eight if you can. Even if half of you pass out, that won't matter as long as someone remains in control. And it may help to keep the leak from spreading, which is the important thing.'

'I'll do that – but if most of us are unconscious, it won't be easy to evacuate the control room.'

There were too many people listening for Franklin to make the obvious reply – that if the control room had to be abandoned it wouldn't matter anyway. Captain Jacobsen knew that as well as he did, but some of his passengers might not realize that such a move would end any chance of rescue.

The decision he had hoped he would not have to make was now upon him. This slow whittling away of the wreckage was not good enough; they would have to use explosives, cutting the fallen derrick at the centre, so that the lower, unsupported portion would drop back to the sea bed and its weight would no longer pin down the sub.

It had been the obvious thing to do, even from the beginning, but there were two objections: one was the risk of using explosives so near the sub's already weakened hull; the other was the problem of placing the charges in the correct spot. Of the derrick's four main girders, the two upper ones were easily accessible, but the lower pair could not be reached by the remote handling mechanisms of the scout-subs. It was the sort of job that only an unencumbered diver could do, and in shallow water it would not have taken more than a few minutes.

Unfortunately, this was not shallow water; they were eleven hundred feet down – and at a pressure of over thirty atmospheres.

CHAPTER 24

'IT'S TOO great a risk, Franklin. I won't allow it.' It was not often, thought Franklin, that one had a chance of arguing with a senator. And if necessary he would not merely argue; he would defy.

'I know there's a danger, sir,' he admitted, 'but there's no alternative. It's a calculated risk – one life against twenty-three.'

'But I thought it was suicide for an unprotected man to dive below a few hundred feet.'

'It is if he's breathing compressed air. The nitrogen knocks him out first, and then oxygen poisoning gets him. But with the right mixture it's quite possible. With the gear I'm using, men have been down fifteen hundred feet.'

'I don't want to contradict you, Mr Franklin,' said Captain Jacobsen quietly, 'but I believe that only one man has reached fifteen hundred – and then under carefully controlled conditions. *And* he wasn't attempting to do any work.'

'Nor am I; I just have to place those two charges.'

'But the pressure!'

'Pressure never makes any difference, Senator, as long as it's balanced. There may be a hundred tons squeezing on my lungs – but I'll have a hundred tons inside and won't feel it.'

'Forgive me mentioning this – but wouldn't it be better to send a younger man?'

'I won't delegate this job, and age makes no difference to

192

diving ability. I'm in good health, and that's all that matters.'

'Take her up,' he said 'They'll argue all day if we stay here. I want to get into that rig before I change my mind.'

He was wrestling with his thoughts all the way to the surface. Was he being a fool, taking risks which a man in his position, with a wife and family, ought never to face? Or was he still, after all these years, trying to prove that he was no coward, by deliberately meeting a danger from which he had once been rescued by a miracle?

Presently he was aware of other and perhaps less flattering motives. In a sense, he was trying to escape from responsibility. Whether his mission failed or succeeded, he would be a hero – and as such it would not be quite so easy for the Secretariat to push him around. It was an interesting problem; could one make up for lack of moral courage by proving physical bravery?

When the sub broke surface, he had not so much resolved these questions as dismissed them. There might be truth in every one of the charges he was making against himself; it did not matter. He knew in his heart that what he was doing was the right thing, the only thing. There was no other way in which the men almost a quarter of a mile below him could be saved, and against that fact all other considerations were meaningless.

The escaping oil from the well had made the sea so flat that the pilot of the cargo plane had made a landing, though his machine was not intended for amphibious operations. One of the scoutsubs was floating on the surface while her crew wrestled with the next batch of buoyancy tanks to be sunk. Men from the plane were helping them, working in collapsible boats that had been tossed into the water and automatically inflated.

Commander Henson, the Marine Division's master diver, was waiting in the plane with the equipment. There was another brief argument before the commander capitulated with good grace and, Franklin thought, a certain amount of relief. If anyone else was to attempt this mission, there was no doubt that Henson, with his unparalleled experience, was the obvious choice. Franklin even hesitated for a moment, wondering if by stubbornly insisting on going himself, he might not be reducing the chances of success. But he had been on the bottom and knew exactly what conditions were down there; it would waste precious time if Henson went down in the sub to make a reconnaissance.

Franklin swallowed his pH pills, took his injections, and climbed into the flexible rubber suit which would protect him from the near-zero temperature on the sea bed. He hated suits – they interfered with movement and upset one's buoyancy – but this was a case where he had no choice. The complex breathing unit, with its three cylinders – one the ominous red of compressed hydrogen – was strapped to his back, and he was lowered into the sea.

Commander Henson swam around him for five minutes while all the fittings were checked, the weight belt was adjusted, and the sonar transmitter tested. He was breathing easily enough on normal air, and would not switch over to the oxyhydrogen mixture until he had reached a depth of three hundred feet. The change-over was automatic, and the demand regulator also adjusted the oxygen flow so that the mixture ratio was correct at any depth. As correct as it could be, that is, for a region in which man was never intended to live . . .

At last everything was ready. The explosive charges were securely attached to his belt, and he gripped the handrail around the tiny conning tower of the sub. 'Take her down,' he said to the pilot. 'Fifty feet a minute, and keep your forward speed below two knots.'

'Fifty feet a minute it is. If we pick up speed, I'll kill it with the reverse jets.'

Almost at once, daylight faded to a gloomy and depressing green. The water here on the surface was almost opaque, owing to the debris thrown up by the oil well. Franklin could not even see the width of the conning tower; less than two feet from his eyes the metal rail blurred and faded into nothingness. He was not worried; if necessary, he could work by touch alone, but he knew that the water was much clearer on the bottom.

Only thirty feet down, he had to stop the descent for almost a minute while he cleared his ears. He blew and swallowed frantically before the comforting 'click' inside his head told him that all was well; how humiliating it would have been, he thought, had he been forced back to the surface because of a blocked Eustachian tube! No one would have blamed him, of course; even a mild cold could completely incapacitate the best diver – but the anticlimax would have been hard to live down.

The light was fading swiftly as the sun's rays lost their battle with the turbid water. A hundred feet down, he seemed to be in a world of misty moonlight, a world completely lacking colour or warmth. His ears were giving him no trouble now, and he was breathing without effort, but he felt a subtle depression creeping over him. It was, he was sure, only an effect of the failing light – not a premonition of the thousand feet of descent that still lay ahead of him.

To occupy his mind, he called the pilot and asked for a progress report. Fifty drums had now been attached to the derrick, giving a total lift of well over a hundred tons. Six of the passengers in the trapped sub had become unconscious but appeared to be in no danger; the remaining seventeen were uncomfortable, but had adapted themselves to the increased pressure. The leak was getting no worse, but there were now three inches of water in the control room, and before long there would be danger of short circuits.

'Three hundred feet down,' said Commander Henson's voice. 'Check your hydrogen-flow meter – you should be starting the switch-over now.'

Franklin glanced down at the compact little instrument panel. Yes, the automatic change-over was taking place. He could detect no difference in the air he was breathing, but in the next few hundred feet of descent most of the dangerous nitrogen would be flushed out. It seemed strange to replace it with hydrogen, a far more reactive – and even explosive gas, but hydrogen produced no narcotic effects and was not trapped in the body tissues as readily as nitrogen.

It seemed to have grown no darker in the last hundred feet; his eyes had accustomed themselves to the low level of illumination, and the water was slightly clearer. He could now see for two or three yards along the smooth hull he was riding down into the depths where only a handful of unprotected men had ever ventured – and fewer still returned to tell the story.

Commander Henson called him again. 'You should be on

fifty per cent hydrogen now. Can you taste it?'

'Yes – a metallic sort of flavour. Not unpleasant, though.'

'Talk as slowly as you can,' said the commander. 'It's hard to understand you – your voice sounds so high-pitched now. Are you feeling quite OK?'

'Yes,' replied Franklin, glancing at his depth gauge. 'Will you increase my rate of descent to a hundred feet a minute? We've no time to waste.'

At once he felt the vessel sinking more swiftly beneath him as the ballast tanks were flooded, and for the first time he began to feel the pressure around him as something palpable. He was going down so quickly that there was a slight lag as the insulating layer of air in his suit adjusted to the pressure change; his arms and legs seemed to be gripped as if by a huge and gentle vice, which slowed his movements without actually restricting them.

The light had now nearly gone, and as if in anticipation of his order the pilot of the sub switched on his twin searchlights. There was nothing for them to illumine, here in this empty void midway between sea bed and sky, but it was reassuring to see the double nimbus of scattered radiance floating in the water ahead of him. The violet filters had been removed, for his benefit, and now that his eyes had something distant to focus upon he no longer felt so oppressively shut in and confined.

Eight hundred feet down – more than three quarters of the way to the bottom. 'Better level off here for three minutes,' advised Commander Henson. 'I'd like to keep you here for half an hour, but we'll have to make it up on the way back.'

Franklin submitted to the delay with what grace he could. It seemed incredibly long; perhaps his time sense had been distorted, so that what was really a minute appeared like ten. He was going to ask Commander Henson if his watch had stopped when he suddenly remembered that he had a perfectly good one of his own. The fact that he had forgotten something so obvious was, he realized, rather a bad sign; it suggested that he was becoming stupid. However, if he was intelligent enough to know that he was becoming stupid things could not be too bad ... Luckily the descent started again before he could get too involved in this line of argument.

And now he could hear, growing louder and louder each minute, the incessant roar of the great geyser of gas belching from the shaft which inquisitive and interfering man had drilled in the ocean bed. It shook the sea around him, already making it hard to hear the advice and comments of his helpers. There was a danger here as great as that of pressure itself; if the gas jet caught him, he might be tossed hundreds of feet upwards in a matter of seconds and would explode like a deep-sea fish dragged suddenly to the surface.

'We're nearly there,' said the pilot, after they had been sinking for what seemed an age. 'You should be able to see the derrick in a minute; I'll switch on the lower lights.'

Franklin swung himself over the edge of the now slowly moving sub and peered down the misty columns of light. At first he could see nothing; then, at an indeterminate distance, he made out mysterious rectangles and circles. They baffled him for a moment before he realized that he was seeing the air-filled drums which were now straining to lift the shattered derrick.

Almost at once he was able to make out the framework of twisted girders below them, and presently a brilliant star – fantastically out of place in this dreary underworld – burst into life just outside the cone of his searchlights. He was watching one of the cutting torches at work, manipulated by the mechanical hands of a sub just beyond visual range.

With great care, his own vessel positioned him beside the derrick, and for the first time he realized how hopeless his task would have been had he been compelled to rely on touch to find his way around. He could see the two girders to which he had to attach his charge; they were hemmed in by a maze of smaller rods, beams, and cables through which he must somehow make his way.

Franklin released his hold on the sub which had towed him so effortlessly into the depths, and with slow, easy strokes swam towards the derrick. As he approached, he saw for the first time the looming mass of the trapped sub, and his heart sank as he thought of all the problems that must still be solved before it could be extricated. On a sudden impulse, he swam towards the helpless vessel and banged sharply on the hull with the pair of wire cutters from his little tool kit. The men inside knew that he was here, of course, but the signal would have an altogether disproportionate effect on their morale.

Then he started work. Trying to ignore the throbbing vibration which filled all the water around him and made it difficult to think, he began a careful survey of the metal maze into which he must swim.

It would not be difficult to reach the nearest girder and place the charge. There was an open space between three I beams, blocked only by a loop of cable which could be easily pushed out of the way (but he'd have to watch that it didn't tangle in his equipment when he swam past it). Then the girder would be dead ahead of him; what was more, there was room to turn around, so that he could avoid the unpleasant necessity of creeping out backwards.

He checked again, and could see no snags. To make doubly sure, he talked it over with Commander Henson, who could see the situation almost as well on the TV screen of the sub. Then he swam slowly into the derrick, working his way along the metal framework with his gloved hands. He was quite surprised to find that, even at this depth, there was no shortage of the barnacles and other marine growths which always make it dangerous to touch any object which had been underwater for more than a few months.

The steel structure was vibrating like a giant tuning fork; he could feel the roaring power of the uncapped well both through the sea surrounding him and through the metal beneath his hands He seemed to be imprisoned in an enormous, throbbing cage; the sheer noise, as well as the awful pressure, was beginning to make him dull and lethargic. It now needed a positive effort of will to take any action; he had to keep reminding himself that many lives besides his own depended upon what he was doing.

He reached the girder and slowly taped the flat package against the metal. It took a long time to do it to his satisfaction, but at last the explosive was in place and he felt sure that the vibration would not dislodge it. Then he looked around for his second objective – the girder forming the other edge of the derrick.

He had stirred up a good deal of dirt and could no longer see so clearly, but it seemed to Franklin that there was nothing to stop him crossing the interior of the derrick and completing the job. The alternative was to go back the way he had come, and then swim right around to the other side of the wreckage. In normal circumstances that would have been easy enough – but now every movement had to be considered with care, every expenditure of effort made grudgingly only after its need had been established beyond all doubt.

With infinite caution, he began to move through the throbbing mist. The glare of the searchlights, pouring down upon him, was so dazzling that it pained his eyes. It never occurred to him that he had only to speak into his microphone and the illumination would be reduced instantly to whatever level he wished. Instead, he tried to keep in whatever shadow he could find among the confused pile of wreckage through which he was moving.

He reached the girder, and crouched over it for a long time while he tried to remember what he was supposed to be doing here. It took Commander Henson's voice, shouting in his ears like some far-off echo, to call him back to reality. Very carefully and slowly he taped the precious slab into position; then he floated beside it, admiring his meaningless handiwork, while the annoying voice in his ear grew ever more insistent. He could stop it, he realized, by throwing away his face mask and the irritating little speaker it contained. For a moment he toyed with this idea, but discovered that he was not strong enough to undo the straps holding the mask in place. It was too bad; perhaps the voice would shut up if he did what it told him to.

Unfortunately, he had no idea which was the right way out of the maze in which he was now comfortably ensconced. The light and noise were very confusing; when he moved in any direction, he sooner or later banged into something and had to turn back. This annoyed but did not alarm him, for he was quite happy where he was.

But the voice would not give him any peace. It was no longer at all friendly and helpful; he dimly realized that it was being downright rude, and was ordering him about in a manner in which – though he could not remember why –

people did not usually speak to him. He was being given careful and detailed instructions which were repeated over and over again, with increasing emphasis, until he sluggishly obeyed them. He was too tired to answer back, but he wept a little at the indignity to which he was being subjected. He had never been called such things in his life, and it was very seldom indeed that he had heard such shocking language as was now coming through his speaker. Who on earth would yell at him this way? 'Not that way, you goddammed fool, sir! To the left – LEFT! That's fine – now forward a bit more – don't stop there! Christ, he's gone to sleep again. WAKE UP – SNAP OUT OF IT OR I'LL KNOCK YOUR BLOODY BLOCK OFF! That's a good boy – you're nearly there – just another couple of feet . . .' and so on endlessly, and some of it with very much worse language than that.

Then, quite to his surprise, there was no longer twisted metal around him. He was swimming slowly in the open, but he was not swimming for long. Metal fingers closed upon him, none too gently, and he was lifted into the roaring night.

From far away he heard four short, muffled explosions, and something deep down in his mind told him that for two of these he was responsible. But he saw nothing of the swift drama a hundred feet below as the radio fuses detonated and the great derrick snapped in two. The section lying across the trapped submarine was still too heavy to be lifted clear by the buoyancy tanks, but now that it was free to move it teetered for a moment like a giant seesaw, then slipped aside and crashed on to the sea bed.

The big sub, all restraint removed, began to move upwards with increasing speed; Franklin felt the wash of its close passage, but was too bemused to realize what it meant. He was still struggling back into hazy consciousness; around eight hundred feet, quite abruptly, he started to react to Henson's bullying ministrations, and, to the commander's vast relief, began to answer him back in kind. He cursed wildly for about a hundred feet, then became fully aware of his surroundings and ground to an embarrassed halt. Only then did he realize that his mission had been successful and that the men he had set out to rescue were already far above him on their way back to the surface.

Franklin could make no such speed. A decompression chamber was waiting for him at the three-hundred-foot level, and in its cramped confines he was to fly back to Brisbane and spend eighteen tedious hours before all the absorbed gas had escaped from his body. And by the time the doctors let him out of their clutches, it was far too late to suppress the tape recording that had circulated throughout the entire bureau. He was a hero to the whole world, but if he ever grew conceited he need only remind himself that all his staff had listened gleefully to every word of Commander Henson's fluently profane cajoling of their director.

CHAPTER 25

PETER NEVER looked back as he walked up the gangplank into the projectile from which, in little more than half an hour, he would have his first view of the receding Earth. Franklin could understand why his son kept his head averted; young men of eighteen do not cry in public. Nor, for that matter, he told himself fiercely, do middle-aged directors of important bureau.

Anne had no such inhibitions; she was weeping steadily despite all that Indra could do to comfort her. Not until the doors of the spaceship had finally sealed and the thirty-minute warning siren had drowned all other noises did she subside into an intermittent sniffling.

The tide of spectators, of friends and relatives, of cameramen and Space Department officials, began to retreat before the moving barriers. Clasping hands with his wife and daughter, Franklin let himself be swept along with the flood of humanity. What hopes and fears, sorrows and joys surrounded him now! He tried to remember his emotions at his first take-off; it must have been one of the great moments of his life – yet all recollection of it had gone, obliterated by thirty years of later experience.

And now Peter was setting out on the road his father had travelled half a lifetime before. May you have better luck among the stars than I did, Franklin prayed. He wished he could be there at Port Lowell when Irene greeted the boy who might have been her son, and wondered how Roy and Rupert would receive their half-brother. He was sure that they would be glad to meet him; Peter would not be as lonely on Mars as Ensign Walter Franklin had once been.

They waited in silence while the long minutes wore away. By this time, Peter would be so interested in the strange and exciting world that was to be his home for the next week that he would already have forgotten the pain of parting. He could not be blamed if his eyes were fixed on the new life which lay before him in all its unknown promise.

And what of his own life? Franklin asked himself. Now that he had launched his son into the future, could he say that he had been a success? It was a question he found very hard to answer honestly. So many things that he had attempted had ended in failure or even in disaster. He knew now that he was unlikely to rise any farther in the service of the state; he might be a hero, but he had upset too many people when he became the surprised and somewhat reluctant ally of the Maha Thero. Certainly he had no hope of promotion – nor did he desire it – during the five or ten years which would be needed to complete the reorganization of the Bureau of Whales. He had been told in as many words that since he was partly responsible for the situation – the mess, it was generally called – he could sort it out himself.

One thing he would never know. If fate had not brought him public admiration and the even more valuable – because less fickle – friendship of Senator Chamberlain, would he have had the courage of his new-found convictions? It had been easy, as the latest hero that the world had taken to its heart but would forget tomorrow, to stand up in the witness box and state his beliefs. His superiors could fume and fret, but there was nothing they could do but accept his defection with the best grace they could muster. There were times when he almost wished that the accident of fame had not come to his rescue. And had his evidence, after all, been decisive? He suspected that it had. The result of the referendum had been close, and the Maha Thero might not have carried the day without his help.

The three sharp blasts of the siren broke into his reverie.

In that awe-inspiring silence which still seemed so uncanny to those who remembered the age of rockets, the great ship sloughed away its hundred thousand tons of weight and began the climb back to its natural element. Half a mile above the plain, its own gravity field took over completely, so that it was no longer concerned with terrestial ideas of 'up' or 'down'. It lifted its prow towards the zenith, and hung poised for a moment like a metal obelisk miraculously supported among the clouds. Then, in that same awful silence, it blurred itself into a line – and the sky was empty.

The tension broke. There was a few stifled sobs, but many more laughs and jokes, perhaps a little too high-pitched to be altogether convincing. Franklin put his arms around Anne and Indra, and began to shepherd them towards the exit.

To his son, he willingly bequeathed the shoreless seas of space. For himself, the oceans of this world were sufficient. Therein dwelt all his subjects, from the moving mountain of Leviathan to the newborn dolphin that had not yet learned to suckle under water.

He would guard them to the best of his knowledge and ability. Already he could see clearly the future role of the bureau, when its wardens would be in truth the protectors of all the creatures moving in the sea. All? No – that, of course, was absurd; nothing could change or even greatly alleviate the incessant cruelty and slaughter that raged through all the oceans of the world. But with the great mammals who were his kindred, man could make a start, imposing his truce upon the battlefield of Nature.

What might come of that in the ages ahead, no one could guess. Even Lundquist's daring and still unproved plan for taming the killer whales might no more than hint of what the next few decades would bring. They might even bring the answer to the mystery which haunted him still, and which he had so nearly solved when the submarine earthquake robbed him of his best friend.

A chapter – perhaps the best chapter – of his life was closing. The future would have many problems, but he did not believe that ever again would he have to face such challenges as he had met in the past. In a sense, his work was done, even though the details were merely beginning.

He looked once more at the empty sky, and the words that the Mahanayake Thero had spoken to him as they flew back from the Greenland station rose up out of memory like a ground swell on the sea. He would never forget that chilling thought: *'When that time comes, the treatment man receives from his superiors may well depend upon the way he has behaved towards the other creatures of his own world.'*

Perhaps he was a fool to let such phantasms of a remote and unknowable future have any influence upon his thoughts and acts, but he had no regrets for what he had done. As he stared into the blue infinity that had swallowed his son, the stars seemed suddenly very close. 'Give us another hundred years,' he whispered, 'and we'll face you with clean hands and hearts – whatever shape you be.'

'Come along, dear,' said Indra, her voice still a little unsteady. 'You haven't much time. The office asked me to remind you – the Committee on Interdepartmental Standardization meets in half an hour.'

'I know,' said Franklin, blowing his nose firmly and finally. 'I wouldn't dream of keeping it waiting.'

SCIENCE FICTION IN PAN

A SELECTION OF POPULAR READING IN PAN

NON-FICTION

Dr Laurence J. Peter & Raymond Hull
THE PETER PRINCIPLE   30p
Peter F. Drucker
THE AGE OF DISCONTINUITY   60p
Jack Olsen
SILENCE ON MONTE SOLE   35p
Jim Dante & Leo Diegel
THE NINE BAD SHOTS OF GOLF (illus.)   35p
Adrian Hill
HOW TO DRAW (illus.)   30p
Maurice Woodruff
THE SECRET OF FORETELLING YOUR OWN
   FUTURE   25p
William Sargant
THE UNQUIET MIND   45p
Graham Hill
LIFE AT THE LIMIT (illus.)   35p
Ken Welsh
HITCH-HIKER'S GUIDE TO EUROPE (illus.)   35p
Miss Read
MISS READ'S COUNTRY COOKING   30p
Gavin Maxwell
RAVEN SEEK THY BROTHER (illus.)   30p

Obtainable from all booksellers and newsagents. If you
have any difficulty, please send purchase price plus 5p postage
to PO Box 11, Falmouth, Cornwall.

While every effort is made to keep prices low, it is sometimes necessary to increase prices at short notice. PAN Books
reserve the right to show new retail prices on covers which may
differ from the text or elsewhere.

I enclose a cheque/postal order for selected titles ticked above
plus 5p a book to cover postage and packing.

NAME ....

ADDRESS ....

....